double moon destiny

LIZZIE STARR

Please note: This is a work of fiction. Names, characters, places, and incidents either are the product of the author's imagination or are used fictitiously, and any resemblance to actual persons, living or dead, business establishments, events or locales is entirely coincidental.

Cover and interior design by Cat & Doxie Author Services

Photo Credits

curaphotography/depositpnotos

korionov/depositphotos

ISBN 978-0-9977542-8-5

We are each other's destiny.

~~ Jacqueline Novogratz

one

Long cycles of focused study and the hard life of the Compound culminated in this moment. Jermanah shuffled her feet to ease her tense muscles. Her slight movements earned a reproving glare from the priestess at her right and a sly grin from the acolyte wedged against her other side. Jermanah froze and though the cool, salty breeze off the nearby sea whipped strands of hair across her face, she refused to push the length back over her shoulder.

She would not give the priestess reason to assign her extra duties. Nor allow the other acolytes the satisfaction of her punishment. Barely contained joy of this night filled her. She was a Child of the Double Moon. Five conjunctions of the moons had passes since her birth and the beginning of her life in the Compound. This night, this moment was the first ceremony where she would participate and welcome another moons blessed child.

An air of expectancy settled around the cottage. A heavily pregnant woman rushed from a grove of dark trees and collapsed before the waiting priestesses. The Highest of the High stepped from her enclosed sedan chair and approached the prone woman. Jermanah's heart sang. The Child of the Double Moon had been chosen.

Guards held an old woman near the cottage door and she cried a warbling denial. The song in Jermanah's heart faded. Didn't the old woman understand the honor bestowed upon the mother of the child, one to be cherished and long remembered within the child's birth family? Jermanah shook her head in wonder and disbelief, receiving a reproving hiss from the priestess.

Taken immediately to the Compound after her birth, Jermanah had no chance to know her birth mother and any information about her family remained hidden from her. She ducked her head and smiled. No matter. She would pay homage to this mother, as the priestesses of the Compound had surely honored the woman who gave her life.

A slender guardsman knelt to carefully arrange the mother in his arms before rising. The woman cried a feeble denial even as he paced toward the cottage. He stopped just outside the doorway and bowed awkwardly before the Highest. With a jerk of one hand she motioned for him to precede her into the dim interior. The old woman's struggles ripped her garments, nearly freeing her.

The door closed with a dull thud and heavy silence settled over the clearing. A shudder ran cold fingers of dread along Jermanah's spine. Her joy shifted, her thoughts turning toward dire possibilities. She caught her lower lip between her teeth and watched the door with trepidation. Where, then, was the song of celebration and welcome? What caused fear in the mother and the old woman's hopeless struggles? Rather than face the swirl of doubt and questions. Jermanah turned her thoughts inward and focused on the man the Seer had her heal earlier that day.

A double hand of fighters crawled over the uneven ground and into the heavy undergrowth beneath a stand of trees. The leader glanced to one side, waited until he caught each man's gaze then signaled with sharp hand movements. The group settled to wait.

Kierigh grimaced. Although his shoulder had been healed of a knife wound earlier that day, an odd vibration had settled deep within the muscle. The tickle of a memory he couldn't quite grasp teased his mind. He rotated his shoulder but the irritation remained. Ruthless, he dismissed the feelings and peered across the small clearing.

A pregnant woman stumbled past his hiding place. He remained still, listening, watching. She fell a few steps from him and black-robed priestesses surrounded her. They were too close. Sweat beaded on his forehead and trickled down the side of his face. He will his solid control into his followers but dared not risk the movement to glance toward them.

Kierigh cursed himself, cursed the clumsy actions that caused the shoulder wound. If he hadn't gone to the Seer or insisted on healing without the sleeping draught, he would have been in time to spirit the woman away and save her child. Now his small band of fighters would have to take the child from the Compound bitches.

He closed his eyes in resignation. The king and the Highest of the High had closed the other Compounds within the last cycle, leaving only the structure nearest the king's Stronghold occupied. For once the king's actions had been helpful. His forces had been spread far too thin watching the numerous, far flung religious centers. How many children had been taken before the Highest's quest for power centralized her control?

A female born under the Double Moon was of little concern to him. A girl child was taken to the Compound and raised under strict guidelines. Although her life would be hard and demanding, still she had life.

Unlike the unfortunate male child who was taken to the Stronghold and sacrificed to increase the power of the king. The grisly ceremony after the last conjunction of the moons remained burned into his memory. Lost in the maze of secret passages within the Stronghold, he'd arrived too late to save the child. Always too late.

Except at his own birth. Then he had been born too soon. He entered the world minutes before the conjunction. His grandmother had hidden him before the priestesses arrived. Yet, he'd shared the womb with a brother who followed him from the birthing passage at the exact time of the Double Moon. His brother... his brother had been taken.

He didn't understand how he felt so certain, how his heart knew, but his brother hadn't been sacrificed as a babe. After six Double Moon cycles his brother still lived. It didn't matter why his brother hadn't succumbed to the sacrificial knife. What mattered was finally finding and reuniting with him. Kierigh repeated his personal vow. Along with his brother, he would protect and spirit away any child unlucky enough to be born during this terrible time.

The priestesses moved from his hiding place toward the small hut. He drew a thankful breath and let it out slowly. A guard came to carry the woman into the cottage. The old one struggled to reach her. A sly smile stretched the Highest's mouth before she entered the squat building. A chill coursed down his spine.

His dispassionate gaze traveled the circle of Compound faithful until the glint of moonlight on long, multi-hued hair held his attention. He drew his brows together and squinted at the young woman covered from neck to toe in a drab, gray acolyte robe. His shoulder muscles twitched as though attempting to jump from beneath his skin. Wishing he could rub at the new scar, he watched the acolyte. Something about her called to him, an almost memory beckoned his thoughts. The throb in his shoulder deepened until it pulsed with the beat of his heart, filling his ears and the silence that had fallen over the clearing.

A ripple of silent command passed to Jermanah from the priestess at her side. She signaled the acolyte beside her. Soon, the women's voices rose in a low chant of praise to the Double Moon. Jermanah fell into the pattern of the slow, weaving dance moving in counterpoint to the chant. In the dry grass she imagined practicing the dance against the braided texture of her rug. Dancing alone in her room was forbidden, she'd wanted her part must be perfect. By increasing the favorable attention she received from one of the High, she might soon be marked for advanced training. Her low, throaty voice joined the second harmony of the chant.

A piercing wail escaped the cottage. The old woman gave a sharp cry and renewed her struggle to free herself from the guards. The Compound faithful showed no indication of the disruption, no change in the tempo of the dance, no hesitation in the melodic chant. Nothing but the dance and the praise existed for Jermanah. She smiled and tilted her face to the light of the Double Moons.

The cottage door slammed against the outer wall and the regal form of the Highest filled the doorway. She lifted one hand and the chanting halted, except for one voice that wavered to silence. Her eyes glittered. She glared from one acolyte to the next. Highest's icy gaze stopped on Jermanah and she shuddered. The Highest pointed one long finger and gestured sharply.

Jermanah shook her head to clear the trance-like effects of the dance. She took a deep breath to steady the weakness in her knees and took a small step forward out of line. She'd hoped for notice, but not when the Highest seethed anger. A snicker sounded behind her followed by a muffled slap. There was no more laughter. But laughter and disparaging comments would be better than the Highest's lowered brows and ominous silence.

Impatience oozed from the Highest and she gestured again before folding her arms under her breasts. Jermanah took another tentative step and swallowed against the tightening of her throat. Why would the Highest of the High summon her now? The shortcuts she'd taken in her duties in order to study with the Seer flashed through her mind. Simply studying with the Seer was one of the most forbidden acts in the Compound. But why might she be called out for that now? Unable to meet the Highest's cold gaze, she lowered her lashes and crossed to the cottage.

The Highest stepped aside allowing Jermanah to enter the dim cottage. Her hopes and aspirations sank into the hard-packed, dirt floor. The shuddering of the slamming door matched the fearful quivering of her heart. She turned to the Highest and lifted her hands in supplication.

"You have studied the forbidden knowledge, have you

not, Jermanah? You know the healing arts?" Pitched low, menace filling each syllable, the Highest's voice strangely carried no hint of anger. Jermanah stared at the floor to hide the flush warming her face.

A long-fingered hand clasped her chin and lifted until she was forced to meet the Highest's intense gaze. "Come now, child. I know you have studied secretly with the old man. While the knowledge of the Seer is forbidden to acolytes of the Compound, the skills are not always unnecessary. You have studied the forbidden arts, have you not? Answer me, Jermanah."

Jermanah nodded against the increasing pressure of the Highest's fingers.

"Answer me, girl. You have studied healing, haven't you?"

"Yes." Long, sharp nails nipped into her skin. "Yes, Highest, I have so studied."

The Highest shoved Jermanah's face to the side. "Good. Punishment will be determined upon your return to the Compound. But for now, I find I need your..." The Highest paused. Her normally controlled features twisted to an ugly sneer. "...arts."

With an imperious wave of her hand she pointed to a corner of the small hut. Jermanah squinted into the darkness then closed her eyes in sympathy. The pregnant woman writhed on a low cot; her distended belly rolling side to side with her movements. Sympathy washed through Jermanah and she lifted one hand toward the woman.

The Highest's fingers dug into Jermanah's shoulder. "You will not heal the woman. You will ease her only enough to make her body give up the child held within. The woman has defied me. Defied the Double Moon and the decree of our king. The child is chosen. It must remain unharmed. The woman is of no consequence."

The Highest shoved Jermanah forward. She stumbled across the room, catching herself on the edge of the cot. At an impatient gesture from the Highest, the priestesses surrounding the woman moved to the head of the narrow bed. Jermanah knelt and rested her hands against the rough blanket.

The Highest cleared her throat. Jermanah focused on the pregnant woman and touched the sweat-drenched forehead. Pain-filled eyes turned to her. "You are one of them?" The woman's raw voice and labored words were filled with accusation.

Jermanah nodded, leaned close to the woman's ear and whispered, "I will ease your birthing pain. You are honored above other women this night, for your child is chosen by the Double Moon. The signs and portents are great for your child. The Seer of the Compound has spoken it so. Let me ease you."

A contraction rippled across the woman's swollen belly. Jermanah stroked lank hair from the woman's damp face then rested her hand over the clenching muscles. "See. The child knows the way of the chosen. It wishes to greet the Double Moon and begin on the path to fulfill destiny." The muscles under her hand twisted. The birth was very near.

The woman jerked from under Jermanah's touch and lifted herself on one elbow. A wad of spittle splatted against Jermanah's cheek. The woman sank back and satisfaction replaced the pain in her gaunt features. ""You'll not have my child while I live. Not you, or the Double Moon. I'll take my child to death with me first, I will. It will not be born."

Jermanah sat back on her calves and wiped her face with the hem of her robe. Confused by the woman's anger, she glanced at her fingers. How could the woman deny her child the joy of being chosen? The soft touch of robes flowed against Jermanah's back. Points of pain dug into her shoulder, pulled her from the cot and tossed her against the wall. Her head connected with hard wood. Dazed, she whispered three rapid syllables to ease her pain and clear her vision.

The Highest arched over the cot. The woman cringed, trying to distance herself from the waves of hatred pouring from the Highest. "Prophetic words, oh chosen mother of the Double Moon. Except the child will not follow you to death. You alone face death, once you deliver the child to me."

A priestess slipped a thin knife into the Highest's hand. She poised the long blade above the woman's belly. "Will you give me the child? Or shall I take it? Either way, the babe is mine." The point of the blade slid against the woman's skin. A line of blood blossomed across her belly. Terrified of the wicked creature the Highest had become, Jermanah shrank against the wall and covered her open mouth with her hand. She wouldn't scream. Wouldn't draw that heated attention to herself.

The door burst open and the old woman hobbled across the threshold chased by a pair of guards. "You'll not have the child of my child." She screamed and ran forward. The sound, old and wavering grated against Jermanah's tattered nerves.

The Highest turned, arched one eyebrow and calmly lifted the knife. A bright flash of metal caught the candle-light before the old woman stopped with a jerk then took a halting step back. Her eyes widened then she stared down at the knife protruding from her thin chest.

Before the old woman fell, the Highest wrenched the

blade from her body, turned and plunged the knife into the woman on the cot. Jermanah's moan of dismay was the only sound as the woman's spirit joined that of her dam. The Highest sliced the knife through the woman's belly with practiced ease, opening the womb. Laughing, she dropped the knife, reached within the bloody wound and pulled forth the child.

Chanting, a priestess nipped the child's life bond with a tiny silver knife. With the same knife, she pricked the child's heel. A startled cry filled the cottage. From outside the cottage, the chant of welcome rose like a cheer to cover the babe's angry cries.

The Highest held the child awkwardly and paced to the door. The guards knelt and each lifted one hand asking for forgiveness. She paused to give each a disdainful glance, the promise of punishment ripe in her eyes. Jermanah tugged the tie from her hair, pulled the length around her to cover her face and crumpled into a ball of misery, allowing her tears to flow unchecked. Whether she wept for the dead women or for the death of her ideals, she didn't care. All she knew was a pain she didn't know how to heal.

When the old woman wrenched from her guards and rushed into the cottage Kierigh's cramped muscles quivered with the need for action. The old woman's shout of defiance was cut short. A chill wrapped around his shoulders. The sudden silence could only mean the old woman was dead. If the mother also opposed the Highest, her life would be taken as well.

A child cried.

The Highest returned to the clearing in triumph, carrying the babe. He closed his eyes and sighed. Nothing could be done now for the women in the cottage. He made a slight gesture to one side and a young man slid backwards through the underbrush. When the women of the Compound had gone, the young man would bring the villagers to care for the women. Such was the best he could do for their spirits.

The Highest held the squalling child before her like an offering and paced around the circle of priestesses and acolytes, allowing each to gaze upon the bloody child and touch the trailing life cord.

She handed the child to a waiting priestess who used a shallow ceramic basin to cleanse the infant. The life cord was trimmed close then shrouded in silk and placed in an ornate bag. He dared not imagine what use the Compound would make of the cord.

Wrapped in a highly embellished piece of cloth, the child was presented to the Highest. Without touching the babe she pulled back the cloth to examine the wiggling form. "This is a fine male child. When the moons are dark, he shall be taken to the king, there to fulfill his destiny."

A chant of praise lifted into the night sky. Kierigh rested his forehead against the dry ground and allowed the pain of this latest failure to wash over him. He and his men had spent the entirety of the last cycle preparing for this night. His first plan had failed miserably, causing the loss of innocent lives. Now using force was unavoidable. He rolled his head from side to side, rubbing dirt into his forehead. How many more innocents might die this night?

Movement in the clearing chased the doubt and failure from his hear. He watched the acolyte and dark-robed priestesses dance for a few moments. Under the cover of the chant he whistled a soft signal. Once his men melted into the night, he followed. Little time remained to prepare their ambush.

two

Soft chanting drew Jermanah to a small window. She peered through the broken shutters, recognized the chant and pattern of the dance to welcome a male child and sighed. She'd hoped to watch a girl-child grow, perhaps even assist in her training. There hadn't been another female child born at the Double Moon since her own birth. Male babes remained within the Compound only a few short days before being taken with great ceremony to the king. After the moment the child entered the king's Stronghold it seemed as though the child was never mentioned again. Perhaps priests trained the chosen there.

The Highest wrapped the child in fur-lined cloths then faced the acolytes who had been trained and prepared to nurse the child. The Highest took a few steps toward them, paused and turned for the cottage. Her gaze bore into Jermanah's. A slow, well-satisfied smile tilted the priestess's lips.

Jermanah shivered and slid to the floor, her robe tangling around her knees. She tugged at the fabric and crawled to the old woman. Nausea rose, nearly overcoming her. She swallowed against the burning in her throat before closing the woman's faded eyes. Moving to the cot, she clenched her teeth, swallowed again and pulled a blanket over the gaping wound in the woman's belly.

The birth of the child of the Double Moons was intended to be a joyous event, not life ending. Insistent, her gorge rose. She did nothing to suppress the pain, vomiting on the blood stained floor. She wiped her face with hem of her robe and rested her forehead against the end of the cot, as far from the gore soaked bedding as possible. She had no strength, nor desire, to move.

Brittle laughter rang from the cottage door. Back stiff, Jermanah brushed her hair from her face. After shuddering at the sticky ends, she wiped her hands on the blanket and faced the laughter.

Holding the ceremoniously wrapped babe in her arms, the Highest tossed back her head. "Jermanah, you are chosen to care for the child while he remains at the Compound. All his needs are yours to fulfill."

"I cannot do as you say, Highest. I'm not able."

"Take the babe." The Highest straightened her arms and held the child well away from herself. "For now, he is yours. You will know what needs to be done."

Jermanah stood and, unsure how to handle a newborn, carefully supported his head and cradled him close to her body. The tiny bundle whimpered and he puckered his small mouth as if searching. She stuck the tip of a clean finger into the child's mouth and marveled at the power of his quest for food. An uncomfortable longing settled low in her body.

Tearing her gaze from the precious bundle, she lifted her gaze to the Highest. "I wasn't instructed or prepared in any way to care for a child. Since I haven't born a child, I have no milk." She glanced down at the boy who still suckled noisily on her finger. Reluctance filled her words. "Other needs I'm able to care for, but I can't feed the child."

A small leather packet fell from the Highest's hand to the floor. "I know what you have learned from the Seer. Although you have yet to study this particular magic, you will know what to do. These herbs induce the flow of milk from a virgin breast. See to it, Jermanah. The babe must feed before dawn."

"I don't—" But she spoke to the Highest's back.

The priestess paused at the door, turned, and smoothed the rustling of her robes. Her expression calm, she arched one eyebrow. "Do not disappoint me, Jermanah. I had so hoped you would advance to one of the High."

Jermanah drew breath to speak. The Highest lifted one finger in a command for silence. Her features hardened to stone and ice flashed in her eyes. "Do. Not. Disappoint. Me."

Once the Highest slammed the door shutting her away, Jermanah sank to her knees, willed the shaking in her hands to stop and reached for the packet. All she'd succeeded doing this day was disappointing the Highest. Following her heart had led to learning healing magic from the Seer. She'd practiced sacred dances alone in her room. And now? Tears welled against her lashes and fell to wet the babe's face.

She lay the boy on the floor and arranged his coverings so he appeared comfortable. The shock of what she'd witnessed and what she'd ultimately lost exploded within her. She curled in on herself and let her sobs wrack her body. Arms wrapped tightly across her chest, she rocked, searching for comfort. If only she could gather the pain into a tight ball and hide it away, never be found. Instead, her mental agony grew and expanded to fill her with hopelessness and despair.

Mingling his angry cries with her pain, the babe wailed. For long moments the sound filled the small cottage. The child's demands imposed themselves on Jermanah's consciousness and her tears dried. The small one would not suffer for her sins.

She lifted the tiny boy in her arms, rocked and patted his back. "There now, child. Your dam is gone, but I am here. I'll care for you as the Highest wills. But you must hush now. I need to concentrate to prepare myself to give you nourishment. Shh, hush now."

The child stared at her with wide, unfocused eyes, but calmed and pursed his lips. She lay him again on the floor at her side, pulled at a corner of his wrappings and placed the fabric against his tiny lower lip. His eyelids lowered closed and he sucked.

Humming a tuneless melody, she rubbed the child's rounded belly. She lifted the packet of herbs to her nose and inhaled. Sorting the fragrances, she recognized each, finding nothing dangerous to her or the babe. She'd need to infuse a tea so glanced around the cottage for a small pot, letting her gaze slip quickly over the still forms of the dead women.

The door eased open lighting the cottage with the mellow glow of the Double Moons. The now silent priestesses hovered at the far side of the clearing. The tall, shadowed form of a guard filled the small doorway. He hesitated then dipped his head to enter.

"Lady? The Highest provides a container of hot water for you. I also brought clean cloths for the babe." He dipped his head again, set the pot and bundle in front of Jermanah and turned for the door.

She grabbed the hem of his cloak. He hesitated before facing her, his expression filled with questions. She recognized him as the guard who had so carefully carried the child's dam into the cottage. He cleared his throat. "Lady?"

"I... I thank you. Your name?"

"Poll, lady. Your servant."

Jermanah shook her head. "I have no servant. But, if you could... might there be something else in the traveling supplies I could wear?" She plucked at the front of her robe and winced at the sticky red that came away on her fingers.

"At once, lady. If there is anything you require, don't hesitate to call for me. I am at your disposal." His smile was gentle and encouraging, so unlike a guard's normal, dour, unchanging expression. He lifted one hand as if to touch her, but stopped short of the contact. Jermanah sighed. Causal contact between guards and acolytes was forbidden.

"No, Poll, I require nothing else. Inform the Highest all will be done as required. The child will be cared for. We'll be able to return to the Compound at dawn." She offered him a weary smile wishing there were a better way to let him know how deeply she appreciated his kindness.

Poll bowed and backed toward the door. His gaze skittered over the bloody scene behind her. Sorrow and disgust swirled in his dark eyes before he schooled his expression.

"You won't be disturbed, lady. I'll remain at the door. Should you require anything, you need only call out."

His muffled orders seeped through the cracks around the closed door. A sharp ring of metal against wood sounded then silence fell. Jermanah imagined Poll stoically guarding the door, his bland expression belying his alert awareness of his surroundings. She envied that ability to block out the world.

Sending sent a prayer skyward that the mixture was

correct and the proportions accurate, she lifted the clay lid covering the cup and dumped the herbs into the steaming water. A single soft knock announced Poll who set a clean robe before her. Not a gray acolyte robe, nor the dark garb of a priestess. The deep blue color fascinated her and she ran her fingers over the rich, soft material.

"This can't be for me." She pushed the robe toward the guard.

"It's what was given to me, coming from the Highest herself. It will be beautiful on you, lady." He ducked his head and turned his back to her. Even in her pain, the reddening of the skin at the back of his neck before he exited the cottage made her lower her brows in confusion.

Then she rose, jerked her stained robe over her head and tossed the ruined material as far from her as possible. She shook out the heavy blue robe, noticing the fasteners down the front. Ah, the robe designated for the one who cared for the child. A slow breath filled her chest. This was now her robe.

After donning the unusual garment, she tested the temperature of the cup of brewing tea. Drinkable. She had nothing to strain the floating herbs, so used her fingers to remove most of the particles, dropping the bits to the floor at her feet.

Jermanah lifted the cup, inhaled and wrinkled her nose. Herbal mixtures were notoriously foul tasting. She took a tentative sip. Not unpalatable, but neither was the flavor pleasant. Holding her breath, she drank the liquid in one long swallow.

Warmth spread outward from her belly to the rest of her body. How long would the changes take? Tightness blossomed below her heart. The cup clattered to the floor. Fierce cramps attacked her abdomen. She clutched her stomach and fell to her knees, bending double to contain the pain. Startled, the child whimpered.

Jermanah bit her lip to stifle her own whimpers. Her breasts grew heavy, the robe's soft fabric chafing against the fullness. She leaned further forward until the material hung away from her body. Tingling filled her breasts, concentrating in the nipples. She straightened, opened the robe and touched the gathering drops of milk. Fascinated, she arched her eyebrows at the sudden and rapid changes to her body. The decoction worked far more quickly than she imagined possible.

Feeling as though her breasts would burst, her thoughts centered on relief. She glanced at the squirming babe. Was this how a mother felt? She lifted the boy and guided his searching mouth to a nipple. A sigh passed her lips when he began to suck then she gasped at the fierce pressure of the small mouth. Holding her breath until the pain lessened, she studied the tiny head at her breast and caressed his soft cheek.

Moments later, she grinned at the child's rumbled response to a full belly. Poll knocked and swung the door open to admit one of the High. Jermanah lowered her head in respect and answered the unspoken question. "The child is sated. We're able to travel whenever the Highest decrees."

Kierigh knelt at the edge of a small stream and dunked his head in the cold water. Sitting back on his haunches, he scrubbed at his face then shook his head and shoved the wet length of his hair over his shoulder. Tendrils of sleep tugged at his senses and he cursed the Seer's heavy hand with the sleeping draught. The old man hadn't wanted him to remember the healer, Kierigh couldn't chase the shimmer of the woman's hair or the press of her body from his mind.

Although the Seer had called the healer 'child', no child had touched him. Despite the sleeping draught, he'd sensed the rough wood of the table beneath his cheek and shock of a wet cloth against his back. He'd strained to lift his head, but couldn't force movement to his muscles. Curse the helplessness.

He took a deep breath and stood. There was no time for personal concerns. No matter ow intriguing the woman's touch had been, there was no place in his life for any woman, let alone a prissy little Compound acolyte.
He had—

A branch rubbed against another. Kierigh whirled, his long knife held at ready. One of his men, a recent recruit, stood before him with his hands held palm forward. A cocky grin lit his young face.

"You take chances." Kierigh scowled and sheathed his knife.

The man's grin faded and he shrugged. "I know. I've told the villagers of the women's deaths and will care for their spirits. The babe's father will be brought to the forest when he returns from fishing."

"The procession?"

"Traveling slowly, but are within a league. We are in position. Once the advance guard passes we attack on your signal."

Kierigh nodded, stalked past the other man and through the forest. He climbed an ancient tree and crawled onto a branch overhanging the road. Once settled in the crook with his back against the smooth bark he peered through the thick foliage and accounted for each of his fighters. Already impatient with the waiting, he fingered his knife and tested the finely honed edge.

A deep throb twitched his muscles, stretching the new, thin scar across his shoulder blade. He rubbed against the bark but couldn't chase the memory of warmth flowing over his skin at the acolyte's skilled healing.

Kierigh blew out a harsh breath and stared down at the road beneath his perch. Squinting, he made out the faint haze of dust rising from the advancing procession. Still distant. He settled deeper into his hiding place, tugging at a thin, leafy branch to complete his concealment.

When the healer's touch disappeared he'd managed to open one eye a mere slit. But all he'd seen was the dull gray of the acolyte's robe. And her hair. Her long, multi-hued hair had glowed in the faint light from the doorway. As physical as her touch had been, her gaze swept over him.

By the moons, he'd actually struggled to rise, his hand grasping toward her retreating figure. The Seer's gnarled fingers had easily pressed him back to the stool. The old man's chuckle and muttered, "soon" broke down Kierigh's carefully constructed defenses, sending him to sleep.

He'd awoken to an empty chamber with barely the time to gather his forces and follow the procession of priestesses. Plans altered by circumstances he couldn't control left him unsettled. He adjusted his position and pushed the unwelcomed longing from his mind. He wasn't here for a woman. Preventing another sacrifice and finding his brother, that was his calling, his duty.

The tip of his knife pricked his finger and he caught back a startled yelp. Staring at the tiny welling of blood, he grimaced. Distraction could easily kill a man. He hadn't kept himself, his men and the small camp of followers safe by being distracted. Now was not the time to fall under the spell of something, of someone, he couldn't have. He squared his shoulders, leaned forward and watched the road.

But the soft glimmer of the acolyte's hair remained fixed in his mind.

Jermanah paced behind the sedan chair carrying the Highest of the High. Puffs of dust from the advance guards' passage tickled her nose. But with her arms weighed down by the infant she couldn't brush away the irritation. She sighed and shifted the child's position. How did such a small creature become so heavy? The how didn't matter. This was now her destiny.

Poll and his huge mount remained no more than a few paces from her side since the procession left the cottage. His presence tempered the isolation placed on her by the others of the Compound. The Highest ignored her completely. The priestesses and acolytes walked far behind, unwilling to be near one who had earned the Highest's displeasure. Though soft and silky, her robe was hot and uncomfortable. She sniffed back a tear.

"I will carry the child for you, lady." Poll shifted in his saddle and leaned toward her extending one hand.

Jermanah shook her head. "This is my duty."

"How then may I help you, lady?"

Grateful for the guard's concern, she shook her head again. "I don't know."

A sharp whistle pierced the still air. Men leapt from the dark underbrush and dropped from surrounding trees. Poll's brows drew together. He glanced from her to the front of the procession, drew his sword, wheeled his mount and galloped toward the advance guard.

The procession erupted in confusion. The slaves dropped the sedan chair. The wooden enclosure broke apart revealing the Highest tossed sideways in a rumpled heap.

Fear rooted Jermanah to the center of the roadway. An odd satisfaction curled through her fear at seeing the Highest disheveled and brought low. She ducked her head lest her emotions be recognized. Though how much more shame could the Highest pile upon her now? Despite the shouts and noise surrounding them, the child wiggled but remained quiet. She should take the child somewhere safe. Where? Indecision froze her bare feet to the roadway.

The Highest struggled from the shattered wood and tangled draperies and brushed dirt from her robes. As she straightened, a man dropped from the branches and pointed a long knife at her chest.

"You will give me the child."

The Highest stood motionless for a moment then arched her eyebrow and laughed. With the tip of her finger, she pushed on the knife, but the blade didn't waver. She sucked her bloodied fingertip into her mouth, tilted her head and, watching the man, and slowly drew the finger from her mouth. "The child belongs to the king."

A few mounted guards broke from chasing men into the surrounding trees and advanced. Shouting and clashing their weapons, they slid from their war beasts. Knife flashing, the man whirled. One guard crashed onto the broken sedan chair.

Swords held at ready, the guards formed a loose, semicircle around the man. Jermanah recognized the ritualistic fighting pattern from the many times she'd hidden behind the training ground wall to watch the men practice. The rebel fighter crouched and waited. Sword high, a guard approached. The rebel's easy, soundless dispatch of the guard, showed her he would easily best any who fought in the way of the Compound.

The Highest backed from the fighting and with an imperious wave signaled to one of the circling guards. Leaving his comrades, he rushed to her side. After her low, urgent words, he gave a sharp whistle. One of the great beasts lifted its head and pranced from the milling mounts. The guard knelt. The Highest placed one food in his cupped hands allowing him to lift her to the animal's broad back. The guard leapt up behind her and urged the animal forward.

At the fringes of the heavy forest undergrowth the Highest jerked the reigns from the guard and dragged back the animal's head to stop it. She watched the fighters for a long moment then focused her gaze on Jermanah. Her harsh laughter rang over the sounds of desperate battle before she wheeled the war beast and disappeared into the forest.

Jermanah clutched the squirming babe. Beyond the blond fighter, Poll waged his own fight with a pair of men. The Highest had abandoned them. The priestesses and acolytes had already run. What should she do?

When the guards noticed the Highest galloping away most called to their mounts and fled as well. Only one member of the advance guard remained warily circling the rebel. Thank the moons Poll remained, easing his mount to where Jermanah stood locked in indecision. He was the only constant in this horrible night. He would know what to do. Heated tension emanated from him when he halted behind her, but all he did was watch the fight in silence.

Run. Every thought focused on the need to run. But where? Even if she left the child behind she'd never be able to escape. She covered the child's face with a corner of the wrappings and swayed to comfort him. And herself. She'd never leave a defenseless babe to the mercies of these rebel fighters.

The blond fighter pushed the last guard away and bent to wipe his long blade on the man's cloak. He turned in a slow, wary circle, stopping when his gaze met hers. He altered his grip on his knife and stepped toward her.

Her hands tingled with the rise of healing power. Startled, she flexed her fingers. She'd healed this man. That morning. He was the one in the Seer's chamber. The one's who's healing had seemed somehow different. Unable to resist the powerful connection, she took a step.

The war beast pressed against her back and Poll's hand at her shoulder stopped her. "No, lady. These rebels are the ruin of the Compound. We must flee with the child."

Jermanah shrugged her shoulder but was unable to shake off his hand. She couldn't, she dared not ignore the pull of the rebel's intense, icy-blue gaze. Poll leaned further, grabbed her about the waist and easily lifted her and the child before him. She uttered one short syllable of denial and squirmed, trying to slide back to the ground.

"No lady, don't. Please, we must save the child."

Ears flicking, the great beast sidestepped. Jermanah struggled against Poll's firm grasp until he spoke close to her ear. "I have sworn to protect you, lady. And so I shall."

With one hand he steadied the child in her arms then rested his sword across her lap. Subtle movements of his legs controlled and directed his mount.

Breaking her eye contact with the rebel, Poll turned them toward a gap in the dense underbrush. The remnants of healing power faded. Feeling as though she'd just woken from a deep sleep, Jermanah blinked. Poll urged the animal into a smooth, rapid pace weaving between the thick branches of the ancient trees.

Unaccustomed to riding and afraid she might fall the great distance from the war beast's back, Jermanah shrank against Poll's chest. He wrapped his arm securely about her waist and whispered, "I apologize for the familiarity, lady."

Bitter laughter died even before escaping her lips. "I thank you for your concern, Poll. But such worries are unnecessary."

"The rebels know the forest. We won't be able to escape by running. When I find a defendable location, we'll stop and I'll stand for your protection there."

Content to let someone else take charge and direct her actions, Jermanah nodded. Poll would do what was best for the child.

three

Poll jerked the reins, bringing his mount to a skidding stop. He lowered Jermanah to the ground then followed. Holding his mount's head, he spoke in its ear. A sharp slap on its wide rump made the animal squeal in surprise. It trotted to the edge of the clearing then stopped to give Poll a reproachful look before retracing their path.

Poll paced the edge of the small clearing. "It won't be long before the rebel finds us. It would be better if you could take the child far from here."

Determination straightened Jermanah's spine. "I won't leave you here alone."

"No, you won't. There is no time. You'll hide and I will fight him. When I'm victorious, we'll continue to the king's Stronghold."

"But, if he—"

"He won't." Poll paced another small circle and peered at a tangle of bushes growing at the edge of a rocky outcropping. He shoved the bushes to one side exposing the entrance to a tiny cave. ""This will do."

Jermanah eyed the opening. Panic settled in her chest, pressed against her lungs. She fought to draw breath. Cold sweat beaded her forehead and ran in a slow trickle down her spine. "I can't go in there."

"Lady, you must hide."

"Not there," she whispered. Although she took a shaky breath, insisting her muscles obey her, she couldn't move any closer than the edge of the bushes. Her arms tightened about the child and he whimpered.

Poll cocked his head to one side and his frown deepened. "But, lady..."

Shame heated her face. "I can't. Don't make me, please."

Poll huffed out a breath and released the bushes to again cover the cave entrance. A doubtful grin stretched his lips. "Perhaps then only in the bushes, lady?"

Edging from the cave, she peered into the thick tangle of branches. "But where?"

Poll inserted his sword and spread the foliage to expose a tiny space barely wide enough for her to sit cross-legged.

"How am I to get in there?"

"Once again I beg pardon, lady." Poll leaned his sword against the outcropping, placed one hand under her knees, wrapped his other arm about her shoulders and lifted her with great care. He pressed against the outer ring of bushes and leaned forward to allow her legs to drop into the open area. When she stood without wavering, he stepped back and retrieved his weapon.

"Oh." Jermanah took a quick breath. She turned in a circle then sat, arranging her robe so the trailing ends were tucked close to her legs. The child gave a soft, sleepy cry.

"You must quiet the babe."

"I know. Be careful."

"I pledge my life to your protection." Poll's features settled into a guardsman's blank expression. "Now I must cover your hiding place."

Terror returned. The dark. No air. How would she—no, she would be brave for Poll. And for the child. "Leave me a tiny sight of the sky and I won't be so afraid."

Poll nodded and braced branches casually over her head, covering the opening. A small spot of the cloudless blue sky remained in her view.

A lump settled at the base of Jermanah's throat and she struggled to swallow her fear and rising hopelessness. She didn't understand how this day had turned her life sideways. First the summons from the Seer for a strange healing. Her joy and delight at her first Double Moon procession had withered, dying with the women in the cottage. Now fear and confusion ruled her thoughts. Not simply fear for herself and what might befall her. Nor only for the child in her arms.

Now her actions brought danger to another. To a good man who had no reason to protect her, except as his duty to the Compound. Her vision blurred. That duty might ring his death knell. Guilt threatened to overwhelm her. How could she continue to exist, knowing her life should have been forfeit instead of Poll's.

The babe's tiny mouth twisted and he drew a long breath. Jermanah stuck the tip of her finger between his lips before he released a cry. After a moment, he sucked and his eyes closed in contentment.

At a soft swooshing sound she peeked through the tiny gaps between the branches. Poll had cut a handful of long grasses to brush away their footprints. He tossed the grasses to one side of the glen and moved to the center of the clearing. He drew his sword and stood in the stiff, awkward, ritual battle posture of the Compound. After a moment he shook his head, repositioned his stance and held the sword loosely, point down. His chest filled with a deep breath. He exhaled slowly. Still and watchful, he waited.

Relieved, Jermanah released her own breath. Poll realized the futility in facing the rebel with the Compound's stilted fighting style. If the rebel still fought with only his knife, Poll's longer weapon would maintain the upper hand. She concentrated on remaining still and keeping the child quiet so as not to be a distraction to her protector. Her silent pleas for their safety rose to the Double Moons.

Kierigh bent with his hands on his knees, drawing in deep draughts of air. But for that moon-cursed guard's interference, he'd have taken the child. He rubbed at his healed shoulder. That woman couldn't be the healer. One who could use forbidden magic to heal wouldn't have been tasked as the babe's caregiver. He shook away his concern and glanced both directions along the empty roadway. The guards were either dead or escaping. The women had fled as well. He didn't care about them. He had one objective, one path to follow.

He sheathed his knife, whistled a series of signals to his men and started after the child. The guard had made no attempt to disguise the direction of their escape. Not that doing so would matter. This was Kierigh's forest. His home.

He wasted no thoughts on what lay ahead, or behind, concentrating only on recovering the babe before it could be returned to the Compound and taken to the king's Stronghold. After a series of deep breaths, he followed the trio with a ground-covering lope he could continue for a great distance.

Kierigh slowed and angled toward a small clearing, listening to the unusual noises. Cautious, he paused before stepping into the open space. A war beast munched leaves from a low hanging branch. The animal watched him warily, but didn't deviate from chewing. Kierigh gave a sharp nod. The animal wouldn't travel far from its companion. The rider, and the child, would be near.

Darting his gaze into the forest shadows, Kierigh jogged past the animal. Signs of the large animal's two-way passage stood in stark relief against the heavy forest undergrowth. The guard would make his stand where there was room to fight. If the guard intended to protect the woman there would be no ambush. A wise man among the Compound guards was a rarity.

Patches of sunlight lightened the forest indicating the next clearing. Hidden by the trees, Kierigh splayed his hands on his knees. He took a few deep breaths and released them out slowly. The usual movement and chatter of small animals and birds was absent. Drawing his knife, he straightened and stepped into the narrow patch of sunlight.

The guard waited in the center of a clearing, sword held in a relaxed hand. His useless ornamental cloak lay in a crumpled heap on the ground. Without moving his head, Kierigh scanned the clearing. Neither the child nor the woman were in sight, but they wouldn't be far.

"I have come for the child." He kept his tone calm and insistent.

"You have no right to the babe. You will not take him."

"The Compound and the king have no right."

"Divine right. The child of the Double Moon will fulfill great destiny."

Sensing doubt in the guard's recitation of the ritual words, Kierigh arched his eyebrow. "Nonetheless, I will take the child."

"You will not."

Managing a sad expression, Kierigh held out his knife, hoping to lull his opponent into a mistake of overconfidence. "A knife against your sword doesn't seem a fair fight."

Impassive, the guard shrugged. Kierigh gave him a grim smile, lifted his knife in salute and stepped forward. The guard presented his sword to mimic Kierigh's salute then lowered the blade to an offensive position.

Kierigh met the guard's thrust with his knife but the force nearly wrenched the weapon from his grasp. Surprise, he repelled a series of rapid blows. He'd underestimated the guard. The man ignored the Compound's formulaic battle training and fought with calm desperation. Reluctant to admit a growing admiration, Kierigh watched the man's shoulder, judging his next moves. They fought in silence with only the rasp of their breathing and grunts from heavy blows mixing with the clang of metal against metal.

Kierigh pressed a small advantage and forced the guard across the clearing near to a stone outcropping. He'd honor the brave man with a swift death.

From the rise and fall of battle sounds, Jermanah knew Poll attempted to keep the rebel from her hiding place. The unfamiliar clangs and shivering slide of metal against metal frightened her as greatly as the hungry dark cave entrance. She gnawed on the inside of her cheek and clutched the child against her chest, covering his head with her palm to block the sounds. Thank the moons the babe remained quiet.

The fighting drew near. The harshness of the fighters' breathing scraped against her sensitive nerves. She ducked her head and bit her lower lip to contain a scream. A sharp gasp, a groan, and the thud of a falling body brought tears to her eyes. No. Not Poll.

She hunched over the child to peek through the sparse lower branches of the concealing bushes. Poll lay on his side, his face turned from her. He struggled to rise, but collapsed with the soft whoosh of escaping breath. He didn't move again.

The rebel pushed at Poll's shoulder with the bloody tip of his long knife. He glanced toward her hiding place, retrieved Poll's sword and slid the blade through his belt. Jermanah pressed against the bushes at her back. The hope he'd leave, allowing her to find her way to the Compound died.

The branches above her rustled and fell. A flushed face appeared, blocking the sky. "Give me the child."

Despite her fear, Poll's bravery inspired defiance to rise within her and she found her voice. "No."

"You'll be unable to move from the bushes with the child in your arms."

"Then I will not leave." She had the patience born of long hours of solitude within the Compound. She could wait until he grew frustrated. Perhaps. She'd never excelled at remaining still, her frequent lack earning her extra chores or punishments.

His eyebrows arched then bunched together over his frown. "You will."

She shook her head.

With a huff of breath, he reached into her hiding place,

grabbed her arm and yanked her to her feet. She clutched at the child, but the rebel caught the slipping babe with one large hand and cradled the boy in crook of his arm. Long strides carried him across the clearing.

Jermanah cried out in denial.

He glanced at her outstretched hand for a long moment before laying the child on Poll's cloak. He returned to bushes, wrapped his hands around her upper arms and easily lifted her from her hiding place. He set her on her feet and kept one hand on her arm until she stood without wobbling. The care surprised her.

Until he issued a command. "Come with me."

Jermanah crossed her arms. "I will not."

He merely looked at her and arched one eyebrow. Unable to stand under the intensity of his expression, she dipped her head. Her gaze fell on Poll's body. She swallowed her dismay, rushed to him and sank to her knees. Without conscious thought she gathered the power to heal.

The rebel grasped her shoulder and hauled her to her feet. She reached for Poll, but her cry of desperation died on her lips. With his long fingers wrapped around her wrist, the rebel tugged her across the clearing. She stumbled when he bent to lift the child.

Jermanah struggled against his firm grip, but the man jerked her along behind him. She reached toward Poll one final time before the rebel forced her under the dark canopy of trees. A faint disturbance of air arched from her fingers, engulfing Poll within a shimmering glow. She prayed it was enough to grant his soul peace.

four

The rebel set grueling pace. Even pulling a reluctant woman and carrying a babe, he moved confidently through the forest. Jermanah strained to catch her breath. Daily walks around the Compound and her assigned physical duties hadn't been enough to prepare her for the night's procession and this headlong rush through the trees. She worked at dislodging a leafy branch tangled in her hair before her captor yanked her forward again and her hair was ripped from her scalp.

The babe snuffled and whimpered in preparation for a full-throated cry. Her breasts ached in response, growing heavy and tender. The child was hungry, triggering the magic controlling her body.

"You, uh, sir?"

"Kierigh."

"Stop, please." Irritation etched deep in his features when he faced her. No matter his thoughts about her, Jermanah's duty was to the babe. "The child is hungry. If you'll allow me to feed him, perhaps he will quiet again."

"You are able to nurse the child?"

Jermanah winced at the harsh challenge. His gaze roamed over her and a strange force twisted her stomach to knots. She ignored the confusing sensation, squared her shoulders and lifted her gaze to the disbelief in his expression. Anger replaced her confusion. Before she thought better of the action, she slapped away his mocking smile.

Astonished at the sharp pain in her palm, she cradled her hand against her stomach. His eyebrows lowered until they met over his icy blue eyes. His lips pressed to a firm line of disapproval. He grabbed her upper arm and his hand brushed her breast.

Arching her shoulders forward, Jermanah moaned. Kierigh took a quick step back, his hand still lifted. Questions stole the anger from his expression.

Jermanah caught her lip between her teeth and closed her eyes. The ache had flashed into pain when he touched her. This must be how the potion insured she'd feed the child. When the pain receded and she was able to catch her breath, she said, "I must nurse the child. There is pain if I don't. I was made to drink a tea to produce milk for the babe. I believe perhaps the mixture was too strong."

Kierigh glanced at the babe. The tiny boy's cries turned insistent, his face red with the effort. Kierigh jiggled the child but the wails continued. "We'll rest here. You may feed the boy."

Thankful for both the opportunity to rest and to ease her discomfort, Jermanah sat on the trunk of a fallen tree. Kierigh lay the babe in her arms and she turned away for privacy.

"No."

Her tangled hair swirled around her shoulders. "You said I could feed him."

"You will not turn from me. I won't allow any

Compound tricks. I'll watch to assure you don't harm the boy." His eyebrows arched and he cocked his head as though daring her to argue.

Righteous anger fueled her reply. "Harm? I'm not the one who prevented him from the joy and privilege of his foretold destiny. I'm not the one who destroyed the sacred procession of the Double Moon. I'm not the one—"

"Who caused the death of his mother? In the name of your sacred Double Moon?" Kierigh spread his legs and folded his arms across his chest.

Jermanah lowered her gaze to the child. Unable to hide her anguish, her voice was wavered. "I am not that one either."

"You are an acolyte of the Compound. As such, you are part of the lie. And so, responsible for the deaths of many."

Tears stung, blurring her vision. The babe wiggled in her arms, full of life and need. The manner of his birth and the empty eyes of the old woman haunted her. Would haunt her for a lifetime. Poll lay dead in the forest. She met Kierigh's harsh gaze. "I know."

Tension drained from Kierigh's neck and jaw and he struggled to distance himself from the woman. He lowered his gaze to block the temptation of her wide, glistening brown eyes. There was no place in his life for softness. He couldn't afford to care. He'd return the child to its father then decide what to do with the acolyte.

He cleared the odd reluctance from his throat. "Feed the child. We must soon move on."

She nodded and gave him her back.

"No. You will nurse the babe so I may protect him from your trickery."

Eyes wide, she stared at him. "I would never harm a child. I am a healer."

He grasped desperately at his fading anger. "What about the boy's mother?"

Her gaze didn't waver. "I was unable to prevent her death. She didn't wish to live without her child. I was given no chance to stop the life flowing from her. I... failed."

An apology formed on Kierigh's lips. Gritting his teeth, he squelched the unusual desire to offer comfort. She was an acolyte and part of the Compound. Even though she appeared innocent and vastly different from the other women sequestered there, he dared not take any chances.

"Feed the child, woman."

The tangles of her magnificent hair swept forward to hide her face. "My name is Jermanah."

She lay the boy on her lap and held him in place with one hand while she unfastened the robe. Kierigh pulled the sword from his belt and rested the hilt against a tree. He sat and leaned into the rough bark, rubbing the itch from the new scar on his shoulder.

The woman slid the robe to one side exposing a pale, creamy breast, the nipple swollen and firm. He licked sudden dryness from his lips and struggled to swallow. She lifted the child and guided his seeking mouth to the nipple. She winced as if in pain, then sighed.

His body lifted in response.

She glanced at him from under the cover of her hair. Fascinated, Kierigh followed the flow of a deep red blush from her face to her smooth breast. Desire and jealousy rose in him. Desire he understood, for once he'd stopped to take notice she was—

He jerked. Dangerous thoughts. But jealousy? Of a babe? He shook his head and angled his body to afford her some small privacy.

After retrieving a flat stone from the pouch at his waist,

he slipped his knife from the scabbard. He spit on the stone and began to hone the knife's long, fine edge. Battle left tiny nicks needing constant attention. He drew the knife across the wet stone. The rasp of metal against stone and the soft suckling of the child filled the clearing with a strange, comforting familiarity.

Kierigh contemplated the easy silence. One day his fighting would cease and he'd have the opportunity to take a woman of his own and create a family. The knife caressed the honing stone and glided over the damp surface then stopped. No, such a dream was beyond obtaining. He would destroy the Compound and the king to save the children of the land. What woman would have him then?

He had nothing to offer. No home but the forest, no property to provide a living. He knew nothing but fighting and fighting held no promise of a stable life.

He glanced at Jermanah. And now any woman would pale in comparison to the acolyte nursing the babe. The power of her healing remained as the constant itch in his shoulder, but now it was the strength hidden beneath her innocence that called to him. Drew him to her.

The knife slid back and forth. He breathing grew shallow and heat radiated through his body. He clutched the stone. To sink his hands into the length of her hair and comb away the leaves and tangles might be the closest he came to heaven. Had he the time, he'd count the myriad of colors of the silky mass as the strands flowed through his fingers. Was the smoothness of her breast as soft as he imagined? The knife moved faster across the stone. Then he'd lift her hair and press his lips to—

"The child has been fed."

He jerked. The stone clattered against a tree root protruding from the ground. An odd rise of guilt heated the back of his neck. He wiped the knife on his pant leg then stood and slid the blade into the scabbard. He picked up the stone and the sword, returning each to its proper place. He spent a long moment adjusting his belt, the sword, the knife, the front of his pants, before turning to Jermanah.

"Are you ready to continue, Jermanah?" He tested her name on his lips and smiled.

The suspicion in her narrowed eyes burned with contempt. "Yes, we're ready. He should sleep now. I will carry him."

Her reaction was no more than he deserved. Still, he stepped closer and held out his hand. She stared at his palm before struggling to her feet. "You don't need to drag me. I'll follow."

Stung by her refusal of his assistance, Kierigh stomped from the ungrateful acolyte. "Then follow."

Much later her soft, wistful, "Are we going much further?" stopped him dead in his tracks. He turned to witness her stumble over an exposed root. She steadied herself and leaned against a thin tree trunk. "I believe I've been walking for days now."

Her weak smile tugged at his heart and the last of his anger drained from him. "It's not far. I'll carry the child now."

Jermanah nodded and waited for him to come to her. After she arranged the babe in the crook of his arm he studied the infant. Unaffected and unharmed after the events of his first day of life, dark crescents of lashes lay against soft, rounded cheeks. The tiny mouth puckered as if still at suck. Kierigh positioned an edge of the cloth over the babe's face and returned to his path.

At the crunch and rustle of Jermanah's footsteps, he rolled his gaze toward the sky. He'd need to teach her the way quiet and stealthy movements if she meant to traverse the forest. An ancient, nearly deaf grandfather would hear her coming. No. He firmed the weakening crack in his resolve. She wouldn't be in the forest long enough to require teaching.

Jermanah's breath came in short, heavy gasps she struggled to hide from her captor. Kierigh continued at a quick pace, but at least he wasn't dragging her. She rubbed her sore wrist and winced at a tender spot. A trio of purple bruises marked the shape of his fingers.

She scanned the forest and found strange comfort in the heavy canopy of trees. The closed-in feeling she'd experienced often in the Compound had disappeared. The air didn't squeeze her lungs. Dark, shadowed places under the trees didn't cause a rise of debilitating panic. She would not to think badly of the Compound. The thick walled, barren enclosure was her home, if she still had a position there.

A sense of the familiar surrounded a grove trees. She peered around a tiny clearing, recognizing the strange animal shapes of the rock formation at the far edge. They'd passed this way already. This time, though, Kierigh turned and led her from the clearing by a different path. Arching her eyebrows, she followed, but paid more attention to her surroundings.

They entered another tiny, clear area she immediately recognized. She stopped, planted her hands at her hips and waited. Moments later the rebel realized she wasn't behind him and returned. Only a small space separated them when he stopped and towered over her.

Too close. She took a step back then poked him in the

center of his chest. At the touch of her finger to the bare skin at the vee of his tunic, a slow, tingling burn flowed from her hand up her arm. Instead of examining the feeling, she poked him again. "We've been through this part of the forest already. Why are you leading me in circles? Are you lost?"

His deep laughter echoed through the trees, startling the child from sleep. Kierigh jiggled the babe until the boy settled. "Most wouldn't notice the circuitous route to my camp. You're very observant."

"This was on purpose? You made me walk extra distance?" She poked him a third time. "You are a cruel man."

Avoiding her finger, Kierigh stepped to one side. "It's necessary. No one takes a direct route to any camp to protect the safety of the men and women there. The safety of these people is my highest priority."

"You made me walk so far for no reason? Why hide your camp from me? You'll undoubtedly kill me as you have so many others this day." Jermanah fell silent. The crumpled form of Poll's lonely body filled her memory.

"I won't kill you." Kierigh's words were soft and laced with sorrow. She chanced a glance into his expressive eyes. He didn't enjoy the fighting and killing. The pain and regret faded, replaced by a dark intensity. Tremors coursed up her spine.

"Unless you give me reason. Come, we'll go directly there."

"Kierigh." Jermanah hurried after him and touched his arm. He froze and brief flashes of emotions she didn't recognize passed over his face. She waited for him to look at her, but he didn't. "I'm sorry."

He gave a sharp nod and angled to step passed between

two boulders. Jermanah caught her breath. Magic? Even after witnessing his passage, she couldn't detect an opening large enough for a man. She tiptoed forward until she was within arm's length of the cold stone. A narrow fissure split the rock.

Too dark. She couldn't follow him there. Neither did she dare risking the anger laying so close to the surface of his emotions. She needed to discover the illusive courage the Seer told her lay hidden within her. But any time she'd attempted to brave a dark, enclosed space, terror had overtaken her and she'd failed.

If her life was the only consideration, she'd refuse to follow the rebel. But he carried the babe. The care and protection of the child of the Double Moon was her Compound-directed responsibility. Should there be a woman within the camp who was able to feed the babe, Jermanah was still accountable for his safety and well-being.

Catching her lower lip between her teeth, she drew a deep breath and stepped into the narrow opening. Tall, deeply shaded rocks surrounded her. She held her hands out to the sides, running her fingers along the cool, smooth surface to keep the stone from crushing her. The edges of her vision pressed in on her like the darkness. A moment before a scream tickled her throat, the faint glow of daylight so like the window in her room appeared. She focused on the small patch of brightness and dashed forward.

She stumbled into daylight and slammed against Kierigh's broad back. He grunted and held his free arm to the side to steady her. A fresh breeze carried the scents of wood smoke. Relief filled her lungs and she clung to his arm to peer around his shoulder.

People dressed in drab clothing of browns and greens moved about tending small, smokeless fires preparing food. The aromas tantalized and her empty stomach complained. Kierigh's chuckle rumbled in response. "Come. We'll find you something to break your fast."

The repeated growling of her stomach made denial impossible, still she found the will to force conviction into her words. "I need nothing from you."

Kierigh angled to stare at her and something—an odd glint she didn't understand—flashed in his eyes. "But I need you."

Throwing back her shoulders, she fisted her hands at her hips. "Oh?"

One of Kierigh's eyebrows arched and he handed her the babe.

five

The Highest took time to bathe, washing the dust of the road and the smell of death and battle from her skin. Naked before the tall mirror in her chamber, she sighed. The rebels had ruined her procession. The child of the Double Moon was lost to her. Her special guards undoubtedly dead. Only a few older priestesses had wandered back to the Compound.

She'd send these elderly women to the Stronghold, keeping a select few of the remaining guards to search for the blasted brat. When successful, she'd move to the Stronghold as well.

She dreaded facing the king with no child to placate his anger. The loss of potential power gained from the babe's sacrifice would infuriate Zigor. Smoothing the frown lines from her forehead, she lifted her breasts in her hands. She'd ease his loss.

For this audience with the king, she chose a form-fitting bodice of sheer golden silk. A long, translucent skirt hinted at the curves of her body. The Highest reached for a small clay pot and carefully rouged her nipples. She applied the same color to the fair curls at the juncture of her thighs. The smear of color across a man afterwards was delightful.

Swaying before the mirror, she dressed with meticulous care. Satisfied with her appearance, she wrapped herself with a long, dark cloak and entered a narrow, empty passageway through a hidden panel behind the mirror. Faint glowing circles from light-producing rocks highlighted the long, underground walk to the Stronghold.

Her determined strides covered the distance to a spy-hole located outside Zigor's chambers. At the low rumble of voices, she blew out an impatient breath and sat on the low, cushioned bench provided for her. Agitated, she tapped one foot.

When silence emanated from the room behind her, she adjusted her clothing for maximum effect, peeked through the small hole, and stepped into the king's private chambers. He stood with his back to her on a wide, stone balcony overlooking a partially covered, enclosed courtyard. "Welcome, Highest."

"Zigor." She wrapped her arms about his waist. After a brief hesitation, she slid her hands beneath his tunic to caress him.

Ignoring her protest, Zigor stepped forward, turned and leaned one hip against the balcony railing. "So. You lost the child."

Heat rose from her chest to her face. His spies got to him before she had an opportunity to control the damage. She'd taken too long in her preparations. She spread her hands in a placating manner. "Zigor, the child was born. A boy as foretold. Rebels attacked the procession upon our return journey to the Compound."

He raked his gaze over her body. She arched to present

her breasts to him. He grinned. "You seem none the worse for the battle."

"What are we to do now?"

Eyes narrowed, Zigor motioned and the Highest rushed to his arms. He held her hands behind her back, preventing further caresses. "I have another for the sacrifice."

"Another child was born?"

"Yes." Zigor chuckled. "Six Double Moons past, shortly after I gained the throne. I have held him here in the Stronghold." He released her to ring a tinny chime then tugged her close, grazing her tender inner lip with his teeth.

A panel on the near wall slid open with a soft whoosh. A tall man with short-cropped dark blond hair stepped into the room and waited. The Highest clutched at Zigor's upper arms. "What is he doing here?"

"This is the one I just told you about."

Squinting at the man's meek posture, she frowned and shook her head. "No, this is the rebel who attacked the procession. He cut his hair."

Zigor gave a disbelieving snort, crossed to the man and clasped him on the shoulder. The man winced. "You are no rebel, are you, Daud?"

Returning his gaze to her, Zigor continued, his back ram-rod straight, his bearing proud and masterful. Ah, then, this was how she wanted him. "Daud has never set foot beyond the Stronghold walls. I have held him apart from all, including you, my dear Highest. At this coming sacrifice Daud holds great power that will be delivered to me."

Cautious, the Highest moved closer. How had she mistaken this man for the rebel? Of course, the hair was wrong. His carriage and demeanor were far from that of the rebel. This man was a magnificent specimen though. She pressed against the king's back and kissed his neck. "So I see. May I examine him more closely?"

"Not at this time. First, I wish to show you how Daud brings immense power to the sacrifice." He angled to tweak her nipple then shoved her to the side. She hid her scowl and offered him her attention.

Zigor pointed to the floor. "Daud, kneel before me." The man did. "Bring forth a child."

Eyes blazing with fury, the man lifted his head. "No child will appear for you to defile. The children are held in safety."

"You defy me?"

"We do."

Zigor's echoing slap snapped Daud's head to the side. He collapsed to the floor. When his gaze lifted to Zigor the defiance had disappeared. Enthralled with the spectacle, the Highest watched his face soften until his features appeared younger. Tears filled his eyes. A high scream burst from his lips. He scrambled backward with frantic kicks of his legs.

After slamming against the wall, he crawled to Zigor's ornate desk and slipped into the knee space. Curled in a tight ball, a high pitched child's voice wailed. "No no no no no no no no no no."

Zigor turned from the noise and shrugged. "You see, Highest, many people inhabit Daud's body. With the sacrifice of that body my power will grow exponentially at the ending of each life. I don't know how many lives are contained within that body, but imagine, Highest, imagine. My power will soar. I will become greater than I would be after many, many cycles of sacrifice. All with just this one body's death."

"I don't understand. How did there come to be many in one?"

"Observe." Zigor crossed to the desk and dragged Daud out by the front of his tunic. The high, childish cries continued until Zigor pressed his palms to Daud's temples. "Be gone."

The instant silence startled the Highest. She moved closer. Zigor arranged the unresponsive body in a kneeling position and signaled her to examine Daud. She studied his face and bent to touch his tear damp cheek. "He appears so much like the rebel. It's uncanny."

She peered into dull, lifeless eyes and shuddered delicately at the emptiness reflecting back at her. "Tell me, how do you gain more power from this?"

After tugging her against his body, Zigor crushed his lips over hers. She welcomed the thrust of his tongue and arched her back when he grabbed her hips and rubbed against her. He bit her earlobe. "What would you desire from this man?"

She glanced at the still form. Possibilities settled low in her body. "Pleasure."

"For you only?"

She smiled against Zigor's mouth and slipped her hand between their bodies to cup him. "Of course not, my king. For us both."

He moved from her embrace. "I shall grant your wish. Watch now as a new source of power grows in Daud's body. One we will control and use to take our pleasures."

Cupping his palms over Daud's head to touch his temples, Zigor gave a command. "I call for..." A smile twitched the king's lips. "How old would you prefer this one to be?"

"A choice?"

"I allow you this one choice. For our mutual pleasure."

"I have always favored younger men."

Zigor scowled. Threat and promise colored his low growl.

Now wouldn't be the time to anger him, not when she was so curious and in need of pleasure. She waved one hand in dismissal. "For the occasional pleasure only. For none can compare with my lord king." She lowered in a curtsy designed to highlight the rouged tips of her breasts.

He ignored her display. "And I have had my fill of boys. Perhaps one freshly into manhood?"

"Yes. He'd have a great deal of stamina then." Anticipation shivered over her skin.

"Agreed." Zigor tightened his grip at the Daud's temples. "I call for a male of five Double Moons to pleasure the Highest and myself."

The man's body jerked and his eyes rolled back in his head.

"Come forth now, Hov." Zigor winked at her. "I prefer to name my creations."

Eyes closed, the body slumped. When the eyelids lifted, awareness brightened the dull eyes, followed by the haze of desire. He straightened and glanced at Zigor before languorously sliding his glittering gaze to her. His lips pulled into a sensuous smile and he drew his tongue across his lower lip. Fascinated, she mimicked his action. His heavily lidded gaze studied her while he pressed his mouth to the bulge tenting Zigor's pants.

six

Jermanah followed Kierigh to a low lean-to at the far edge of the clearing. The heavy weight of the camp's curiosity followed them. Hatred hovered like a shimmer of heat in the clear air. Surely their hate was directed at the Compound. Or did they hate her? Not that the focus of that hatred mattered. To most, she and the Compound were be one in the same. Refusing to meet the heated glares, she ducked her head.

Kierigh rummaged through a few sacks and bundles stored under the rude shelter. He held out a crumpled pile of cloth. "Give me the babe and take these. You'll be less... conspicuous if you remove the Compound robes. There is a private area behind the lean-to. Don't attempt to escape."

After exchanging the babe for the clothing, she moved behind the structure. She sagged against a rough post and bit her lip. She'd become lost in the forest before she'd taken ten paces from the camp. And then only if the rebel was slow in coming after her. The only recourse—be strong and face her destiny with composure and dignity. There was no time for mourning what she'd lost, what more might be taken from her. No time for fear and weeping. She took a deep, fortifying breath and inspected the bundle.

A pair of loose leggings, a long, sleeveless tunic and a soft short-sleeved under tunic that opened down the front. Suede slippers and a small wooden comb.

She didn't understand this rebel leader. He was harsh and angry, determined in his action. A hard man. She rubbed her fingers along the teeth of the comb. Then he offered her a small kindness.

Neither did she understand her unusual reactions to him. Being near him made her forget the Compound and everything she'd worked for her entire life. His silent presence eased the pain of the long night. When death surrounded her, he made her feel alive.

She'd never worn anything but loose Compound robes. The serviceable clothing felt odd against her skin, but having her arms nearly bare to the slight breeze seduced her exhausted senses. She studied the slippers from many angles. As an acolyte she'd never worn foot coverings. Those were reserved for those honored as high priestesses. The forced trek through the forest hadn't really harmed her feet, so she shrugged and carried the slippers and comb and returned to Kierigh. The robe remained in a discarded pile behind the lean-to.

The rebel hadn't moved except to lay the child on a blanket at his feet. He stood, arms crossed, watching the lean-to, waiting for her. She offered him a shy smile. "Thank you. I've never worn such fine clothing."

Kierigh clenched his teeth. There were no fine garments in a rebel camp. All clothing was rough and uniquely colored, enabling his followers to melt into the forest shadows. He drew breath for a sharp retort, but the happy glow of Jermanah's expression halted his words. She was serious.

She held her arms out to the sides and looked down at herself, the movement stretching the cloth tightly over her full breasts. He closed his eyes but the tantalizing sight remained lodged in his mind.

"This clothing allows more freedom than the Compound robes." She twirled in a circle, her hair swirling in a vibrant cloud. "And I do need the comb. But, I've lost the tie for my hair. Would you have something I might use?"

Without considering his actions, he stepped around the babe and tugged at the twine holding a bag closed. With a gesture of one finger, he encouraged her to turn. He lifted his fingers to her hair. The multi-colored strands were as soft as he'd imagined. Steeling himself against the sensations, he gathered the length at her nape and secured the long tail with a loose loop of string.

"That will do until you have time to contain it properly." He allowed his fingers to linger at the base of her neck then brushed the tips along her shoulder. She turned toward him. Her warm skin trembled under his hand. Or did he tremble against her skin? He wasn't sure. He didn't care.

As if forming words, her lips moved. But if she spoke, he couldn't hear over the pounding of his heart. His chest tightened as though he'd run many leagues. His breath stalled in his throat. Her tongue darted out, wetting her lips. A groan rumbled through him.

At the questions in her eyes and the tilt of her face, he accepted her unknowing invitation. Maintaining the distance between their bodies, he lowered his mouth to hers. Desire coursed through him, hotter than the summer sun. He allowed himself only gentlest of pressure in his kiss. More. He wanted, needed more of her. But she was a bitch of the Compound. He didn't care. He forced himself to lift his head bare inches from her.

Her eyes had fallen closed. Her lips parted. The soft breath of her sigh caressed his cheek. Her fingers twitched against his shoulder and she leaned closer. She offered—why resist? Slanting his mouth across hers, he touched the fullness of her lower lip with his tongue. Tension quivered his muscles at the sweet taste of her innocent kiss. Her mouth softened, offering him the growing honey of newly awakened passion.

Her restless fingers moved over his heart and a rush of power flowed to his shoulder. He jerked stepped back. She stumbled but his hand on her arm held her steady. He couldn't do this. To be an acolyte meant she was untouched and innocent. He wouldn't take advantage and lose himself in the process. He turned from the questions filling her dazed expression and knelt to pick up the babe. When he rose he held the child against his chest. The tiny body was an ineffectual shield.

He cleared his throat and turned away before the luminescence of her confused brown eyes pulled him further into her innocence. "Come, I will show you where you can rest. Food will be brought for you. Should you need anything, you must ask."

No. He couldn't afford to lose his convictions, his direction now.

Jermanah took a shaky breath and followed Kierigh. Her knees felt weak and wobbly. Delightful tingles danced over her skin. The new clothing rubbed her breasts increasing the tight aching of her nipples. Perhaps the time neared to feed the child, but she wasn't sure. Without the proper training, how was she to know what to do?

She touched her fingertips to her lower lip. Sensations

gathered there and the pulsing intensity made her pause. She ached so. Kierigh said she must ask for what she needed. But how did she ask for something she didn't understand? She willed calm to her overcome senses and rebellious body. But when she looked at Kierigh's back, the play of his muscles under his loose tunic—oh, the tingles.

He led her across the small camp to another sturdy lean-to set against a rocky outcropping. A rickety table sat partially under the slanting roof, with two squat benches fully under the open sky. Kierigh pulled a roll of blankets from near the rock wall and spread them over a low, grass-filled pallet. He smoothed the wrinkled surface.

"Rest here. I'll send food."

Unsure her legs could hold her upright much longer, she sank to the end of the pallet. Kierigh placed the child in her arms. Curling on her side, she rested her hand on the child's belly, holding him close. "Thank you. I'm so tired."

Silent, he nodded. Even when she closed her eyes, she sensed him watching her for a long moment before exhaustion carried her to sleep.

Jermanah woke with the late afternoon sun warming her feet. She reached for the child and patted empty blankets. Gone. Panic surged from the pit of her stomach and she lurched to her knees.

An old woman sat on the bench with the babe resting across her lap. She smiled and beckoned to Jermanah. "The boy was awake, but you needed more rest. So I bathed and cared for him while you slept."

She waved a gnarled hand indicating the table. A round loaf and a small chunk of soft cheese sat partially covered by a clean cloth. "This should fill your belly until the evening meal."

Jermanah tore off a hunk of bread and dipped a large portion of honey from a small wooden bowl onto the bite. Leaning sideways, the old woman poured her a mug of water.

"Thank you. It's been a long time since I last ate. I'm very hungry."

"Eat up, dearie. You need extra when nursing a wee one."

"Is he hungry?" Concern for the babe stole her hunger and set the bread aside to focus on her body. The ache hadn't returned. Perhaps it wasn't yet time. Or had the herbs worn off? She had no more of the herbs if she needed to replenish the magic.

The woman chuckled. "He will be when he wakes. Eat. I enjoy the feel of a young one on my lap."

While she nibbled on her bread, Jermanah scanned the camp. Kierigh stood nearby and she watched him from under her lashes. A second man paused at his side then started toward her. Kierigh used one arm across the man's chest to hold him in place until Jermanah finished her meal. Then the men stepped forward together and she smiled a welcome.

"Jermanah, this is the child's father."

Odd disappointment caused a sharp ache in her chest and she struggled to maintain her smile while indicating the bench across from her. The scruffy man sat.

Refusing to meet her gaze, he spoke quickly. "I just returned from the fishing at sunrise. I'd been home sooner but the seas roll treacherous this season. I could have saved my mate...and her dam."

Jermanah reached across the table and rested her palm

against the man's arm. He jerked. His furtive actions disturbed her. But no, he was the babe's father and had lost his mate, his family. It was possible he'd never been to a rebel camp before, and was nervous. This she understood. "No, the Compound is too strong. More likely you would be upon the pyre as well."

Loyalty to the Compound warred with Jermanah's love for the child she'd had under her care for less than a day. The will of the Double Moon had chosen this boy. Yet just this short time away from the overbearing priestesses made her question her own convictions. Experiencing this tiny bit of a much different life, and the freedom found in a hidden campsite offered her the ability to make her own decisions.

Tension drained from her neck and shoulders. The babe was too young to be offered choices, and she—despite her ability to provide nourishment—she was a stranger. No longer compelled to return to the Compound with the child, she listened to her heart.

A child needed his own kin.

She motioned to the old woman who gave the man his son. "Your son is strong. Protect him well."

"I will, lady. I'll leave the village. Move far away. None will know of his birth."

Awkward, he held his son and stared at the small swaddled bundle. A slow, incredulous smile lit his dirty face. He rose to kneel at Jermanah's feet, dipped his head in respect and asked, "What is the child called?"

"He has no name."

"Bless him with your choice?" Hope filled the man's request.

But she'd been part the Compound procession. She'd been there when his mate died. The agony Jermanah felt at her part in the woman's death returned and she shook her head. "You shouldn't honor me."

The man dropped his gaze. "I'd be grateful for my son to bear the name chosen by the one who saved him from the Compound."

She glanced at Kierigh who simply watched her with a confusing intensity burning in his light, blue eyes. The father didn't know she was an acolyte. As if knowing her thoughts, Kierigh shrugged one shoulder. Her heart beat faster. He had no reason to protect her or keep that knowledge from the boy's father. She took a steadying breath. "Are you certain this is what you want?"

"Yes, lady."

The babe should bear a special name. A name of strength to honor, not her, but the guard who had died protecting them. "Poll. His name is Poll."

"Poll. Yes, thank you, lady." The man grinned and stood. All too quickly he was gone and the child with him.

The old woman sighed. "Perhaps soon my own grandbabies will fill my lap." Placing her palms against the tabletop, she rose. "I must see to the meal. Remain here and I'll send word when it's time to eat. Perhaps later Kierigh will take you to the springs." Her old eyes glittered with mischief.

Kierigh shooed her away with a wave of his hand and sat in the spot she vacated. He drew his knife and sliced the cheese. He offered part on the tip of his knife but Jermanah shook her head. Tears burned her eyes and the lump growing in her throat wouldn't allow her to eat.

"Are you rested?"

The sudden loss of the child who had been hers such a short time brought the rise of strange grief. Unable to ignore the questions in Kierigh's gaze and not wanting to search within herself for those answers, she replied, "Yes, thank you. Did you rest?"

"No. There is much to do."

Sounds from the camp filtered through the silence surrounding them. She studied the muscles of his jaw and throat while he chewed and swallowed. He seemed deep in thought and oblivious to her presence. A question burned in her mind and she had to ask, "Why do you fight the Compound and the king?"

Kierigh choked on a bite of cheese. He glanced at her from the corner of his eye while taking a long swallow of water. "You're very forthright."

"Yes, it's gotten me in trouble many times. The priestesses say I'm too curious."

"Asking questions is the best way to learn."

"So the Seer told me. Many times."

Kierigh shoved his food to one side and leaned toward her. The intensity in his gaze intrigued her and she attempted to catalog the emotions she imagined there. "I fight to save children from my brother's fate. As is the...custom, he was taken to the king's Stronghold. I don't believe he was sacrificed. We were born of the same womb. Somehow, I would know of his death."

"Sacrificed? No, Kierigh, you're wrong. Children born under the Double Moon are cherished and honored, both in the Compound and the Stronghold." But as she spoke, Jermanah wondered why no one ever spoke of the male children. She'd never seen a priest or a male acolyte. But her place in the Compound was honored and... Her thoughts lost conviction. "I am a child of the Double Moon."

"While instructing you in their ways, the Compound has kept you innocent of the world and far from the machinations and the power both the king and your Highest struggle to obtain. If I could show you all this, show you the recent history of this land, you would see both the good and the bad. This knowledge would allow you to make your own decisions."

"You're very certain of yourself. Sure that your way is right."

"Perhaps not right, but true and honest."

Kierigh held her gaze and she dared not look away. She found no desire to look elsewhere. His face was strong and angular, the muscles moving just below the surface of his skin. Her lips tingled at though his pressed there again. She touched her mouth. Were these curious feelings part of his true and honest world?

A grin softened his expression. If this was his world, she ached to experience the sensations again. Longing filled her heart and her breasts grew heavy. She closed her eyes savoring the unusual feeling. Until pleasure turned to pain. She gasped and hunched her shoulders.

Worry filled Kierigh's expression. "Jermanah? What—"

Hot agony shot through her breast arrowing to her nipple. Cold sweat beaded on her forehead. Muffling a sob of pain, she bit her lip.

"Jermanah?" Kierigh leapt to his feet, toppling the bench.

"No, don't touch me. Pain." She grimaced and rested her forehead against the rough, wooden table.

Panic settled hard in Kierigh's gut. Drawing startled glances, he sped through the camp. Grandmother was working at the cook fire. He grabbed the old woman's arm. "Grandmother, Jermanah is in pain. I don't know what to do."

Her eyes narrowed. She peeled his fingers from her arm and patted his hand. "Go. I will follow."

After she disappeared into her hut, Kierigh whirled and returned to his lean-to. He skid to a stop behind Jermanah, reaching toward her shoulder but he jerked his hand back before he touched her. He let his fist drop to his side. She remained hunched over the table. Deep, ragged breaths shuddered through her slender body. In her distress, she didn't even recognize his presence.

He didn't care for the helplessness and didn't know how to respond to not knowing what to do. The feeling—far too close to failure.

Grandmother shoved his hip and keeping his gaze focused on Jermanah, he took Grandmother's small bundle and circled the table. Grandmother rested her wrinkled hand on Jermanah's arm.

A haze of anguish filled Jermanah's eyes. Grandmother brushed damp strands of hair back from the young woman's face. "What is it, child?"

"To nurse the babe... tea... too strong. Now... no child. Pain." Agony twisted her features.

Planting both hands on the sun-warmed table, Kierigh cleared his throat, but his voice remained gruff and filled with the concern he'd wished to keep hidden. "What is she talking about?"

Grandmother reached for her leather bundle. "Such is the way acolytes are prepared to nurse the newborn child. None will have born a child, for the legends say the chosen of the Double Moon must be nursed on milk from a virgin body. A tea filled with deep magic is given the young woman. She produces milk. Isn't that right, child?"

Jermanah dipped her head once in agreement. "Can't nurse... pain."

Grandmother's astute, understanding gaze touched

Kierigh's rising panic. The faintest hint of calm washed over him. She would know what to do. She always did.

Glancing at Jermanah for confirmation, Grandmother continued her explanation. "There is then a magical reaction in the acolyte's body that bonds her to the child. When the child becomes hungry her body fills in response. If the child doesn't nurse, the woman's body reacts with pain. A cruel way to ensure the babe will be cared for."

Jermanah whimpered and caught her lower lip between her teeth. Grandmother took her shoulders and forced her to turn until they were face to face. She lifted Jermanah's chin with a gnarled finger. "I may be able to prepare an infusion to wash the effects of the nursing tea from your body."

Kierigh didn't wait for Jermanah's response. "Do it."

seven

Careful in her movements, Jermanah straightened her shoulders and gave Kierigh and his grandmother a wan smile. Thank the moons the treatment had worked as quickly as the original infusion. "I'm sorry to cause so much trouble."

"Why didn't you tell me about this?" Kierigh's question was soft, as though he feared the strength of his voice would cause her pain.

Jermanah shrugged. "There wasn't any reason while the child needed me. I wasn't prepared to care for the child, I didn't receive the needed training. I didn't know. The Highest gave me the herbs after the child was born. As a punishment for angering her. After his father took him, I didn't think about nursing. Until the pain."

The muscles in Kierigh's neck stood in sharp relief although his expression remained calm. He was angry, angry with her for disturbing his camp. Or because she didn't understand enough to have known about the pain.

Interrupting her thoughts, Grandmother patted her shoulder. The old woman held her gaze for a long moment.

"Clear. My herbs have worked completely." She turned a smile to her grandson. "Her muscles are exhausted from fighting the pain. She'll be sore and miserable on the morrow unless you take her to the spring tonight. The warm water will sooth her."

Kierigh bowed his head. "Yes, Grandmother."

No, she'd been too much trouble to the rebel already. "I don't need—"

A weathered hand slapped the table. "You do. I insist and he will take you. I don't want you trying to find your way by yourself. You're too weak. Now, both of you go. I'll prepare a meal for your return."

She rose and strode away, her head high. Kierigh chuckled. "We'd best do as she advises. No one in camp argues with Grandmother and wins."

Pressing her forearms against the table, Jermanah stood. She took two shuffling steps and lurched to her knees with a soft cry. Kierigh knelt to lift her in his arms. Her ineffectual struggles made him growl low in his chest. "Hold still, woman. I don't wish to drop you."

He sat her on the table, retrieved a small bag and a large square of cloth from the lean-to and tossed them to her lap. She wrapped the bag's cord around one hand and, when he lifted her again, curled her other hand over his shoulder. She tangled her fingers in the soft, ragged ends of his dark blond hair.

His pace was smooth, and she floated toward some unknown destination. Warm and secure, her body tingled where his fingers flexed against her ribs. She inhaled his strong, earthy scent, the forest and something she liked but couldn't define. With her cheek resting against his shoulder she allowed his essence to flow through her. Fleeting thoughts slipped into words. "Am I too heavy?"

He grunted.

Jermanah wiggled until he loosened his hold and she could look past the firm angle of his jaw to his expression. The movement threatened to unbalance her and she clutched at his shoulder. "I said I could walk."

The straight line of his mouth softened. His gaze raked over her and she shivered with strange delight. "No. You're no burden. And we're at the springs."

Kierigh lowered her to a large, flat rock. He took a few backward steps, turned and pulled at his belt, letting it drop to the ground. "The water of this spring is hot and will ease your aches. When you're ready, I'll take you elsewhere to bathe. We don't sully the water in the springs."

"Where are you going?" Paralyzing fear filled her. He would leave her alone in the forest. She should have paid attention to their path. How would she find her way back? Or did he expect her to find her way from the forest alone?

"I go to the cold spring."

"You would bathe in cold water?"

He paused and angled the top half of his body to speak to her. "I will wash in the bathing place. I seek the cold water to..." Deep red colored his neck. "...to calm myself."

Admiring the play of muscles, she watched his long strides until he passed from sight. She'd overheard other acolytes discussing the attributes of the guards, and after discussing her concerns with the Seer, understood the concept of mating. Now, watching this man, she also understood the admiration and longing in the girls' voices. Those acolytes had soon disappeared from the Compound, one disgraced by pregnancy.

No, her thoughts about Kierigh weren't appropriate. Yet she found no censure resounding in her mind, no harsh priestess's voice promising punishment.

In less than a day she'd changed. Her thoughts, her dreams felt different now. Unknown, yet filled with the excitement of discovery. How could she return to that cloistered way and face a lifetime of having others choose her thoughts and direct her destiny?

Untangling her fingers from the bag, she stood and stretched despite the ache and pull of her muscles. The water bubbling from a multitude of tiny cracks in the rocks at the far side of the wide pool called to her. A soft haze of steam hovered inches above the rippling water.

She glanced toward the undergrowth where Kierigh had disappeared. A loud splash followed by an even louder gasp sparked her grin. The water must be cold indeed.

She dipped her toe into the spring, testing the heat. Ah, much warmer than any bathing tub she'd been allowed to use. This water was just at the edge of being too hot. After undressing she stepped into the silky water, holding her breath and moving carefully until the water reached her waist. At the far side of the small pool a large flat stone sat before a long fissure releasing a spray of bubbling water. She sat, wiggled in the slight depression in the stone and leaned forward to allow the water soothe her tired back and shoulders. She rolled her head from side to side and arched in delight.

When her back was thoroughly tingly, she slipped off the ledge to a second, lower rock where she sat with only her head above water. Her hair swirled and danced in the moving water. The length would tangle terribly, so she gathered the length to one shoulder, leaned back against an angled rock and allowed her eyelids to drift closed. This was contentment.

Frigid water lapping at his chest, Kierigh stood in the exact center of the cold spring. Chill bumps covered his arms and legs. The water was so cold he could barely draw breath.

He'd rushed to the pool and ripped his shirt over his head, but had to fight to lower his pants before diving into the frigid depth. He squinted down through the clear water. The cold hadn't provided the desired effect. Desire was the effect. Shaking his head at his folly, he sank lower into the icy water, swimming back and forth across the spring.

Shivering, he crawled from the water and rubbed at the blue tinge of his skin with his shirt. He squeezed water from his hair and tugged his pants over his damp legs. He tucked his shirt under his arm and picked up his boots. He was reluctant to leave Jermanah alone for too long.

After a moment of indecision, he stole through the trees to the hot spring. An overhang of thick branches concealed him while he studied the woman reclining in the steaming water.

She'd tilted her head back against the rock exposing the creamy skin of her neck and chest. Bubbling water hid her breasts but allowed tantalizing glimpses of her smooth, heat-pink skin. He devoured the sight of her. He clenched and unclenched his fists then backed further into the forest and rubbed his damp palms on the front of his thighs. His hand brushed against his body's insistent response and he choked back a gasp.

The cold spring again? Would the cold water shrink his desire this time? He was at a loss. Cold water, directing his thoughts elsewhere, losing himself in his plans. Nothing worked. No, there was only one way to find relief. One impossible way.

Splashing shattered the silence of the forest twilight and he imagined Jermanah rising from the pool. His sensitized hearing caught the soft swoosh of the drying cloth over her body. No. Don't think about the feel of her skin against his.

He broke a small twig between his fingers with a sharp snap to announce his presence. Jermanah gave a startled gasp and his heart dropped for frightening her. After breaking another stick, he stepped into the open, holding his shirt loose at his waist.

She hastily wrapped the cloth around herself, tucking the end securely before turning with a smile.

Unsure he'd survive the experience, Kierigh cleared a lump from his throat before he could make words a reality. "Are you ready to bathe?"

She clutched the top of the drying cloth with both hands. "Yes. Relaxing in this bubbling spring was wonderful, but I do wish to cleanse the dirt from my hair."

Best get to it. He indicated her pile of clothing. "Leave that here, but bring the bag."

Turning on his heels, he rushed headlong through the trees. He paused listening for the sounds of her following then forced himself to a slower pace. He led her past the cold pool to a third spring. Water bubbled from the ground, filled a small pool then flowed away as a gurgling stream.

When she moved to his side he said, "The water isn't as warm as the other pool, but is comfortable enough for bathing. There's a small gourd in the bag."

Brows drawn together, she fumbled with the bag. The cloth slipped precariously and she dropped the bag to grab the falling cloth. Kierigh retrieved the gourd. "Give me your hand."

He removed a tight stopper from the side of the gourd and poured a tiny amount of a fine, granular powder into her palm. She lifted her hand to eye level and curiosity filled her expressive face.

He couldn't stop his grin. "Soap. Wet what you have in your hand."

Awkward, she clutched the bathing cloth and knelt by the pool. She dipped her hand in the water. A rich lather bubbled in her palm and she laughed. But when she glided the foam along her arm, Kierigh jerked his gaze past the tree tops.

"Oh, this is so much nicer than the soap we make in the Compound. That leaves my skin rough and irritated."

Unable to imagine her skin reddened, unless it was from the rasp of his hand, Kierigh closed his eyes. He shouldn't think of her skin, of how soft it might feel to his touch or he'd find himself lost in a sensual distraction neither he nor his goal could afford. Distance. He needed distance. And a plan.

He ran his tongue over his dry lips. Giving her his back, he sat cross-legged on the ground. "I'll wait here."

The drying cloth dropped beside him in a damp heap. He bit back a groan. Focus. Focus on the next move against the king. Jermanah's splashing brought the grace of her movement to his inner vision. Grace and damp skin and— No. the king.

The child was safely with its father so the king had no babe to sacrifice. A rush of satisfaction lifted his chest. The tiny, helpless boy had been saved. By Jermanah.

The soft splashing urged him to turn. Like a fool, he'd refused her privacy when she'd nursed. He wouldn't deny her that honor now. He'd deny her nothing, feared he never could. Denying the image of her invading his mind, however, would do much to ease his discomfort.

"Won't the soap be harmful to the stream?"

Kierigh jerked, eased the tension from his shoulders and shook his head. "Grandmother makes it from plants. In less than a quarter-league, the water will clear leaving no remaining evidence of the soap. This, too, helps keep our campsite hidden."

"I could never imagine such an amazing thing."

The soap was such a small part of his life, one he took for granted. The joy she found at such a simple thing humbled him. In concentrating only on his fight, he'd forgotten appreciation of what he did have and the small comforts others offered him. "It is but one of the wonders of this world."

Jermanah moved beside him to gather the cloth. Droplets of water fell to his bare back, each a kiss against his skin. He shivered and somehow found his voice. "Life in the Compound has always been one of simplicity and denial. There is much in the world you would consider wondrous."

"What would you know of life in the Compound?"

Hiding a grin at the accusation underlying the light tone of her question, he angled to face her, raising his gaze to her flushed face. "I know. The life of an acolyte is little but work and study. With little of the comforts offered to the priestesses. And their lives pale in comparison to the decadence of the Highest."

Determination firmed her jaw but doubt dulled the golden brown of her eyes. "You lie to me."

His determination matched hers. "I do not lie. To you. To anyone."

Tugging the cloth tighter around her body, Jermanah lifted her chin but the surety of her conviction faltered with the words that had governed an acolyte's life as long as the Compounds had existed. "Life in the Compound is the same for all. Each has a duty and serves as is required. I could exchange my life for that of the Highest of the High. Except for the level of responsibilities...the conditions of living would be the same."

Kierigh snorted and shook his head. "Jermanah, you've been pulled and used for the power of others. How is it, then, you studied with the Seer? That magic is forbidden to women, isn't it? Especially to an acolyte."

"I had no choice. The power to heal called me, led me to the Seer. I've prayed often for forgiveness but I'm unable to deny the magic."

"Hmm." His lips thinned.

His doubt sparked her own, thoughts she buried, discovered and reburied time and again. She was different. Flawed. Her self-image had been reinforced by the taunts and separation from the other women of the Compound. "If I have a destiny, I fear I'll never discover what my life may be."

"Perhaps the reason is because your destiny doesn't lay within the Compound. Perhaps you'll find it here or in some other land. In the freedom to choose as you wish. To do what you will."

"Freedom?" She sat on the soft grass, pulled the cloth under her then up again over her breasts. "You're trapped in a secreted camp, hunted by Compound guards. How can you call this freedom?"

His bright eyes sparkled and his easy smile made her heart dance. She resisted the urge to cover the fierce beating with her palm by clasping her hands in her lap.

"You forgot the king's soldiers. They hunt me as well. Even so, here I am free to choose to do what I wish. I create my own destiny. When I complete my quest, that freedom will allow me to choose another way of life. Just as each man and woman who joins in my fight will make their own choices. No one directs my actions or controls my thinking."

Tight cords of muscles stood in stark relief in his fore-arms. She didn't believe he was angry, but she'd over-stepped some boundary. She touched his arm in apology and slid her palm over the soft golden hairs. "I didn't mean..."

He ducked his head. "I know. Each day I question my actions. Time grows short. My brother."

"You've spoken of a connection with him. Help me understand."

"I don't understand it, nor how to explain. I only know, here, in my heart, I must find him and release him from captivity. Every moment he grows stronger in my thoughts. Each day the danger he faces grows." He twisted the shirt wadded in his hands. "I don't know what to do."

The reverberations of a long, undulating howl swirled around them. Seeking safety from the unknown, Jermanah cringed against Kierigh's solid form. "What was that?"

He chuckled. The movement shot a delightful ache through her, not unlike the call to nurse. Yet, so wonder-fully different. She longed to extend the feeling, but didn't know how, or how to ask for what she wanted.

"A wild dog. They're noisy, but rarely attack."

"Attack?" She pressed closer. Kierigh wrapped his arm around her waist and eased her onto his lap. She snuggled against his chest. She tugged at the cloth to cover her exposed hip but the material remained bunched beneath her.

Kierigh's short breaths puffed past her ear. Did he fear the wild dogs? No. He feared nothing. His lips grazed her cheek, firm against the heat rising there.

"Even with the coming darkness?" Her breathless question lingered on the air, uneven, like the pounding of her heart.

She followed his gaze through the open tangle of overhanging branches. Clouds glowed orange and pink with the setting sun. His lips slid to the corner of her mouth and her eyes drifted closed.

"We're safe here."

"Am I safe with you?"

He stilled. Jermanah's eyelids felt heavy as her breathing. His breath mingled with hers. Was this what the others had whispered about? This odd combination of lassitude and delight?

The barest of whispers tickled her ear. "I." His lips brushed over hers. "Don't." Firmer, another touch, then his tongue swept a damp trail over her lower lip. "Know."

A violent shudder shook his body and he turned his face from her. She slid her hands up his chest, tested the tense muscles of his neck with her fingers then traced his high cheekbones and the firm line of his lips. Unsure whether she answered an unspoken question or spoke only her own desire, she used gentle pressure to turn his gaze to her. "Yes."

A lazy grin stole the tightness from Kierigh's mouth. She waited for him to return to kissing her, but he only stroked her hair, watching her mouth with longing and desire. She understood wanting something desperately. Her desire to rise to one of the Highest within the Compound had shone as a similar look in her eyes when reflected in a cup of still water.

Now a different desire coursed through her body. But what did she want? An end to the swirling ache within her? Or something that she didn't yet fully understand?

The bright blue of his eyes darkened, glittering with the fading light of the sun. A slow drop of his eyelids hid the wonder from her. She touched his lip with her finger.

A deep groan rumbled from his chest, vibrating against her to create both pleasure and an increase in the odd agony of need. Kierigh covered her mouth with his, touching the seam of her lips with his tongue. She gasped and he held her close to stroke the silk of his tongue against hers.

The kiss pulled such intensity from the center of her being she doubted she'd ever feel again. She dared to meet the touch of his tongue with hers then joined his slow, twining dance. She couldn't breathe, but wasn't sure she wanted to if doing so meant stopping the delight.

To her dismay, Kierigh eased from the kiss and drew a long, harsh breath. A swirl of emotions danced through his expression, encouraging her to float in the fathomless depths forever. A flash of clarity blazed in her mind. Kisses wouldn't be enough to conquer the ache within her. Nor within him.

She leaned close to his ear, welcoming the slight tremors of his skin against hers. "You're offering me a choice."

"Yes."

"So I may choose the path I wish to follow."

"Yes." The movement of his throat when he swallowed fascinated her. He tangled his fingers in the length of her hair, his expression both cautious and hopeful. "Little one, what destiny would you choose this night?"

If she chose to return to the Compound—no, that wouldn't be a choice she'd make ever again. This choice, the first she'd make without another directing her thoughts was important. It would set the course for her future. The correct action was hers to take. She captured his face between her hands. She nibbled on his lower lip and slid her tongue across the surface. "This."

Hands clasping her shoulders, Kierigh studied her. "You don't know what you're asking."

"No, not completely. I am not innocent of the ways of men and women, but I haven't experienced desire. Until now. There is an ache, a pain—"

"The pain returns?"

Confusion warred with Jermanah's desire until she realized his concern. She hurried to reassure him. "Not the nursing pain. Different. Can you heal this?"

With a relieved grin, he caressed her cheek with the back of his fingers. "Jermanah, you're the healer."

"Do you also experience an ache?"

He slid her from his lap, reclining next to her on the short grass and taking her hand. After touching his lips to her palm, he curled her fingers around the firm length that had pressed against her bottom. "Yes."

She felt the intensity of his gaze as she watched his body twitch in her grasp. "And my choice heals you as well?"

He chuckled, a rough sound with little humor. "Yes. But doing so comes with a price. Jermanah, are you willing to pay that price?"

Knowing the answer, she asked anyway. "What price?"

"You'll no longer be welcome in the Compound."

The feel of him, the throb against her palm deepened the need. "Yes, I know. But, I ache so. I need... I need you. Can you take away this desire and ease the ache?"

"Perhaps. This night may create a greater need. The desire, the ache may return." He tensed under the caress of her hand.

Touching him was near bliss but she focused on what she wanted, needed to say. "Kierigh? This day I held the painful decision of the Compound in my arms. Nursed him at my breast. Also this day you've given me a taste of what life could be when I make my own decisions. I can fill my life with choices. Now is my first choice. Kierigh, now I need you to fill me."

"There will be pain."

"I've known pain. I choose this price."

Kierigh covered her lips with his, using varying pressures to persuade her to respond, then deepened the kiss. Her sensual bravery humbled him. He pulled away, kissed her eyelids and trailed his lips down her neck to the hollow at the base of her throat. Her rapid pulse tickled his tongue.

Rising to one elbow, he peeled away the drying cloth to expose her body. Lingering sunlight filtered through the branches to bathe her skin in a warm glow. He'd never imagined skin so soft, so inviting. Had never believed he'd touch glorious beauty. Hadn't realized his hand could know the flow of such pleasure.

She speared her fingers through his hair. At her not so subtle tugging, he returned to the temptation of her mouth. He allowed her to control the kiss, delighting in her innocent exploration. Her hands moved to his back, tracing the muscles, touching the scar at his shoulder. He jerked and arched back drawing a shallow breath.

No experienced lover lay with him. Jermanah believed

she understood what would happen between them and offered him her body. Taking advantage of her—choice—might change more than just her status at the Compound. He should stop. While he was still able.

Jermanah touched his lips with her fingers and smiled sweetly, her chest lifting with a deep sigh.

Matching her sigh, Kierigh exhaled. Or he could show her, teach her pleasure and ease his own raging discomfort. Silent in his indecision, he held her gaze until her smile softened to sultry desire.

Lost, he trailed a soft breath down the length of her neck then inhaled to imprint the fresh, floral scent of her on his mind. He exhaled to return the scent to her trembling skin. Moving lower, he brushed his lips over a swollen nipple. She gasped, the movement lifting the dusky peak to his mouth. Mindful of her earlier pain, he caressed with his tongue and sucked gently.

Scraping her fingers against his scalp, she pressed his head closer. Her low moan enticed him to fill his palm with the softness of her other breast and circle the pebbled tip with his thumb. Despite her whimper of protest, he trailed his fingers down her quivering belly, pausing when his hand covered the thatch of hair protecting her innocence.

And her womanhood.

What right did he have to take her innocence? He was stronger than this temptation.

She'd worried her lower lip to a deep red. Her mouth, the sweetness of her kisses demanded he return to sooth the redness before fully covering her mouth with a demanding kiss.

No. He wasn't.

The arching of her hips to his hand made him smile against her lips. He stroked and teased until her legs spread. When he discovered the nub of her desire, he flicked his finger against it.

Jermanah clutched Kierigh's shoulders. He was her lifeline, keeping her from floating away with the rising pleasure. She danced tongue with his, frantic to ease the ache growing at her breast, and lower still. With her feet planted flat against the ground, she lifted her hips to his wonderful fingers.

Merciless in teasing and touching, he created a tight, winding spiral that threatened to undo her. Unable contain the wondrous feeling, she moaned. He paused, but before a heartbeat passed, his assault on her senses continued. She couldn't stand more. She ached for more.

His relentless tongue twined against hers in a slow counterpoint to the movements of his fingers. The increased torment would make her explode. Please. This wasn't pain. It was...exquisite.

Cradling her head in one hand, he trailed nibbling kisses to a tender spot just below her ear. He sucked her earlobe into the warmth of his mouth and grazed the flesh with his teeth.

The air flashed, vibrating against her body. Lights swirled behind her closed eyelids. She spun, thrashed. Her sharp cry lifted through the trees, echoed by startled, night-roosting birds.

Kierigh gathered her close, holding her, protecting her new sensations. Strangely afraid, she kept her eyes closed. Surely the world had altered in that flash of glory.

Kierigh studied her flushed face. Faint tension lines still creased her brow. The same tension pressed his body painfully against the confines of his clothing. When her hands slipped from his shoulders, he inched away and tried unsuccessfully to ease the tight material at his groin. He leaned back on his elbows, stared into the growing darkness.

"Do you ache?"

He turned his head. Lingering desire filled the deep brown depths of Jermanah's eyes.

"An emptiness remains within me."

He blew out a long, shaky breath. "Yes."

"There is a way to fill this emptiness?"

Her innocence was both frightening and incredibly stimulating. He clenched his teeth. "Yes."

"It is one of the choices I am able to make."

The statement wasn't a question, but he would answer anyway. He leaned toward her, his voice a raw whisper. "Yes."

"If I make this choice, will you choose this as well?"

With a groan, he gathered her close and kissed her. "Yes."

"I must be free. I willingly make my own decision." She reached for him, but he lifted his hand to hold her in place.

"I might not be able to stop should you change your mind."

A flicker of fear flashed in her eyes then a flare of desire burned away the fear. "If this ache isn't eased, I fear I'll die from a longing I don't understand." She held his gaze and stroked him.

Kierigh strained into her caress. While he could still think clearly he had to be sure she understood how her life would change if she gave herself to him. "You must be sure."

The agonizing, wonderful caress stilled. Dread shivered over him. She'd refuse him now.

"Yes, Kierigh. I'm sure. You've asked again and yet again. Perhaps it is you who is unsure."

The rising moons spread cool light across the clearing. The multitude of colors in her hair glowed like a halo around her head and shoulders. The softly bubbling spring water created a sensual musical backdrop, blending with the chirping of night insects. Struggling from his pants, he kicked the clothing to one side, gave a sigh of relief and rose to his knees.

She rose as well, and moving closer, captured his erection between them. Sensation flooded his body. He skimmed his hands over her, frantic to touch, to discover every inch of her skin. The glide of her hands burned his skin with pleasure. He could no more refuse her now than live without breath. Raining kisses over her face, he stretched beside her on the cool grass.

The taste of her kisses, the flavor of her awakening desire... He'd never experienced, felt, needed this much. He dipped his finger into her, testing then drawing his finger to touch the throb of her desire. At her whisper of his name, he returned his finger to the warm sheath.

Clawing her fingers, she pulled tiny clumps of grass from the loose soil and tossed her head. She was ready to accept him. Afraid to frighten her, he shook, barely controlling his passion. Soon, soon they would heal these aches. Together.

He settled in the warm cradle of her thighs and positioned himself. Using one hand, he lifted her hips and she opened to him. His pulse throbbed. He strained to remain in control as he eased the tip of his erection into her welcoming heat. Shaking with effort, he denied the powerful urge to thrust deep and remained still. "Little one?"

She wiggled, surrounding a bit more of him in bliss. "Jermanah, the pain?

Desire heavy lids rose. “So you have said.” She cupped his buttocks. Her fingers twitched and his muscles quivered in response. “Make it a quick pain then, or I’ll surely die.”

He managed a tight grin, but his words were heavy with restrained passion and promise. “You won’t die.”

Jermanah barely registered his words through the haze of sensation. He held her still, safe, yet wanting. Part of him throbbed within her. More. Wanted, needed more. His fingers tightened on her hips.

A sharp piercing pain. She bit back a startled cry.

Kierigh froze. The rising moons reflected in his eyes highlighting regret. And pain.

“You shared my pain?”

One harsh bark of laughter escaped his lips then his voice softened. “My pain is that I caused you pain.” Moving within her, he kissed her forehead. She gasped. He stilled.

If he refused to move, then she would. She tilted her hips. The inner stroke of his body encouraged her to arch closer. Wonder filled her as he did. Her pain faded, but concern remained in the tight set of his lips. She smiled and touched his shoulder. “The pain is a memory. But I’ve not been healed. There is more?”

With a slow smile Kierigh braced his forearms close to her sides. Sliding her fingers through the silk of his hair, Jermanah urged him to kiss her. His tongue dove into her mouth as he arched back then pushed into her. Each adjustment of his hips filled her with powerful sensations. Like the rise of healing magic, but more. More than she’d dare imagine. Something changed within her.

Then thought dissolved and she was lost in the power of Kierigh’s mating. She kissed his face, his neck, caressed his chest and sides, marveling at the play of muscles under her sensitized fingertips. Power surged through her with the deep sounds of his pleasure.

Building urgency twined through her before concentrating at the point of the joining of their bodies. She muffled her cries against his shoulder and exploded.

Drained and panting, she lay back and gazed into Kierigh's face. His eyelids remained squeezed closed, his face frozen in a tight expression she'd never seen. His arms shook as he held himself above her. He hadn't yet found relief from his pain.

She wrapped her arms around his neck and he collapsed on her. She bore the joy of his weight and although he struggled to move, she arched her hips to his, repeating her insistent movement until he joined her rhythm.

He rose to his forearms and cradled her head in his hands. His dark pupils filled his eyes with an intensity that renewed the need and desire at their joining. A wild coil of sensation drew her tighter. His lips drew back from his clenched teeth in a feral expression that delighted her.

The tempo of their mating increased and their rasping breaths filled the clearing. With a sharp cry he pulled nearly free then surged into her, touching far more deeply. Wrapping her legs around his hips, she surrendered to the spirals of sensation, welcoming the hot, pulsing tremors of his release. Her breath escaped in a single, pleasured moan.

"Ah, Jermanah." Kierigh pressed his damp forehead against her shoulder then rolled to his side, pulling her with him. Cooling her fevered skin, he caressed her. Their breathing slowed. The frantic beating of her heart calmed. Silent, she snuggled into the warm security of his embrace.

When the light of both moons shone through the branches directly above them, Kierigh sat. Tears stung her eyes at the tenderness of his gaze. He captured a tear on his finger and studied the tiny droplet. His brows lowered. "Are you well?" The soft, low timbre of his voice carried the same tenderness.

Her heart melted at his concern. "Very well."

His sober and thoughtful expression tempered to a smile filled with regret. "I shouldn't have—"

"You did only as I requested." She didn't regret her decision nor would she allow him to dwell on useless remorse.

"You don't realize what is lost to you now."

She sat and shrugged. "Perhaps not, but I've also discovered something amazing. I'll survive." She glanced at him from under lowered lashes. "If you will help me."

One corner of his lips twitched. "Yes."

She offered her hand and he enclosed it in the warmth between his palms then kissed her knuckles and stroked her fingers. She bit her lip to hide her reaction to the subtle caresses but her body betrayed her and she trembled.

Kierigh chuckled, rose in a fluid motion and helped her stand. She winced at the strange pull of her muscles. Concern tempered his expression. "Perhaps you should return to the hot spring. The warmth will ease your muscles and prevent aches."

Bending, she tugged at a corner of the discarded drying cloth. "I don't believe I wish to prevent the aching when the healing is so wonderful."

A hearty laugh burst from Kierigh. She frowned. Why did her words cause the odd reaction?

Wrapping an arm about her shoulders, Kierigh leaned close to whisper, "That ache will return. I meant only the stiffness of muscles which haven't been used so before."

eyes at the tenderness in his gaze. He captured a tear on the tip of his finger and studied it [illegible]. His eyes lowered. "Are you well?" The soft, low timbre of his voice carried the same tenderness.

Her heart melted at his concern. "Very well."

His solar and thoughtful expression transformed to a smile filled with [illegible]. "[illegible]"

"[illegible]?" She didn't require [illegible].

"You don't realize what it [illegible] you now."

She swallowed hard. "There [illegible] much to learn and something [illegible]. [illegible] lowered lashes. "If you will help me."

The corners of his lips twitched. "Yes."

She offered her hand and he enclosed it in the warmth between his palms. [illegible] his thumb [illegible] and stroked her [illegible] and she trembled.

[illegible] and helped [illegible] the music.

[illegible]

[illegible] and dying [illegible] when the [illegible]."

[illegible]. She [illegible]

"[illegible]" she [illegible] only the [illegible] used to before."

eight

Kierigh perched on a boulder high above the hot spring. At his insistence, Jermanah had remained longer in the steaming water. Now, he drank in the sight of her. He tugged tangles from his hair, reliving the feel of her fingers stroking over his scalp.

Jermanah climbed from the pool. He gave a low whistle and she followed the sound to smile at him while she wrapped the cloth around herself. Kierigh skidded down the narrow path, clasped her hand and led her to the low stone. He sat behind her, tugged the comb from his belt and drew it through her hair.

The strands flowed through his fingers. He attempted to count the colors reflected in the moonlight. A myriad of browns and reds, striking silver and a few odd strands of gold and black. He divided her hair in thirds and braided the length, tying the end with a leather strip. Draping the long braid over her shoulder, he kissed the back of her neck.

Despite her low hum of pleasure, she winced. How had he not noticed the bruises marring her fair skin? He knelt before her and took her hands in his, discovering purple marks wrapping her wrists. He matched his fingertips to the bruises. “I didn’t mean...”

“It doesn’t matter. I was your enemy then.”

He hesitated then touched the bruise on her shoulder. “And this?”

Jermanah lowered her gaze, her reply soft. “I don’t know.”

“Jermanah?” Cupping her chin with his fingers, he lifted her face. “I didn’t touch you here. Who did this?”

“The Highest.”

“I’ll—”

Water-puckered fingers covered his mouth. “You won’t. It’s past. The bruises will fade. The memory... will remain longer.”

She rested her forehead against his shoulder. The rise of anger faded. He couldn’t change the past, but he could protect her future. Her stomach rumbled and he grinned. “Are you hungry?”

She straightened and pressed her hand to her stomach. “It would appear so.”

“Come. We’ll return to camp. Perhaps Grandmother saved something for us.”

“I must dress.”

The rumble of her stomach sounded again so Kierigh gathered her in his arms and hugged her close. “There’s no time. If you don’t eat soon, the noises from your stomach may call the wild dogs.”

“You said they wouldn’t attack us.” A gentle shiver trembled through her.

He grinned and leaned to the side. “Gather the bag and your clothing.”

“I’m able to walk.” Her ineffective struggles made him clutch her tighter.

"Yes."

"You don't have to carry me."

"No. But the way is treacherous. I don't care to lose you in the darkness."

Kierigh's steps were sure and quick, and soon they left the forest and crossed the clearing to the lean-to. The moons had begun their downward path in the sky, light fading so the stars shone more brightly. The dim glow of a shaded lamp illuminated the area.

The table had been pulled from the lean-to. A rough curtain now hung from the sides and front of the structure. When he leaned forward, Jermanah shoved the curtain to one side. Two pallets lay side by side, a single blanket tucked over them.

"Grandmother has been busy." Kierigh stood Jermanah next to him.

She arched her eyebrows and tossed her clothing to the pallets before turning toward the table. "Here's food, too. But I fear it's cold. We may have taken longer to return than expected."

"She hoped we would be long. See, the meal is meant to be eaten cold." He chuckled and lifted a loaf stuffed with thinly sliced meats and cheese. "Grandmother is ever hopeful."

Jermanah sat and reached for the bowl of fruit. "Is she truly your grandmother?"

"Yes. She's the last of my family, except for my brother."

"Why is she hopeful?" She spoke around a mouthful then hid her lips behind her hand. Faint pink covered her cheeks.

Ignoring her embarrassment, Kierigh cut the sandwich into smaller pieces. "She wishes for her family to continue, desiring grandchildren playing at her knee. I haven't been helpful since I have no time to devote to a mate."

"Oh." Jermanah lowered her head.

Kierigh gave himself a mental slap. Fool. Take a woman's innocence then claim you have no time. He should have taken the child and left her in the forest. He should have resisted the temptations of her willing body.

With his emotions wrapped in a tight knot, he dipped his head, waiting for her tears and accusations. But only the night sounds of the camp filled the clearing. Finally he peered at her from under lowered lashes.

She chewed and swallowed. "I understand. Your destiny is to find your brother. To rescue him from the dangers you see in the king's Stronghold. Perhaps when you've fulfilled that destiny, you'll have the freedom to build a family for your grandmother. And for yourself."

Kierigh collapsed to the wobbly bench.

Jermanah gave him a confused frown. "Aren't you going to eat?"

He nodded. Then shook his head in disbelief. This woman was truly innocent. Innocent of the wiles and clinging ways of most women. A self-satisfied grin stretched his lips. But no longer innocent of passion and desire.

"Well, which will it be? Will you eat, or not?"

"Yes."

They cleared the platters in silence. Jermanah leaned back and rubbed her stomach. "Wonderful. We weren't ever allowed so much at one time."

Was this, then, the time he'd been dreading? For her accusations that his irresponsible actions caused her to lose any chance of position within the Compound? Perhaps, but he wasn't prepared for her to make light of his camp's meager hospitality. Anger teased the edges of his tired mind. Anger at her? Or at himself and his failings?

Jermanah stacked the bowl on the platter. She rose, pulling at the drying cloth to bring it higher under her arms. He shook his head. She didn't disparage his offerings —either food or passion. She spoke the truth as she knew it. He ached to offer her a feast of tender meats and fine pastries. To love her on a soft bed. To offer her his devotion.

He needed to face the simple fact she would soon be gone. From the camp, and from his life. He took a determined breath. "You may sleep in the shelter."

"And you?"

"I'll pull a pallet out here. I often sleep under the stars."

Jermanah's expression dimmed. "I had hoped to sleep at your side."

The need to kiss the sadness from her voice vibrated through him. Instead, he gripped the table edge. Hard. Then spoke his truth. "If I lay next to you, I won't sleep. I'll want you again. And yet again."

"This is part of what you've shown me this night. To be able to choose."

"Yes."

"Then I choose to lay next to you. To heal the need that even now grows within me. Again and yet again." Her innocently coy grin faded. "You have awoken this passion within me. Please don't take it from me so soon."

Kierigh stumbled to his feet and into her embrace. He lifted her off her feet and pressed his lips to her forehead. She kissed the hollow at the base of his neck.

After a quick breath to blow out the lamp, he carried her into the dark lean-to, letting her tug at the makeshift curtain until it fell closed behind them.

Daud rose to awareness, the taste of the king burning in his mouth. He opened his eyes then let his lids droop in defeat. The many inside the body had attempted to stand against Zigor. They'd tried to protect the body from his abuses. They'd failed. Again.

Attempting to make sense of his surroundings to adjust to the proper behavior when he opened his eyes again, he held his breath. He lay on silk surrounded by pillows. Inhaling, he sorted the scents of sex. More than one person. They'd been shared.

A soft hand rested on his chest, long nails moving across his nipple. Cautious, he opened one eye and turned his head. A woman slept curled next to him. The Highest of the High. Until this day, Zigor had hidden them from her.

Another hand clutched possessively at his thigh. This hand he knew. Zigor snored at his other side. Daud shuddered. He slid from between them to the end of the wide bed and glanced at his body. Bites and scratches marred his skin. Turning his thoughts inward, he searched the shared mind. There. The new one, a young man, stood stroking his erection. Another one created for sex only. Zigor was cruel. At least this one wasn't a child.

Calling out to the recesses of the mind, Daud concentrated and others appeared. Of all ages, both male and female, they gathered around the newly created one to lead him to a safe place. Daud wished him peace within the darkness of the crowded mind.

The external world intruded. The woman moved and caressed the king. The bed shifted. Daud slipped to the floor and ducked behind the screen obscuring the bed alcove. *He* wouldn't participate in shared sex. Nor would he stay, tempting Zigor to further creations. He glanced behind him. The Highest mounted Zigor.

Daud scooped up his fallen clothing and disappeared through the silent doorway known only to him and the king.

The faint, dusty light of early morning filtered through the curtain. Kierigh stretched and lifted his arms. Jermanah mumbled softly and snuggled closer to his side. He stroked long strands of hair from her face and smiled. Her responses during the night filled him with pure, male satisfaction. As he remembered, so did his body, stirring to life.

He eased to his side and lowered his lips to brush Jermanah's but a soft cough sounded outside the lean-to. Closing his eyes, he waited. Without an answer perhaps the intruder would leave and he could begin again with the woman at his side.

"Kierigh?" The low whisper vibrated with urgency.

Kierigh groaned, moved from Jermanah's warmth, tucked the blanket over her and stood. Wrapping the crumpled bathing cloth around his waist, he stuck his head through the overlap of curtains. "What?"

"The man who came for the child..." The young man's words faded into silence and he spread his hands.

Taking care to close the gap behind him, Kierigh stepped from the lean-to. Grandmother had left a covered flagon of fresh water and a bowl of whole fruits. He reached for the water. "What problem?"

"The man has taken the child..." Looking down, the man cleared his throat.

His focus narrowed to an impatient glare, Kierigh faced him. The man stumbled over his words. "He's taken the child to the Compound."

"What?" Kierigh slammed the flagon on the table, shook water from his hand and towered over his compatriot.

"Once we released him, he traveled toward his village. But once he left the forest, he turned toward the Compound. The guards are holding him until the Highest will see him. I don't believe he told anyone about the child yet."

"Can he lead them here?"

"I don't think so. As always we followed your instructions. Blindfolded both ways. The paths were different and twisted. I've set additional watchers at the edge of the forest and along the road. The camp is alert and prepared to move on your word."

The young man cringed when Kierigh lifted his hand, then blew out a breath when Kierigh clasped his shoulder. "You've done well."

The young shook his head. With a flat-lipped smile Kierigh gave a single nod. "You could have done no more. Gather our fighters and send word to the villages. Test the safety of our hidden places, then direct the moving of the camp."

"What of the child?"

"I'll retrieve the child. If one can be found willing to care for the babe, bring her to the second camp. I'll take the child there."

"What about the acolyte?" The harsh undertone of hatred tainted the man's casual question.

Kierigh squared his shoulders. "She will go with Grandmother to the second camp."

"She could care for the child until a *better* woman is found."

The short hairs on the back of Kierigh's neck bristled. "She isn't able to nurse the babe. She's no longer a part of the Compound."

"Once an acolyte—"

Kierigh wrapped a fist in the man's tunic and lifted him to his toes. "You will not speak so. She has forsworn the Compound." Kierigh shoved the young man, making him stumble before falling to his knees and bowing his head.

"As you say, Kierigh. I meant no disrespect. I'll do as you order. Who goes with you to the Compound?"

"I'll go with him." Both men turned at Jermanah's soft, determined words. Fully clothed, she stepped from the lean-to. Kierigh moved toward her and the other man scrambled away without standing.

"No."

"I know the Compound. I'll help find where they've taken the babe."

"No. I will go alone. I know the hidden passageways." He folded his arms across his chest. Intimidation cowed many a man.

Jermanah drew her brows together and matched his stance, planting her bare feet in the dirt. "I will go with you. I don't have much, but there are a few things I wish from my cell. I must speak with the Seer. I won't stay within the walls. I will keep this freedom."

"It isn't safe for you."

"Is it safe for you?"

He hesitated. "No."

Jermanah arched one eyebrow and tilted her head.

Kierigh opened his mouth to argue, then snapped his lips together. He paced in a tiny circle before stopping to tower over her and scowl. She would go with Grandmother and be safe.

"You won't intimidate me, Kierigh." She smoothed the wrinkles in his forehead with gentle fingers. "I'm going with you."

He backed from her tempting touch. "You will not." He turned toward the rest of the camp and roared, "Grandmother."

Moments later the old woman strolled into the clearing. Kierigh sat at the table, gestured for Jermanah to join him and offered her the bowl of fruit. She took a small piece and nibbled, her gaze never leaving his face.

Why did she defy him? Not listen to reason? Danger lurked everywhere within the Compound. Danger for them both should they be discovered, as well as for the child. Better for him to face this challenge alone. Kierigh held back an impatient huff and let his gaze drift to hers. Did she have to look at him like that? Like she understood his thoughts?

"You, ah, bellowed, Grandson?"

He forced his gaze from Jermanah and turned to his grandmother. "You've have heard about the child? I'm going to the Compound to retrieve him. Jermanah will go with you to the second camp. She is your responsibility." Rising, he touched his grandmother's arm and strode toward the activity at the center of the camp.

"You may wish to dress first," Grandmother called after him. Jermanah hid a chuckle behind her hand.

He stopped short, whirled on his heels and stalked back to them, his lips twitching. He bowed before entering the lean-to. Moments later he reappeared tugging his belt tight. He bowed again, kissed both women on their cheeks and strode from the lean-to.

Jermanah sighed. “I need to go to the Compound. I must let the Seer know I’m alive, and that I won’t return. Perhaps there will be some way for me to continue my lessons with him.”

“Kierigh will leave the camp soon. We’ll wait a bit longer before I show you another trail from camp.” Grandmother grinned and nodded with a wink. “Women always find their way around the wishes of their men. It’s the way of the world, dearie, and you’ll learn. Now, eat. You must replenish your strength before facing the Compound.”

“You’ll go against his wishes? For me?”

“I sense something special within you, young woman. Something involving my grandson. I do what I can to further my cause.”

Jermanah took the older woman’s wrinkled hand and pressed it to her cheek. “I’ve never had a family other than for the Compound. May I call you Grandmother?”

The old woman’s smile grew wide and her deep blue eyes sparkled. “It will be my honor to include you in my family.” Grandmother glanced over her shoulder. “Ah, good. He’s gone. The other men are attending to their duties. Only a few will remain here to protect and move the camp to a new location. No one will notice us slip away.”

She paused. “I’m not sure how to help you return to the forest and find the second campsite. That area is seldom used. I’m not sure of the paths.”

“I’ll find a way. And if I don’t, Kierigh will find me.”

Grandmother chuckled. “Judging from the way he looked at you, I’d agree. He’d go to the ends of the land and over the seas to find you. He just doesn’t know it yet.”

Jermanah found Grandmother certainly difficult to believe. "I don't think it will ever come to that."

They talked for a few moments then Grandmother rose and glanced from side to side. She beckoned to Jermanah and led the way through the forest to the bathing pool.

Jermanah stared into the clear, bubbling water and let memories of the past night flow over her. Grandmother cleared her throat. Deep heat rushed to fill Jermanah's face but Grandmother turned with a wink and pointed.

"Follow the stream. Once you reach a narrow canyon there will be two paths. The one on this side will lead back into the forest. Cross the stream and follow the other path. It will fork many times, but if you continue to take the path on the far side of the stream, you'll reach the Compound. The water flows into a small tunnel and through the lower kitchens."

"I've spent many hours scrubbing vegetables and pots there as punishment for my curiosity. My way will be easy from there." Thankful for Grandmother's belief and assistance, she hugged the old woman.

"Wait, child. Take this." Grandmother held out a narrow leather sheath. After taking it, Jermanah pulled a knife from the oiled leather. The thin blade was finely wrought with strange markings running down the center. The bone handle fit perfectly in her hand. She returned the blade to the sheath and shook her head.

"I can't take such a fine blade from you."

"You may need protection. This blade is designed to be worn either on your arm or calf, beneath your clothing. I think the leg would do best for you." With stiff care, she knelt, lifted Jermanah's pant leg and fastened the sheath.

Jermanah assisted her to her feet. "I'll return the blade to you soon."

Grandmother gave a sharp nod. "I'll hold you to that promise, child. Now go. Using this path, you'll arrive at the Compound near midday. Perhaps you can be in and out before Kierigh even gets there. Men must always make so many plans before they take action."

Jermanah kissed Grandmother's dry, wrinkled cheek. Then she leapt over the tiny stream, but stopped after a few paces to turn and watch Grandmother. How would she explain Jermanah's disappearance?

With the camp on the move, she imagined Grandmother could easily convince the fighters the disappearance of a woman they didn't trust anyway was of little importance. How the acolyte would easily lose her way and be unable to lead anyone to the camp—if she ever made her way out of the thick trees.

A day ago, that would have been true. She would have remained lost and terrified among the trees. The freedom to go as she wished still frightened her, as did the possibilities of making her own decisions. Hopefully, Kierigh would continue to teach and encourage her. She would prove to herself to those who discounted her.

Now, the forest would be her home.

nine

Kierigh entered the Compound through the dark passageway he'd used the previous day to visit the Seer. He paused to listen by the old man's chambers, but no sound of the mystic's industry emanated from the room. No herbal aromas tickled his nose. He frowned. The Seer rarely left his rooms.

Pacing the silent halls, Kierigh's frown deepened. The usual busy sounds of the Compound were missing. No timid acolytes rushed on the priestesses' business, no chimes called the women to ritual prayers. The rebel attack shouldn't have decimated the Compound.

He shrugged away the concern. Now it would be easier to retrieve the child and return to the forest. And his acolyte. No, Jermanah wasn't his. Recent satisfaction faded with the onset of desire. Nor was she an untouched acolyte.

He pressed the heel of his hand against his temple. No time for these thoughts. The child would have been taken to the Highest of the High as soon as she deemed an interruption worthy of her attention. He'd find a secure hiding place to wait, and when the opportunity arose, he'd relieve the Compound of the chore of the young one's care.

The soft jingle of a guard's ornate uniform sounded behind Kierigh so he slipped into the shadows of a darkened doorway. No reason to take unnecessary chances. The guard passed him. Stunned, Kierigh narrowed his gaze.

He knew this man. Had fought him yestern, deep within the forest. Had fatally wounded him and left him to die. But now the guard showed no evidence of the mortal wound, his broad shoulders showed no sign of weakness or subterfuge.

Determined to understand this new mystery, Kierigh slipped from the shadows to follow the guard.

As Grandmother predicted, Jermanah reached the Compound by mid-morning. Despite the fear of what she might face happen at her return, she'd enjoyed the brisk walk. She'd never imagined the dark shadows shrouding the trunks at the base of the trees she'd glimpsed from her narrow window could contain such beauty.

But darker thoughts had clouded her enjoyment. Doubts sprang from hidden depths like the small animals she'd startled with her passage. If Kierigh was correct, the male children of the Double Moon were sacrificed. Her blind devotion may have only furthered the Highest's power. Dim memories twisted through her mind. With each step, pieces of overheard conversations, the Seer's teachings, and hidden objects fit together like a puzzle.

Determination fading, she stood at the wall watching

the stream disappear into the tunnel. So dark. No light eased the heavy oppression of the passage. Her mouth dried. She knelt and cupped her palm to bring water to her lips. Though refreshing, the cool water did nothing to lessen her fear.

The only other way into the Compound was through the gates. Not an option open to her now. She took a deep breath and stepped into the darkness. Dragging one hand along the cool, damp wall, she reached toward unseen light. With a single sliding step forward her fingers no longer touched the light behind her. Even though she remained frozen, the light faded with each of her breaths.

Darkness pressed her against the wall, stole the air from her lungs and clawed thought from her mind. She slid her foot forward. Dark. The harsh rasping of her breath fought the tight need to scream in her throat. She wasn't brave. Her muscles trembled.

The memory of Kierigh's face brightened behind her closed eyelids. He was brave and she couldn't allow her fears to endanger him. In one night he'd given her a light to follow in her discovery or a way to live without the Compound. Another step. The vision of him beckoned her forward. A step. His mouth curved in the smile that touched his lips before he kissed her.

The overbearing dark pressure gave way. Another step, then two. She opened her eyes and strained to see in the darkness. A faint glow outlined the end of the tunnel. In her rush to reach the safety of light and an open space, her foot landed in the stream with a loud splash.

Panic froze her advance, her breath stilled. But no call of warning sounded. No face appeared at the end of the tunnel searching for the cause of the noise. For her.

Jermanah lifted her foot and wiggled her toes before hugging the wall and peering into the dim kitchen.

No women bent over low tables to prepare the Compound's simple meal. No small girls rushed to bring fresh ingredients to the master cook. Even the large cook fires were cold and silent. Only the distant sounds of scurrying rodents willed the void.

Confused and disoriented, Jermanah moved into the room. Even if the priestesses hadn't returned after the procession and those who never left should still be here. Only one person could assuage the rise of curiosity. She'd ask the Seer. Palms damp with new, unreasonable fear, her hands shook. She dashed from the kitchen and up a flight of steep, narrow stairs.

Pausing in the entry to the Seer's public outer chamber, she cocked her head to listen. Like the kitchen, this room was too quiet. The silence sensitized her skin, making her jittery and unsure. She drew breath to call to her mentor, but the words died in her throat. To break the silence would alert the Compound to her presence. Pressing her lips together, she wadded the curtain separating the two rooms in a tight fist the she pulled aside the heavy material.

The Seer's organized and meticulously labeled herbs and decoctions lay tossed about the room though if caught by a whirlwind. The heavy table rested on one side. Rude markings had been carved deep into the polished surface.

The burn of tears blurred her vision. She crumpled to a heap, crushing a small pottery bowl under her knee. The fragrance of the herbal mixture offered strange comfort and her tears dried. Crying wouldn't bring the Seer to her, nor answer her questions.

A conversation with the Seer while she assisted him in storing and marking hers many days past intruded on her thoughts. He'd spoken of a time when an occurrence such as this would happen and had given her instructions. She was not to grieve, but how could she not? After a shaky breath, she returned to his instructions. She was to look for something. What? A message?

Jermanah glanced around the room. It was imperative she recall the Seer's exact words and the inflections of his voice. She closed her eyes and wrinkled her brow in concentration but no answers, or even a clue appeared to guide her. Leaning against the wall, she pulled the end of the drapery into her lap to caress the tight weave. The simple repetitive motions helped her think.

Her fingers stilled. The curtain. The message was in the curtain.

She gathered the thick fabric and stroked her fingertips along the sides and hem, then over the carved wooden rod holding the panel in place. Nothing. She crouched in the doorway and examined each stone, each minute joint between them. Still nothing appeared as a message.

Where was the Seer? He'd promised a message would be left for her. A single, frustrated tear trickled over her cheek and she lifted the curtain to dab away the wetness and froze

The cloth. The message was woven within the fibers of the fabric. Lifting the material to the light from the window, she discovered and read the Seer's words.

But the message made no sense. Shaking her head, she chuckled. So many of the Seer's teachings made no sense until the event or need came to fruition. Then she'd wonder why understanding hadn't come to her sooner. Now, as always, she'd do as instructed without question and ponder the actions and results later.

First, she passed her fingers over the message and the

barely discernible words faded further into the cloth. She brushed the crushed herbs and crockery from her clothing and straightened her spine. She'd never been called to the Highest's chambers, but if that was where she'd find a book, the subject of the Seer's final message, then there she would go.

A muffled thud drew her attention to the tall window. She'd always admired the wide sill, the high arch, and especially the light the opening provided the room. She crossed to the window, squinted into the sunlight and took a deep breath. Holding the fresh air within her lungs made her fret for the cool breeze and open spaces of the forest. And for the one who had shown her so much in one night. How rapidly her life had changed.

A thud sounded below her. She glanced down to where a rough rope swung from a hook imbedded in the Compound wall. The Seer's thin, white hair blew about his head in the light wind. His body bounced against the wall with a dull, empty sound.

Jermanah jerked from the window and covered her mouth to hold back her rising scream of protest and denial. But even as her mind filled with the echoing cries, she knew nothing could be done for the gentle Seer.

Tentative, she returned to the window, closed her eyes and reached over the sill toward the hook. Even stretching dangerously far out the window, she couldn't reach the rope.

Holding her flat palm above the Seer, Jermanah sent a silent vow to the beloved man. She'd return to honor him. Somehow, she'd find the way to send his spirit to the fires and into the sky.

. . .

Kierigh shadowed the guard through the rabbit warren of hallways. Occasionally the man would slow and step casually from his usual pace. The resounding echoes of his steps left silences where Kierigh's footsteps would fall had he not paused when the guard's shoulders tensed and his head tilted slightly to listen. The guard suspected.

This man seemed more intelligent than the usual brutes guarding the Compound. Kierigh had also noted a difference when he'd fought the man. He would have made a formidable and welcome addition to Kierigh's forces had his allegiances not lay with the Compound.

As though he knew he was being contemplated and discounted any danger, the guard shrugged with a short lift of one shoulder then turned toward the large center courtyard. He crossed to a small cage set against the far wall.

Impatient to see past the guard's back, Kierigh shifted from one foot to the other. Fingering the haft of his knife, he settled against the dark, shadowed wall and squinted across the sunlit courtyard. Finally the guard moved to one side.

The cage wasn't large enough for standing, so a man sat hunched on the ground. A rag wrapped bundle lay in the dirt beside him.

The guard motioned urgently toward the bundle. The man shook his head and placed a protective hand over the rags. The guard gestured again. Kierigh strained to hear the low spoken words but understood the meaning well enough. The guard wanted the bundle. The prisoner refused, clutched the bundle to his chest and lifted a defiant sneer to the guard. A babe's angry cries mocked the silence.

A heavy breath filled Kierigh's lungs. The child's father

still had the babe. If the child could be liberated before being taken to the Highest, Kierigh's time in the Compound would be shortened. And nearly bearable.

A sparkle of light bouncing from the walkway high above the courtyard captured his attention. Someone moved along the covered passage, avoiding the patches of bright sunlight. Pausing before a wide sunny area, the figure crouched out of view then reappeared well past the light. One corner of his mouth tipped in a smile. He wasn't the only prowler taking advantage the nearly empty Compound.

The brightness highlighted a long braid. His smile died. The remembered feel of the multi-hued strands falling through his hands made his fingers twitch.

White-hot anger flared along his veins. He told Jermanah to go with Grandmother to the second camp, insisting she was not to return here. Told Grandmother as well. The anger blossomed to rage, heating his skin. He wasn't accustomed to being disobeyed. Now, not only had she gone against his orders and returned, that elevated walkway led only one place. The chambers of the Highest.

Kierigh pressed his forehead against the wall. When she willingly gave herself to him, he'd believed she had forsaken the Compound. Despite the anger churning in his belly, his body responded to the memory of her beneath him, surrounding him. He closed his eyes and let heavy defeat crush his soul. She said he'd given her freedom. Now she'd taken his precious gift and thrown it back in his face.

The ringing of a chime tingled along his spine and Kierigh returned his gaze to the courtyard. The guard glanced over his shoulder, spoke a few harsh words to the prisoner then turned on his heel. Within moments he crossed the courtyard and disappeared through the wide doors of the worship center.

Moving each joint in practiced succession and sighing at the faint pops, Kierigh stretched his cramped muscles. His body ached for action. His mind as well, if only to wipe away thoughts of the woman betraying him. He stilled. There would be no action until he was certain the courtyard would remain empty.

He'd taken only three breaths before the guard returned, followed by a second who pulled back a beaded panel to expose the doorway. The Highest of the High strolled from the dim interior. A third guard lifted a feathered fan above her head to block the sun.

Kierigh eyed her dispassionately. She'd forgone the modest clothing of the Compound. A tight band circled her ribcage to lift her bared breasts above a flowing translucent skirt. Kierigh arched his eyebrows. The skirt covered nothing. And she'd applied bright color to her nipples and the pale thatch of her pubic hair.

He bit back a chuckle. Jermanah had insisted all were equal here. But an acolyte would be beaten if she allowed a glimpse of a leg or arm to show. How soft Jermanah's skin had been, how succulent her breasts to his touch. She didn't need artifice to be appealing. He wrenched his thoughts back to the moment and focused on the woman regally crossing the courtyard.

The Highest stopped before the cage and leaned so her breasts were eye level with the prisoner. Her low, sultry voice filled the expectant silence. "You have brought something for me?"

The man stammered, cleared his throat, and moved his mouth. The Highest gave an impatient wave and the guard handed the man a water flask. Water dribbling from his chin, the man drank in loud gulps.

The Highest tilted her head in a practiced, coy manner. "Now, what have you brought me?"

"My lady. Here is the child chosen by the Double Moon. I've brought him from the rebel camp, directly to you."

The Highest gripped the bars of the cage.

"Can you take me to this camp?" The words dripped venom.

"No, my lady." The man cringed in the far corner of the cage. "I was blindfolded and led in circles. But, I brought you the child."

Relief tempered Kierigh's tense focus. The camp was safe, but the move still necessary.

The man lifted the bundle and unwrapped the rags as if displaying a great treasure. A tiny hand waved in the warm light. The Highest nodded. The malice in her expression when she turned to her guard flowed across the courtyard to Kierigh's hiding place. He shivered at the near physical touch of evil.

"Poll, take the child and its father to my chambers. They shall await me there."

The guard nodded once, unlocked the cage and held out his arms for the babe. Denying the unspoken command, the father clutched the babe tighter. Poll sighed and stepped from the opening to allow the man to crawl awkwardly through the door.

Once the father had worked stiffness from his back and legs, Poll gestured for the man to precede him to a flight of stairs. At the prodding of Poll's fist against his back, the man climbed the steep steps, disappearing through an open archway.

Kierigh studied the woman as she silently watched the men. The rise and fall of her chest grew more pronounced with each breath. Smiling, she motioned to her shade bearer and ambled through to the worship center entrance.

Now the child was in the Highest's chambers, making it much more difficult to retrieve him. The Highest wasn't the mothering kind, so perhaps she'd send the child from her. He'd make his move then. For now all he could do was wait. Kierigh chewed on the inside of his cheek. Waiting was never an easy task.

A guard reentered the courtyard, flipped the feathered fan over his shoulder and strode toward the guard's quarters. The man at the curtain had also disappeared. Only the one guard remained with the child. Kierigh firmed his lips. He had no wish to face that one again in battle.

He scanned the courtyard and the upper level walkway. The sun had passed the zenith and layers of shadows shrouded the walkway.

Realization slammed into his chest with enough force to steal his breath. Jermanah. She wasn't there to betray him. She'd said she would come with him then return to the forest. With him. Unlike so many others of the Compound there was no deceit in Jermanah, only truth. Instead of keeping her safe under his guidance, his insistence had placed her in grave danger.

He pushed from the wall, scanned the courtyard and sprinted toward the stairs. Waiting for a shout of alarm, he crouched on the bottom step. But the Compound remained eerily silent. Relieved, yet focused on remaining hidden, he took the narrow steps three at a time.

If he barged into the chambers like an unprepared fool, he risked three lives. How should he proceed? Ah, yes. The

Seer told him once of a secret door opening from the hall behind the chambers into the Highest's clothing storage. That would have to do. Plan set, he sank into the shadows and followed the memory.

ten

Astonished the Highest had so many books in her possession, Jermanah skimmed her fingers over a long shelf of leather-bound volumes. A second shelf held haphazard stacks of tomes interspersed with herbs, flowers and strange, noxious substances in tiny jars. She wrinkled her nose in disgust. The room was filthy with every available surface covered with stacks of parchment and spilled ink jars.

She searched through the books with single-minded determination. The Seer's message stated she would find the *Book of Futures* in the Highest's chambers. The Seer had said the book was a history of the ancients, a book telling of a time long before the rise of the Compounds. Unfortunately, the Seer's cryptic message gave her no clue to the size or appearance of the volume beyond a binding of deep purple.

After a fruitless search of the outer chamber, Jermanah paused in the doorway of the bed chamber. This room was uncluttered. Thick furs covered the floor. A canopy-draped bed filled the center of the room. Accustomed to the narrow cot provided an acolyte, she paced from one side to the other touching the soft coverings draping to loose piles on the floor. The bed appeared larger than her tiny room and big enough for four or five restless sleepers.

Jermanah shook her head and tucked loose strands of hair behind her ear. *The Book of Futures* couldn't be in this room. She turned and a speck of purple among the stark white furs caught her eye.

She stepped on to the furs, wiggled her toes and let the long hairs tickle the sides of her feet. She closed her eyes with a sigh. The soft caress filled her with renewed longing for her forest rebel.

Sharp noises from the outer chamber jerked her from the sensuous contemplation of her feet. She couldn't be discovered here. No longer an honored child of the Double Moon, or an acolyte of the Compound, she dared not imagine what punishment she'd incur. An amazing thought settled with strange contentment in her heart. She'd be considered one of the rebels.

Increased noise spurred her to action. A small table stood beside the opulent bed, one of the legs propped with the thin book to level the top. She knelt, peered at the binding and smiled. This was the book the Seer sent her to find.

Tugging on the book set the table rocking. She worried the edge of a torn fingernail with her teeth. She had to retrieve the book without anyone knowing it was gone. But how would she keep the table level?

Heavy footsteps pounded down the hallway from the outer chamber. Panic flared in her chest. She'd be discovered unless she found a place to hide. Somewhere. Where?

Two openings faced her on the far wall. The wider led to a small room filled with piles of clothing strewn across the floor. No place to hide there unless she covered herself with the clothing. Not a safe option.

The other opening was a dark recess behind a low chest. She could crouch behind the chest. No one would find her there. Then she'd take the book and return to the freedom of the forest.

And Kierigh. Unfortunately it was too great a hope to believe he wouldn't be very angry with her. Or with Grandmother.

The reverberations of a baritone voice sounded beyond the door. She slipped behind the chest and set her back against the wall. The alcove loomed beside her, dark and enclosed. She cringed away from the tiny space.

A tall guard shoved a man in tattered clothing into the room. He fell to his knees on the thick furs. Jermanah drew herself into a tight ball, ducked her head against her knees.

"You should have given me the babe," the deep voice whispered.

She blinked. She knew this voice. Cautious, she lifted her head and leaned forward to peek around the edge of the chest.

A small bundle held securely in his arms, Poll stood over a cowering man. "Now you must face the Highest of the High."

The man rose to his knees and held out his hands, defiance filling his rough features. "Give me back my child. This is no concern of yours."

Poll shook his head. "Once I vowed to protect this child. But I wasn't able to save the one who cared for him. Now I have been given this second chance and I will see the child to its destiny."

The man grunted. "You mean that pretty little thing

with the strange hair? She seemed mighty cozy with the rebel leader."

A tick in Poll's cheek was his only response.

Jermanah caught her lower lip between her teeth. Poll was in the Compound, alive and hale. She'd been positive the deep wound just below his heart had been mortal and he'd died protecting her. Kierigh hadn't allowed her to heal him, yet here he stood. Was there an unknown healer in the Compound or forest? Her fingers tingled.

Poll's eyebrows lowered. He lifted the child in one arm and rubbed at a spot just below his ribs. Questions whirled in his eyes and he shook his head as if to clear a fuzzy memory.

The kneeling man smirked. "So, you remember her, too. Lusting after an acolyte isn't a good thing, guardsman."

Poll's thick eyebrows formed a level line. "Neither is facing the Highest's wrath."

"But, I am not angry."

Poll whirled to face the door and bowed his head.

The Highest pointed a long-nailed finger at the kneeling man. "No, my loyal guardsman, I have no anger toward this one." She tilted her head, inspecting the man. "In fact, I believe I may reward him."

The man rose to his knees to offer a feeble attempt at a bow. "My lady, it's my pleasure to serve you."

"No, it shall be mine."

Jermanah wondered at the odd smile the Highest bestowed on the man, but shivers of dread traveled the length of her spine and she cringed back against the wall. This woman wasn't the honored Compound leader she'd followed all her life.

In the past two days the Highest had frequently acted in a manner confusing to Jermanah. When the child... the

Highest had ended two lives. Jermanah pressed her palm against the ache in her heart. Lives were precious, sacred. How different this past day might have been had the Highest shown compassion.

A new thought startled her and she covered her mouth. Had the Highest always been so evil?

Perhaps this new observation was because Jermanah, herself, had changed. Could one day of freedom from the strictures and harshness of her life bring so drastic a change in how she saw others? Were there other changes she might notice in others? Or in herself?

The Highest turned her back on the kneeling man. "Poll, I want—"

The child's father sat with a thump and roared with laughter. Poll and the Highest turned to him. "Poll you say? Poll is it?" Barely intelligible, the words tumbled through his laughter. "Poll is what the little beauty named the babe." He wiped tears from his eyes with dirty fingers.

The Highest grabbed a handful of his hair and pulled until his neck arched. His laughter died with a squeak. "Who named the child?"

He swallowed and licked his lips. Poll stood nearly motionless behind the Highest, one hand comforting the child in his arms. "My lady, it was a strange-haired girl. At the rebel camp. They said she cared for my child."

"Jermanah." The name squeezed between the Highest's taut lips.

Jermanah's head jerked and she nearly stood in answer to the commanding voice. How did the Highest still hold power over her? Drawing on meditations taught to her by the Seer, she tried to take deep, quiet breaths. But sorrow tightened her breathing. If she were discovered now, there would be no one to honor the Seer.

The Highest turned to Poll. "You, guardsman, will care for this child until the time he is presented to the king. Where the child is, there will you be. The child will never be from your sight. Find some woman for a wet nurse." Her words dripped with honey and barely concealed threats. She pointed to the fur piled against the chest. "Place the child there and guard the door."

Jermanah scooted into the alcove. Darkness closed around her. She told herself not to fear, it was only darkness like the night, the dark of sleep.

Poll lay the child next to the chest, touching the babe's soft, rounded belly before rising. His gaze slid over the alcove. Jermanah held her breath until he gave a negative shake of his head and turned to the door. Once she had her breathing under control, she peered out of the darkness and returned to the light-filled safety behind the chest.

Arms loose at his side, eyes facing straight ahead, Poll stood at the door. The guards took great pride in maintaining their stoic expressions under the teasing of the young acolytes. Jermanah had never been able to draw even a muscle twitch from any of the beleaguered men.

With a swirl of skirts, the Highest knelt before the child's father and lifted his face with her hands. "What do you wish as a reward? The Compound has no money, no jewels or finery to offer."

"A reward's not necessary, my lady. The honor of doing right is enough."

She laughed. "You don't fool me, man. You have no honor. But, even so, I believe I shall reward you." She tilted his head so he looked directly at her breasts and arched her back. "Would you like to bed me, man?"

He made inarticulate sounds and licked his lips. His tongue flicked out to rasp against her nipple.

The Highest gave a low, throaty chuckle and backed from his seeking mouth. “Is this what you wish, man?”

She stood and unfastened the clasp between her breasts, letting her skirt pool around her ankles. She speared her fingers through the man’s tangled hair and held him close to her powdered curls. “Or is this what you want? Remove your clothing and I shall determine if your reward is worth my time.”

Reclining on her bed, the Highest watched the man strip off his dirty clothing and tapped her finger against her cheek at the sight of his thick member. She motioned him closer and wrapped her hand around him. He grunted then gasped as if in pain. With a smile, the Highest dragged him onto the bed and between her thighs.

Jermanah pulled her knees to her chest and pressed her forehead against them. She covered her ears to block the grunts and sighs, the sharp, pained cries. This was nothing like the joy Kierigh had shown her. This was vile. Disgusting.

If she sank back into the black alcove, she wouldn’t be able to see the bed. But which would be worse—the dark terror of being closed in or watching. She couldn’t face the terror nor block out the sounds. Silent tears trailed down her cheeks. She should have listened to Kierigh and remained in the forest.

She chanced a glance at Poll. He stared straight ahead, his gaze fixed on a point high on the wall above the bed. How did he remain so unaffected?

The babe hiccupped and began to cry. Ignored, his wails grew louder. She focused on the cries and for a brief moment forgot the rhythmic squeak of the bed.

“Guard. Stop that infernal noise.”

“My lady, perhaps the child requires food.”

"Take it. Watch it as I ordered. Send another guard to my door." Sharp and staccato, the Highest's words were echoed by the man's grunts and moans.

"My lady." Relief colored Poll's response and he strode across the room and lifted the wiggling child. Wishing she could escape with him, Jermanah chewed on her lip and watched until he exited.

The snap of a hand meeting flesh jolted her gaze to the bed. The man held one palm to his face. A dribble of blood trickled down his chin through the rouge rubbed from the Highest's body.

"Man. You are too gentle. Harder." The Highest grabbed the man's ears and forced his face against her breast. "Yes, there. Bite me, man."

Closing her eyes hid the sight of the man's pale buttocks jerking between the Highest's thighs, but couldn't remove the memory of long scratches and bloody half-moon imprints from the Highest's sharp nails.

Was this the true way of mating? After a time, would she act in this manner? Better to never heal the ache of desire again than to behave in this way.

After peering through a crack in the stacked-stone wall, Kierigh slid a wall panel to one side, stepped over a top-heavy pile of clothing and closed the panel. Tense, he strained to sense Jermanah's presence. He cast his gaze to the low ceiling at the squealing bedsprings and the slap of flesh against flesh. His heart heavy, he paused. Surely it wasn't Jermanah who cried out with such pleasure.

He crouched at the opening into the chamber, took a

deep breath and leaned to one side to scan the chamber. Relieved Jermanah didn't occupy the bed, he flexed his fists. If she'd been there he would have stormed into the room and—and what?

The Highest lay with the man who claimed to be the babe's father. Perhaps he was, but his stated intentions of fleeing with the child were obviously false. Kierigh huffed. It wasn't often he was fooled. And he refused to believe Jermanah had been a planned distraction.

Where was Jermanah? She hadn't returned down the passageway while he'd watched and no other chambers occupied this level. He studied the room and arched his eyebrows. The luxury and decadence was far more than he'd suspected.

The scar on his shoulder tightened, an odd irritation he now recognized as remnants of Jermanah's healing, present only when she was near. He leaned further to the side to peer into a dark alcove partially hidden behind a low chest. The tip of a bare toe wiggled before disappearing behind the heavy chest. When he recklessly shifted so his head and shoulders were exposed to the Highest's chamber, the top of Jermanah's head came into view. Her hands covered her ears and she pressed her forehead to her knees. Her shoulders rose and fell. She wept.

The ache to hold her trembled along his arms. He would calm her and kiss away her tears.

He spared a quick glance at the bed. The wild mating continued, the man's moans louder than the ecstatic cries of the Highest.

Knowing himself a fool for taking a fool's chance, he dug through a pile of clothing and discovered a heavy broach. He tested the weight, willed Jermanah to silence and tossed the jewelry behind the chest.

The broach landed on her foot. Her head jerked up and she covered her mouth. She darted her gaze about the room. Kierigh waited until she looked toward the door then held out his hand, palm facing her, motioning for her to wait. She nodded. Thank the moons she understood and followed his command.

The cries from the bed increased, a mix of pleasure and pain resounding through the chamber. The ruckus would cover any noise Jermanah might make. She'd risen to her hands and knees, waiting at the edge of the alcove. Worrying her lower lip, she watched him with wide-eyed intensity. Kierigh glanced at the bed.

The man threw back his head and howled. Kierigh gestured. Jermanah crawled forward and he motioned her to greater speed before slipping deep into the clothing storage area.

Jermanah sped around the corner and launched herself into his arms. He covered her mouth with his palm to contain her sobs. Trying to silently convey his meaning, he arched one eyebrow and pulled her further into the recesses of the room. She nodded and he moved his hand, letting the back of his fingers caress her soft, damp cheek.

She drew breath so he pressed one finger against her lips and she nodded again. Settling her against his side, he wrapped an arm around her shoulders. They tempted fate remaining here, but he couldn't resist delighting in the feel of her head resting against his chest or the silkiness of her hair beneath his palm. After a moment he eased from her, touching her lips again with his finger when her enticing mouth formed a protest. Remaining low, he peered into the bed chamber.

The man had flopped to his back, panting. The Highest stretched languorously, lifted a thick metal rod and struck a small chime. The door opened to reveal a guard. A slight lift of one eyebrow betrayed his interest in the scene before him.

"Guard, take this one away." The Highest paused. "Kill him."

Mouth gaping wide, the man lurched to sit. "My lady?"

The Highest jabbed him in the chest with the rod. "You will not speak. You've served your purpose. Unfortunately, it doesn't bear repeating. Take him, guardsman, and return to me in the outer chamber when your task is completed. I may wish to discuss—my security with you."

Smiling, the guard nodded, and grabbed the man's arms to drag him from the bed. Unable to struggle from the guard's grasp, the man sighed and hung his head. "Is it permitted to face death clothed?"

The Highest studied the metal in her hand before running the rod across her stomach. She shrugged.

The guard gave the man a stern expression and pointed to his pile of clothing. Once dressed, the man exited with his head held high. The Highest stretched and tossed the metal to one side. She rose, donned a fur wrap and followed the guard from the chamber.

Kierigh breathed a sigh of relief and returned to Jermanah. He spoke softly in her ear. "I told you to remain in the forest."

Her forehead wrinkled but before she opened her mouth to respond, he pressed his mouth to hers in a soft kiss then nibbled a path to her ear. "We'll speak of this later." He grinned at how she trembled from his kisses.

Foolish tears welled in her eyes and Jermanah bit her lip. Kierigh was kind, so patient with her.

He grasped her shoulders and gave a gentle shake. Her tears continued to flow and he brushed them from her skin with the hem of a discarded robe. One of his brows lifted in question.

Aching for his lingering touch, she wanted nothing more than to sink into the comfort and security of his arms. The ache, this need of him, spun through her body, making her feel weak and boneless. Fear seized her heart until each beat throbbed against her chest. Stricken from her by rising terror, need and desire vanished. Shrugging off Kierigh's hands, she scooted deeper into the storage room.

"I won't become like that, will I?" She covered her face with her hands willing an end to her tears.

"Quiet. There are guards nearby." He crawled closer. "We need to leave. Discover where they've taken the child."

Grabbing the front of his shirt, she twisted the fabric between her fingers. "Answer me. I won't become like her. Tell me I won't."

"The Highest?"

Jermanah's breath stalled in her throat. She nodded, watching Kierigh's face, but she couldn't decipher his expression.

He gave a dismissive slice of his hand. "You're nothing like that woman. Come. We must go. Now."

He untangled her fingers from his shirt. She snatched back her hand to cradle his palm against her stomach. Finally, the tears had ceased, but the damp tracks on her cheeks were as cold as her dread. She had to know. To understand.

"You showed me desire, along with the need to ache so. Because of you I understand I may choose to heal that ache. Tell me, Kierigh. Tell me I won't become like her. For if I shall, I don't wish to live."

Kierigh stared at her for such a long moment she knew he would surely confirm her fear. The length of the slim scabbard at her calf gave a strange comfort. Grandmother had been correct, she might have need of the sharp blade.

"What are you talking about?" Kierigh glanced into the bedchamber before lifting his hands in question. His gaze was intense. Confused. "What?"

She drew her gaze from him and stared at her toes. He didn't understand her fear, her concerns. Or perhaps he was waiting for her to change, to create pain with pleasure. She gasped. He *had* been concerned at the pain the first time.

He rested his hand on her shoulder. She bit the inside of her cheek to keep from flinching. "Tell me what troubles you, little one. Quickly. We risk discovery."

Heat burned across Jermanah's cheeks. He was making her say the humiliating words. Squaring her shoulders, she dipped her head. "The way the Highest mated..."

The warmth of his hand jerked from her shoulder. "Did you enjoy it?"

Hating what she might see, she lifted her gaze to his face, but no mockery filled his expression. No flare of interest in his intense, blue eyes. Only cautious concern. What answer did he expect from her?

He'd told her he only spoke the truth, so she would speak true as well. "It was vile, disgusting. I don't understand finding pleasure in such a way. How does it happen? Does desire grow to a place where—that—is the only way to ease it?"

Disbelief dawned in his gaze and she turned her face from his. So, it was true. Determined to keep her fear hidden, she sniffed. When she was alone—

Strong, gentle fingers lifted her chin. His face hovered close, his breath a warm caress across her cheek. "Little one. Such innocence."

Stiffening at the condescending words, she attempted to pull from his touch. She might well be innocent of the interactions between man and woman. But she wouldn't allow that lack of knowledge to control her life. Wiggling, she struggled to free herself but Kierigh held her still and rubbed his thumb along her jaw. Her body betrayed her determination and she sighed.

He continued to stoke her cheek as he spoke. "There are many ways a man or woman may find pleasure, both alone and with another. Some are beautiful. Others you may find dangerous or ugly. If you had no interest or curiosity, you won't become as she is. Your love making comes from the purity of your soul."

Kierigh's soft words and the touch of his fingers fascinated her. Warmth and wonder filled her with hope. "You speak the truth?"

"Yes." His eyelids lowered. Perfect crescents of lashes rested against his cheeks for a moment before he looked at her with fierce determination sparkling in the deep blue depths. "We must go."

He tugged her to her feet but she struggled against his hand until he tightened his fingers around hers. She twisted until he turned to face her, his free hand fisted against his hip.

"You wish to remain?"

"No. But, I must get the book."

"Book? There aren't books here."

"There is. *The Book of Futures.* The Seer told me."

"The Seer isn't in the Compound."

"No, he isn't." Now wasn't the time to weep for her mentor so she brushed at fresh tears with an impatient swipe of her hand. Kierigh cast her an indulgent grin and she frowned.

"I'll show you."

She whirled and entered the bed chamber without checking to see if the room was safe. The rumble of a deep growl vibrated Kierigh's throat. He'd have to teach her to be more careful. For the safety of them both. Despite his misgivings he followed her swaying hips to a small table near the bed.

She knelt, pushed at the furs piled against the leg, turned her face to him and pointed.

He crouched beside her. A thin volume propped one of the table legs. This was why she endangered their lives? He set his mouth in a firm line meant to intimidate and scowled. Her lower lip pulled to a pout and he softened his expression in response. When her wide eyes pleaded with him, he let his shoulders slump in resignation and gave a single, sharp nod. Training would come later.

She pulled on the book, setting the table rocking. He glanced around for something to replace the book. The metal rod? No, too rounded. Ah, there. A small scrap of wood had fallen from the underside of the bed. He gauged the thickness. It would be close.

Senses focused on any sound or movement from the hallway, he crawled to the bed and slid the scrap into his hand. With a triumphant flourish, he presented the wood to Jermanah. Gratitude sparkled in her smile and the fear he'd do anything to have her look at him that way again shook through him. She was a dangerous distraction.

He grasped the edge of the table and lifted. A soft grunt of surprise passed his lips. The small table was far heavier than he expected. Jermanah slipped out the book and set the wood in its place. When he lowered the table, it tipped a tiny bit to one side.

Jermanah clutched the book to her chest and pointed to

a small jar sliding toward the lower corner. Kierigh caught the stone container at the table's edge. Cupping the jar in his palm, he rocked the table. They couldn't leave any evidence of their presence. After a moment's thought, he handed the jar to Jermanah, felt through the floor coverings and pulled his long knife from the scabbard.

He sliced a thin strip from the edge of a soft, tanned skin. After testing the leather with his fingers, he folded the strip in half. He inserted the folded skin between the wood and table leg, gestured with his head and Jermanah returned the jar to the table top. Neither drew breath when he pushed tentatively at the table. The jar remained solidly in place.

Jermanah's released breath blew across his arm and lifted the fine hairs. He struggled to restrain the tremor running rampant over his skin. His scattered thoughts centered on the softness of the furs beneath him, and the woman at his side. He stroked the fur, comparing the sensation to the smoothness of her skin. If he lay her back against the furs, would she welcome him? Invite him to... Drawn inexplicably, he leaned toward her.

A sharp bark of deep, masculine laughter from the outer chamber shattered his fantasy. His preoccupation with Jermanah endangered them both. He jerked to his feet. At the door to the storage room, he glanced over his shoulder. Jermanah hadn't followed him. Instead, she still clutched the book and had bent to rearrange the furs around the table leg.

He glared and gave a sharp gesture to capture her attention, but she didn't look at him until satisfied with the casual effect of the pile of fur. She rose and after a final glance at the table and minute adjustment of the small jar, ran past him into the shadowed room.

The Highest's throaty laughter sounded just beyond the bed chamber door. Kierigh melted into the darkness as the door slammed open and a guard entered carrying the Highest. He tossed her onto the bed and crawled across the resilient surface after her.

Kierigh blocked Jermanah's view of the room. They needed to be far away before the Highest began again. The woman's low, seductive whispers spurred him to action. He pushed past Jermanah, found the hidden latch and opened the panel. He wrapped his fingers around Jermanah's hand, wincing at the haunted look glazing her eyes. If she'd remained in the forest as he'd ordered, she wouldn't have witnessed the depravity. If he would have followed her to these rooms sooner, they would have been gone long before she'd been forced to learn of the Highest's perversions. He feared Jermanah would long remember what she'd witnessed.

Distracted by the dire thought, he stumbled. Jermanah's tight smile as she passed him to lead the way did little to ease his worry.

An unwelcome possibility caught the breath in his chest. Would she turn from him? Refuse his love? What would he do if he couldn't calm her fear and ease her concerns?

eleven

An insistent nudge lifted Daud to consciousness. The Custodians, those within whose purpose was to keep the body alive when no others could deal with life, called mentally to him. He rose to the surface of the body's control and blinked to adjust the eyes to his vision. The chime calling him to Zigor's presence jingled in a long stream of metallic sounds. How long had the king been calling?

Daud stood and stretched. The body had been immobile for a lengthy period of time. He took a few steps and lurched at the agonizing pull of his thigh muscle. Rubbing the cramped, knotted muscle, he wished there was some way to note the passage of time when he wasn't in control.

The chimes rang, spurring him to movement before the cramp fully relaxed. In the passage to Zigor's chambers, he passed under a high window, no more than a mere slit in the thick wall. A shaft of sunlight pierced the constant gloom. At least it was day. Daud lifted his face to the tiny slice of sunlight. One of his greatest wishes was to give the children an opportunity to play outside in the sun. They'd never had the chance to be children.

He paused before his personal entrance to Zigor's rooms and rubbed his fingers through his short-cropped hair. What would Zigor have them do this time? He sent a silent plea into the dank air. Please, no more children.

The door slid to the side with well-oiled silence. Zigor faced the opening with his ankles crossed on the surface of his large desk. An empty bottle lay on its side by his booted feet. He tipped a second bottle to his mouth, took a long swallow then lifted the bottle in salute to Daud.

"Took you long enough to get here."

"I beg pardon, my lord."

"No matter. Sit. I wish to talk."

Daud lowered himself onto a stool. A frightened, huddled knot of inner children watched. He told them Zigor was deep in his cups and couldn't function sexually at that time. Relief spread through his mind as the children returned to their places of safety and their play. He focused his full attention on the king.

Zigor twirled the bottle in his hands then held it out to Daud. When Daud shook his head, Zigor shrugged and took another swallow. His feet dropped heavily to the floor and he sat forward, propping his elbows on the desk. "You know why I keep you as I do."

Daud nodded once. He knew the perversions Zigor enjoyed with the body. He understood how each new being the king created within him was thought to increase the power Zigor would gain at the body's sacrifice. Daud also knew that soon the pain would end.

"I had hoped to avoid your sacrifice until another Double Moon cycle had passed. But it seems the brat has disappeared. Unless it is brought to me within the next two days, I'll be forced to renew my power—with your life." Zigor hiccupped and shook his head with drunken sadness.

"I understand, my lord." Daud ducked his head and smiled at his clasped hands. Two days and their fear and pain would be over. If the Captain's plan worked, their sacrifice would end Zigor's lust for power. No others would be created and abused by this man.

Taking a deep breath, Daud calmed the rise of the angry ones and listened to Zigor's wandering speech, his regrets and plans. The king became maudlin under the influence of drink and Daud had heard these false woes many times. So he also listened within to the plans and questions swirling in his head. Arguing voices fought to be heard. The innocent pleasure of the children at play. The peace of the sacrifice called to him. Others within also felt the call and longed for relief.

"Daud, my Daud. What will I do without you?"

"My lord?"

"Who will I talk to, tell my troubles to? Things could have been different had your birth been other than it was. Did you know there are times I'm sorry for what has to be done to increase my power?"

Daud arched his eyebrows in disbelief and barely controlled the sarcastic laughter bubbling beneath his calm demeanor. Zigor sorry? He projected the thought inward and listened as others were free to laugh. He allowed himself a smile.

"Why do you smile, Daud? I would that this sacrifice wasn't necessary."

"Yes, my lord." More empty bottles must be stashed from view. He'd never seen the king so repentant, so... human. Unfortunately, once his mind cleared, Zigor would not remember his remorse.

A light knock sounded on the wall at the far side of the room. Zigor's eyes sparkled. He stared at Daud as if seeing him for the first time and wiped his hands over his face. "Ah, my half-sister pays me a visit. You may go, Daud. I don't wish for the Highest to see you at this time."

Daud snorted. Zigor had forgotten the Highest had already seen him, as well as learned the control the king had over the body. Grateful for the reprieve, Daud stood, bowed to the king and retreated before Zigor changed his mind. Once the panel closed behind him, Daud pressed his ear to a tiny opening drilled through the thick wall.

Zigor called, "Enter, my dear."

Even though a thick wall separated them, Daud sensed the strong, commanding presence emanating from the woman. He waited patiently, cataloging the sounds until the Highest gave a sharp exclamation of frustration. Satisfaction settled in Daud's chest. She would find no pleasure with the King this day.

"You shouldn't drink, Zigor. It debilitates you."

"So? I'm not your only pleasure, am I?"

The Highest remained silent. A loud crash covered Zigor's laughter. "My bottle. Now what shall we do?"

"You're a fool, Zigor. I've found the child and placed it under guard. The boy will be presented to you for sacrifice at the appointed time."

Zigor noisily swallowed a hiccup. "The child? Ah, see how the moons support my plans. You've brought me glorious news."

The scrape of wood over stone and Zigor's stumbling footsteps gave Daud a picture of the king's movements. A muffled thump sounded.

"Zigor, get off me. The floor is too hard."

"But we must celebrate." The sound of wet, sloppy

kisses made Daud cast his gaze to the ceiling. “To bed then?”

The Highest laughed her agreement. Daud turned from the wall. Let them try. The Highest would be sorely disappointed.

Contemplating what he’d heard, Daud returned to his room. The fated child had been found. The body’s sacrifice would be delayed yet another cycle. In truth, Daud didn’t believe the body would survive that long, no matter how many others Zigor created. They needed to discover where the child was held and free the babe. Then their sacrifice would again be ordered.

The adults had been unable to save the children inside, couldn’t protect them from Zigor’s lusts. So, the body would save this outside child. Daud needed to speak with the Captain and the Council. Filled with purpose, he strode to his room, sank onto his narrow bed and closed his eyes. His breathing slowed as the Custodians took charge of the body, regulating the breathing, holding the muscles still.

Daud entered the council chamber. The Captain sat at a table, pouring over the parchments spread before him. Daud slapped his palms against the wooden surface and leaned forward on straight arms. He gave a single, sharp nod.

twelve

Poll watched as Treenie nursed the child at her full breast. She lifted her head and smiled at him.

Poll's chest tightened. She stirred his body with no more than a glance. Unfortunately his duties hadn't allowed him many visits lately to the Stronghold, or to the beautiful kitchen maid.

He'd missed her strong arms around him, her legs locked about his hips. He'd been afraid to hold her when she became heavy with child and even more afraid of hurting her after her daughter was born.

Her girl-child lay in a cradle at his side. He stroked the silky, fine hair covering her tiny head. Her rosebud mouth puckered then relaxed in the sleep of a sated child. She was a tiny thing, hardly larger than the boy Treenie now nursed, even though she was months older.

Treenie rested the boy across her lap and closed her bodice. She placed one hand protectively over the babe's full belly. "You can't give him to the Stronghold."

Poll hesitated. "It is my duty."

Treenie gave a snort of disgust. "Where has that duty

gotten you, Poll? How has your devotion helped the people of this land? The Compound and Stronghold grow more powerful each cycle, the people more oppressed. You should fight for the people instead."

"Join the rebels?" He stared past her shoulder. This was an old argument between them. He'd long stood firm against her thoughts. But now? Now, his beliefs rapidly crumbled around him.

Treenie lifted the babe to her shoulder and rubbed his back. Poll turned his gaze back to her and tried to smile. "It's true, Treenie. I no longer feel a compulsion to serve the Compound. The destruction and depravity I've witnessed in the past days eat at my soul. I must guard this child, but I don't know how. Do I give him to the king? Or follow the calling of my heart and hide the child away?"

He searched for comfort and strength in her face, but Treenie kept her expression calm and neutral. He had to make his own decision.

"Has the babe a name?"

Heat filled Poll's face. "My lady Jermanah called him Poll."

"Oh. Her."

"Yes. She was chosen to care for the babe and I vowed to protect them both."

Strange emotions swirled in Treenie's eyes. He drew his brows together, but before he recognized and named the emotions, her neutral expression returned. "And what of the lady now?"

"She's held by the rebels."

Treenie searched his face then held his gaze. "Do you love this woman of the Compound?"

Surprise made him blink. He wondered at the hint of fear filling Treenie's expression while she waited for his answer. "When I began my service I vowed my life to the Compound, and as such, to her. She's unlike other acolytes, for she is gentle and kind. To me. To the child. She's like a dream, a dream of what I once believed the Compound would be. I love her as a servant loves a gentle master. Perhaps even as a friend. But not as a man loves a woman."

Grinning at the tiny burp in her ear, Treenie nodded. She rose to lay the boy beside her daughter then startled Poll by sitting on his lap. She leaned close to his ear. "How will you protect this tiny Poll? See him sacrificed to Zigor, or help him grow to a free man?"

"There is no sacrifice." The statement wasn't as convincing as he'd hoped.

"There is. A male child of the Double Moon is killed to provide power for the king with an ancient magic the king discovered long ago."

"How would you know this?" Poll leaned back to stare into Treenie's face, judging the honesty of her words.

"How I know isn't important. What will you do?"

Poll shook his head. "You're right, of course. I'm unable to watch this, or any child die. But, how can I hide him? Treenie, what do I do?" His anguished plea was soft. He wrapped his arms around her and buried his face against her soft breast.

Treenie stroked his hair. "We'll take him to the forest. The rebels will find us. They watch all coming and going. He'll be safe and protected there."

"Too much risk. I won't put you in danger. I won't take that chance."

After a moment, she sighed. "I face danger each time I enter the forest. Poll, I do what I must, for every fighter is important in some way."

He cupped her cheek. "You risk much in admitting this to me."

"No, I don't believe I do. Your heart tells you to fight the Compound." She kissed him and rested her hand over the rapid pounding in his chest. "Listen to your heart."

"Will you help me? To save the child?"

She kissed him again. "Yes. But later."

The girl-child moved restlessly. Poll stroked her cheek with the back of his finger until she quieted. Silent, he repeated the vow that now included this small one. Treenie's lips hovered close to his ear, her breath sweet and warm against his cheek. "She is yours, Poll. I have been with no other."

Poll held Treenie so he could search for the truth of her words deep in her beautiful face. Her smile softened and she nodded. He studied the tiny bundle that was his—his daughter—then pulled Treenie into a fierce hug. He kissed her until she melted breathless against him.

Together they watched the sleeping babes. Now more than ever, Treenie deserved to understand, so Poll gave voice to his vow. "I've made my decision. No child will be sacrificed to another's power. Nor for any reason. Not Poll. Not our child. None."

Treenie captured his face in her hands. "This is the decision I knew my love would make. For how could I love you otherwise? Come. The children will sleep now. We have time for ourselves. I'll take you to the forest tomorrow."

She stood and tugged on Poll's hand. His body ached for the return of her softness against it, but he held back. He glanced at his daughter. "It's not too soon?"

Treenie's low, seductive chuckle eased his fears. "It's not. In fact, I've waited far too long."

Jermanah trotted behind Kierigh, following his swift passage through the Compound. Her breath came in little gasps. Did the man run everywhere? He navigated the twists and turns without pause, showing her he must have spent time here. But how? When? The only men allowed within the inner walls were the guards and the Seer.

Jermanah slid to a halt. She'd vowed to honor her teacher. But Kierigh had lost her in the maze of unknown hallways and now she didn't know which way to turn. She stomped her foot.

Kierigh returned to her side and touched her shoulder. "We must hurry. The child—"

"I know who has the child."

Kierigh grasped her upper arms. "Why didn't you tell me right away?"

Even though she needed the contact, she shrugged off his hands. "I didn't think about it. And you rushed off too quickly. I can't leave the Compound now, I must go to the Seer."

"He isn't here."

"The body vessel is, but no, his spirit is not. He's been desecrated. No one remains to mourn him but for me. I will not leave until I've done so."

"Honor the man from the forest."

"No." She stomped her foot again. "Kierigh, they hung him from the window."

Disbelief colored his expression. "Who would dare?"

Jermanah arched her eyebrows. She didn't need words, he'd understand.

Kierigh's lips flattened. "The Highest would if she believed he stood in her way."

He took off and turned down a side hallway. Jermanah shook her head at his rapidly changing moods. He held great concern for the Seer. But then, the Seer had obviously known Kierigh well enough to allow her to heal his shoulder. There was much she didn't yet understand.

They reached hallways she knew and the Seer's chambers in a short time. Kierigh swung his arm to the side to hold her in place while he peered into the room and allowing her to enter. She motioned toward the high workroom window. Kierigh gave her a doubtful look and leaned far out over the broad sill. His shoulders slumped.

He turned to her. "I'm sorry, Jermanah. I didn't believe you. Can you right the table so we have a place to lay him?"

Bracing his upper legs against the sill, he leaned out the narrow opening, stretching downward until his feet left the floor. Jermanah backed from the window. Struggling to right the heavy table, she kept her gaze on the taut muscles of Kierigh's thighs. He wiggled and slid over the sill tipping too far forward.

With a sharp cry, she ran to the window and lay across his thighs to hold him in place. He shifted and her feet left the floor. "No, Kierigh. It's too far."

"I have the rope. Be ready. I'm handing it back to you."

Balanced on the smooth rock sill, they rocked precariously. Afraid to move, or even breathe, she stretched one hand toward the window. Kierigh's shoulder muscles stood in stark relief, the strain outlining his strength. His forearm appeared and the back of his fingers grazed the sill. He slipped a loop of rope into Jermanah's waiting hand.

She twisted her wrist to wrap the prickly rope around her fingers.

Kierigh grunted. "Off."

Sliding to one side from his legs, she kept her free arm across his hips. He squirmed backward into the room and when his feet touched the safety of the floor, she released a relieved breath. The tension of the rope wrapped around her hand cut into her skin but she refused to acknowledge the pain. Kierigh motioned for her to stand behind him and wrapped the rope around his forearm. She mimicked his action, braced her feet against the cold stone floor and curled her toes for a more secure grip.

"Now." The strain of lifting the Seer's body bunched Kierigh's muscles. After a long pull, he grabbed further along the rope. Keeping the tension as well as she could, Jermanah took up the slack after each long tug. They pulled slowly. Wind buffeted the Seer's body and the rope swayed. Anger did nothing to keep tears from filling her eyes.

Kierigh spared a glance over the window ledge. "Hold tight." He wrapped the rope across his shoulder and around his other forearm before lunging forward until half his body hung suspended out the window. "Pull."

Jermanah swallowed her desperation and leaned back until only the tension in the rope held her upright.

Kierigh stumbled from the window. With the sudden loss of tension, she landed hard on a broken jar. Ignoring the sting, she clamored to her feet to help him lift the Seer through the opening.

Kierigh carried the body to the table. Lower lip caught between her teeth, Jermanah removed the rope from around the old man's neck. Her tears fell unchecked while Kierigh reverently arranged the body. Even with the violence of his death, the Seer's expression have remained peaceful and full of joy.

Standing at the Seer's feet, Kierigh spread his hands.

"What must we do? Consigning his body to flame here would be dangerous."

"There are herbs to guide his way. As long as they haven't been taken or fouled." She glanced at the broken mess surrounding the Seer's workbench, patted his cold, gnarled hands and went of search of what she needed. Kierigh crossed to the doorway and peered into the hall. When he returned Jermanah had discovered a packet of herbs and stood staring at them in her hands.

"This was attached to the underside of the workbench. It contains the exact herbs I need. Do you think he knew?"

"Yes."

"You're worried we've been here too long."

"Yes."

"I'll hurry. Will you help?"

Kierigh nodded and followed her lead sprinkling herbs over the Seer's body. Together they placed the crushed leaves in the Seer's mouth and over his closed eyelids. Jermanah knelt beside the table and pressed her forehead against the scarred wood. Kierigh stood behind her, one hand on her shoulder, his fingers moving in a gentle caress.

When she lifted her head, her eyes were dry and determined purpose filled her. "I know you want to leave immediately, but I must return to my cell."

Kierigh stared at the high, wood-beamed ceiling. He wouldn't argue with her for it would take less time simply to let her do as she would. He took her hand, but paused at the door and turned back for a final farewell. He'd miss the old man and his confusing bits of wisdom. A shaft of sunlight highlighted the Seer's serene expression. Tiny dust motes and bits of the dried herbs danced above him before swirling out the window. They'd done what they could.

Jermanah held onto his arm and sighed. He wrapped

his free arm around her, holding her close to his side until she straightened. She was ready to leave.

After a final glance around the room Kierigh retrieved a small amulet from a hook on the wall. At Jermanah's questioning expression, he said, "For Grandmother."

The look Jermanah gave him was full of questions, but thankfully, this time she remained silent. She led the way through the silent halls to the lower level and made no apology for the tiny, dark room, hurrying to gather her belongings.

She stripped a thin blanket from the bed and retrieved a few small bags from hooks on the wall. After creating a small pile on the blanket, she pulled the book from under her tunic and placed it on top. Once she tied a tight, four-cornered knot, she lifted the small bundle in her arms.

Satisfaction settled in Kierigh's chest. She'd completely disregarded the dull gray robe hanging at the foot of the narrow bed. Then sadness replaced the pride. Even as a rebel forced to move camp at a moment's notice, he had more belongings, more personal items that held meaning for him. The uncomfortable realization most of what she'd packed in her bundle was only to have possessions made him ache to give her beautiful, useless things. More than she could ever carry.

She slipped past him into the hall and waited until he stood behind her. Her shoulders were warm and trembling under his palms. "Don't fear, little one."

"Not with you, Kierigh." She turned in his embrace and lifted her face. He closed the short distance and kissed her soft, welcoming lips.

He'd barely lifted his lips from hers before he smiled. "Are you now ready to leave?"

"There is nothing more to hold me here."

Kierigh led her directly to the nearest safe exit. They stepped from the Compound into a late twilight. They'd remained for too long. He leaned to speak in her ear. "We can't reach the second camp tonight. But there is a safe hiding place nearby. The walk isn't long."

Intending to ease her burden, he reached for the bundle but Jermanah clutched the bulky blanket tight against her chest and shook her head. His hands fell to his sides with soft slaps. "Use caution, little one. The ground is uneven."

After a lengthy distance, Jermanah stared at Kierigh's back. She should have known his idea of a short walk was far different than hers. She was so tired and her eyelids drooped lower with each heavy step. She stumbled over a tree root and pain shot through her toe. A soft grunt passed her tightly compressed lips.

Kierigh turned and touched her arm. Moonlight highlighted the concern in his expression. She hurried to reassure him. "I stubbed my toe. I'm fine."

Silent, he swept her into his arms. The comfort was such she had no wish to struggle, so snuggled against his broad chest and closed her eyes in relief.

"Jermanah, wake, little one." Kierigh's whisper intruded on a pleasant dream that floated away before she could capture the memory. She blinked. The moons' light barely penetrated the thick forest canopy. "We'll be safe here. Can you stand?"

Why would he ask such a silly thing? "Of course."

He chuckled and lowered her feet until she stood upright beside him. He gave a low whistle followed by the call of a small bird. The call repeated from nearby. "I told the watchers who we are. They'll guard the area until morning."

"Where are we? No, don't tell me. Do we sleep here?" Darkness hid the heat filling her face. Sharing her single blanket, in the open, with others nearby—

"Come." Kierigh held out his hand. She rested her palm in his and he led her toward the deeper dark of a towering bluff. They walked a few paces along the steep, rock-strewn face before he indicated a narrow opening. "A cave."

"I can't go in there."

"You'll be safe."

"No." Panic tightened her chest. The dark opening allowed no shine of moonlight. The space beyond would be small, the walls too close. Already the heavy rock pressed against her chest. Terror shivered over her skin and her voice wavered. "It's too dark. Too small. I'll be crushed."

Kierigh cocked his head at and brushed the back of his fingers over her heated cheek. "Jermanah, what are you afraid of?"

Embarrassed to admit weakness to him, she stared at her toes. "I fear closed spaces. It feels like the walls will crush me, as though a great weight presses on my chest. I can't go in there."

"If there is light?"

"At times, but not if the space is small. Confined."

Kierigh chuckled and she slapped his chest. "Don't laugh at my fear. Even with the Seer's instructions and special meditations, I've never conquered the fear. I'm—I was the only acolyte assigned an outside cell, a room with a window. The others couldn't bear my nightly screams."

There. Now he would turn from her. She may not have knowledge or experiences outside the Compound, but no fighter would logically burden himself with one who suffered from unconquerable fears.

Cupping her cheek, Kierigh leaned closer. "I'm not laughing at you. Everyone has fears. Close your eyes and I'll carry you."

"That won't help. I'll still know. Still be afraid."

But he covered her lips with his fingers and lifted her. She struggled against his gentle hands then bit the inside of her cheek until she tasted the copper of her blood. She wouldn't scream. She wrapped her arms around his neck, hid her face against the beat of his heart and whimpered. Kierigh stroked her back and spoke low, meaningless words of comfort.

"Open your eyes now." He stood her on her feet but she clung to his arm and kept her face hidden from the darkness.

He turned her, holding her so her back pressed against his body. "Open."

She couldn't resist the command in his tone, although she only opened one eye at a time. They stood inside a large, high-domed chamber. Flickering light illuminated the area with a cool brightness, reminding her of moonlight. She took a hesitant step forward. "Oh."

"The light emanates from the natural rock, so it never fails. We haven't explored the entire expanse of this cave system, but as you see, it's far from a small space. Do the walls close in on you?"

Jermanah searched the far reaches of the cavern then shook her head. "I don't think so. The light is bright enough to chase away the overpowering shadows. Why couldn't I see the light from outside?"

"The entrance is winding and the many turns block the light, and the cavern, from prying eyes."

Kierigh led her to a tiny, open alcove where thick pallets lay on the smooth rock floor. He sat, placed his knife on the floor and toed off his boots. She turned back to the cavern. Multi-colored sparkles danced from the crystals dotted over the surfaces of gigantic rock formations. "You'll be more comfortable over here."

Jermanah's squeak of surprise echoed across the sparkling chamber. Her heart pounded in her ears. "Please, don't startle me. The panic still lies just below the surface of my control."

Kierigh dipped his head in apology and she sank wearily onto the pallet. Her fingers lingered a moment on her bundle before she set it at her side. Her past, nearly everything she knew, was wrapped in the small parcel. Helpless sadness filled her. The future lay before her. She had no time to be unhappy. She propped a folded blanket behind her back and leaned against the wall.

"Are you hungry?"

Hungry? She didn't believe she could eat after the experiences of the past day so shook her head.

Kierigh eyed her then reached into a small box. "You must eat to regain your strength." After handing her a jagged hunk of hard cheese and a wrinkled apple, he waited until she nibbled at the cheese. He set a flask of water between them then attacked his own meager meal.

After he disposed of the apple cores, Kierigh joined her in leaning against the wall, their shoulders touching. He drew a deep breath. "You know where the child is?"

"I said I knew who had the child. I don't know where they are."

"Who?"

She barely understood how Poll was alive. Now she needed to explain the fact to Kierigh. She cast his a sideways glance. "The guard who tried to protect us from you in the forest."

"He was an excellent fighter." His calm statement gave her the courage to continue.

"I believed he was dead. But he was in the Compound, in the Highest's chambers with the babe and—" She shuddered. "—the babe's father. When the child cried, she ordered Poll to take him away and find a woman to care for him. He's to never allow the child from his sight." She paused. "He was relieved to leave."

Nodding, Kierigh spoke as if to himself. "How did he survive? I gave a mortal blow. Yet, I saw him as well."

"You wouldn't allow me to heal him." Jermanah's tone was flat and emotionless.

Kierigh cringed. She didn't accuse him yet the heavy weight of guilt filled his chest. To cover his discomfort, he swung around to lean over her. "He was my enemy. You were also an enemy."

"I'm not your enemy now." Dark eyes, wide and luminescent held his gaze without fear.

"No." Her lips parted under his, her kiss tasting of sweet apples, her tongue dancing silk against his. Unfortunately, this wasn't the time for love. He still had questions. Needed answers.

Nestling her against his side, he rested his back against the cold wall. "You have no idea where he may have taken the babe?"

"Only that he needed someone able to nurse."

He thought a long moment. "I didn't see anyone in the Compound except the Highest and her guards. However, a handful of women in the Stronghold have recently given birth. Rather than search a village for a woman, he would take the child there."

Jermanah wrapped her arms around her bent legs and turned her face to him. "Are you certain?"

"Yes. He wouldn't be able to take the child far. I doubt the boy has been fed since you last nursed him."

Jermanah sighed and he searched for the emotions she kept hidden beneath her calm expression. Did she miss the child? He kissed her forehead. "In the morning I'll go to the Stronghold to search for the child."

"I'll go with you."

"No."

Jermanah poked his chest with her finger. Her lips twitched. "Last time you told me 'no' I followed. I'll do so again."

Exasperation flowed over Kierigh, prickling his skin. If he thought it would help, he would shake her until she realized the danger of behaving foolishly. "You will not."

Determination firmed her features but Jermanah silenced him with a sweet kiss. "I will."

Grandmother often wore the same expression when she believed right was on her side. He shrugged. He seldom prevailed with Grandmother. Now it appeared Jermanah would have her way as well. "You will. But you will do as I say while within the Stronghold."

"I'll try." She chuckled and he smiled in return. Despite her easy words she didn't fully understood the danger the morrow would bring. A low growl rumbled through his chest. He eased her to her back and stretched at her side.

Taking her face between his cupped palms allowed him to stare into her eyes. He could lose himself in the darkening depths. He blinked and focused on making her understand. "This is serious. And extremely dangerous. I don't wish to worry about you. I'll have no time to worry."

"I will be careful. You have my word." She sealed her

promise with a kiss. Her fingers smoothed over his cheeks until she held his face as he held hers. "I don't want to worry about you, either. You must also promise to be careful."

Kierigh moved his mouth over hers and nipped at her full lower lip. The warm curve of her arched neck captured his attention. He pushed at the neckline of her tunic with his chin and darted his tongue along her collarbone. She shivered and clutched his shoulders.

He slid his hand under her tunic, filling his palm with the weight of her breast. Her nipple peaked under his teasing fingers.

"Kierigh?" The fear in her voice froze his movements. "You spoke the truth? I won't become—"

He stopped her words with a lingering kiss and spoke against her lips. "I've said I will never lie to you. You will not."

Her silence lasted a long moment before she took a deep breath that pressed her breast into his palm. "Then love me, Kierigh."

I do, little one.

thirteen

Light and shadows filtered through the trees at the edge of the forest. Jermanah wrapped her hands around Kierigh's upper arm and peered at the king's Stronghold. She'd seen the Stronghold from the walls of the Compound, but even that short distance had masked the sheer height and magnitude of the walls. Whipping from tall poles, banners snapped in the breeze. The smooth walls towered over a few ancient trees at their base. Other than the occasional barred gate, the only openings were a few tiny slits high above the branches. The structure had been created to make any approaching the structure feel infinitely small and insignificant.

The builders had been successful.

The tiny figures of guards watching the roads leading to the Stronghold moved along the top of the wall. How were they going to cross the short distance from the forest without being seen? She glanced at Kierigh. His face remained immobile, his jaw clenched.

She pressed her cheek against his arm and he shifted,

pulling from her grasp to take a step forward. “I can feel my brother.”

“If he’s there, we’ll find him.”

Kierigh turned to her. “You don’t have to come with me.”

Heart leaping at his concern, she nodded. “I know. But I have vowed to protect the child much as you’ve vowed to find your brother. We’ll face the danger together.”

“And you’ll do as I say? Listen to me?”

“Yes.”

Kierigh’s skeptical expression came from under lowered brows. Then he tucked a long strand of her hair under the cap he insisted she wear to conceal her braid. “There’s a change of guards soon leaving no one on the wall. We’ll have only a few minutes to cross the clearing.” He glanced at her bare feet.

She curled her toes. “I’ve never worn shoes. The run won’t be troublesome.”

“And last night?”

“It was dark and I was tired. I don’t yet know the pathways through the forest. This morning I can see my way.”

A grim smile pulled at his somber lips. A single horn blast from the Stronghold startled her and she caught her gasp behind her hand.

“The signal for the guards. Be ready.”

Prepared to face whatever unknown she raced toward, Jermanah watched the man at her side. He held up one hand and adjusted his knife at his side with the other.

She patted the blade strapped to her calf, took a deep breath and slowly let the air flow past her lips. The run would be longer than any she’d attempted and much different than running errands for a priestess. After another deep breath, she was ready.

Kierigh's hand slashed the air and he ran without checking if she followed. She stumbled forward but after a few paces, found her stride and ran smoothly. Still, Kierigh's longer legs carried him further ahead. Panic slowed her stride. She wasn't fast enough. She'd cause them to be seen. Captured.

Kierigh glanced over his shoulder and jerked to a stop. He motioned and grinned encouragement. Even if it endangered him, he wouldn't leave her behind. A burst of energy increased her speed. When she passed, Kierigh grabbed her hand and loped at her side.

She was gasping for breath by the time they reached the deep shadows at the base of the wall. Bent forward, Jermanah fought to draw breath into her burning lungs. Kierigh rubbed her back and she glared at him. He was hardly winded. He crouched so his face was level with hers. "The guards won't see us as long as we stay in the shadows. When you're able, we'll enter."

She nodded, straightened then pressed her palm against the pain in her side. Trailing her hand along the wall for balance, she paced a few steps and returned. The pain lessened and her breathing returned to normal. The cap had slipped during the run, so she pulled the rough covering from her head, wrapped her braid into a knot and set the cap firmly to hold her hair in place. "Ready."

"I don't know my way around the Stronghold as well as the Compound. If we can find Treenie, she'll help."

"Treenie?" An unaccustomed irritation rose in her chest. Who was this woman to Kierigh?

Confusion cleared to grim humor with the slight curl of his lips. "She's a kitchen maid who has often given me information about Zigor. She's a loyal friend. To me and to my followers."

Ashamed of her assumptions, Jermanah ducked her head. She had no right to be concerned over others in his life. He lifted her chin with a curled finger and waited until she looked at him.

"Are you ready?"

Remaining silent, she nodded. The deep shadows hiding their presence, they hugged the wall and soon reached a small wooden door set into a shallow recess. Kierigh tested the handle then with slow caution opened the door. After a deep breath, Jermanah followed him into a narrow hall lit by piles of the light-producing rock in niches cut into the wall.

Kierigh glanced back, concern for her fear evident on his face. The ceiling was high enough above them and the way more brightly lit than the hallways of the Compound. The priestesses would have benefited if these amazing rocks had been used there. With a smile, she motioned for him to continue.

They passed low doorways and panels she imagined might also provide entrance to other passages. Kierigh paused before a door, touched the thin strip of cloth knotted to the handle and shook his head. He moved to another door. There was no knot. A signal? He opened the door, scanned the room and entered. Jermanah followed on his heels.

Tumbled stacks of boxes and bulky bags littered the floor of a cramped storage room. High, thin windows provided dim light filled with swirling dust. The musty smells attacked Jermanah's nose. She rubbed at the irritation, attempting to force the tickle away before falling into a fit of sneezing. She made so much noise. "Someone must have heard me. What do we do?"

A wide grin lit Kierigh's face. Her breath stalled and her

concerns faded. He should smile more often. The expression softened the rugged angles, making his face so very appealing. Or, perhaps he shouldn't, for she didn't want another to feel as she did when he smiled.

"Don't worry. This is a seldom used storage area. Unless someone is right outside the room, they won't hear you sneeze." Despite the soft tones, his deep voice filled the room and rumbled through her. She held the wonderful feeling fast in her heart. Until she sneezed.

"I'll find Treenie and bring her. You'll remain here."

Jermanah arched one eyebrow and folded her arms across her chest. Kierigh blew out a short breath. "Please."

Relenting, she nodded and he pressed a light touch of his lips to her forehead. That wasn't enough to seal her promise, so she wrapped her arms around his neck, stood on tiptoe and lifted her mouth to his. Their deep, lingering kiss burst her senses to life. Every inch of her body knew his. Their hearts beat the same rhythm. Amazing, wonderful tingles—she jerked away and sneezed, barely covering her mouth with her hand.

Kierigh chuckled. "I hadn't thought to have such an effect on you, little one. It's dangerous to tarry, so I must go. But I won't be long." He turned, crossed to the door on the far wall and was gone.

Unaccustomed to having no duties to keep her occupied, Jermanah wandered aimlessly around the storeroom, opening boxes and bags to discover an extensive assortment of dried herbs and flowers, labeled carefully and stored according to type. Small wonder the room was so dusty.

Unable to shrug away the feeling of unease building with each moment Kierigh wasn't with her, she dragged a sack of sweet smelling flowers to where she could sit in the shadows and watch both doorways.

Poll hefted the basket and settled the handle securely over one arm. If the basket tipped, their plan might be discovered. Treenie peeked under the blanket at the two sleeping babes. Their tiny faces were soft and relaxed. She adjusted the blanket to cover them completely.

"What if the babes wake?" Poll winced. Concern made his voice overly loud.

Treenie ducked her head and glanced at him from under her lashes. "I gave them each a small portion of Zigor's wine." At his sharp intake of breath, she held up her hand. "It won't harm them. A tiny amount of wine is often given to a babe when they fuss. They'll sleep now and wake with no ill effects."

Poll adjusted the basket so the handle was padded by his sleeve. "I confess I have no knowledge of babes. In this, as other things, I trust your judgment."

Her bright smile wrapped around his heart. Aye, Treenie was his soul. She peered out the door to the quiet kitchen. Only the cooks' soft mumbling as they prepared vegetables for the evening meal indicated any presence there. She signaled Poll and when he moved next to her, wrapped her arm about his waist and leaned intimately into his side. Taking his free hand, she planted a kiss in his palm.

They ambled through the kitchen and past the cold storage areas. Once free of the cooks' sight, they hurried toward the farthest storage rooms. Poll stared at the openings lining the hall. "So many. How do we leave the Stronghold unnoticed?"

Treenie gave his hand a squeeze. "There are many halls and even more hidden passageways behind the walls of the Stronghold. The cooks now believe, as will any who see us outside the walls that I'm taking my lover to the forest for a tryst."

She held his hand between her breasts. "And so I am. However, the special meal we carry isn't be what they expect." She patted the blanket-covered basket.

"How do we find the rebels?"

Treenie covered his lips with her fingers. "Hush. It's not wise to speak so, even far from the kitchen. There could be someone in a nearby passage. The king has many spies." She glanced both ways then whispered, "There is a place I've been before. We'll be safe and they'll find us there. The babes will grow in freedom."

"I'm unsure..."

"I understand, my love. You've been loyal to the Compound most of your life, caught in the lies an illusions. But now you've seen the evil and watched how they destroy life and all that is good."

Poll nodded. He'd seen and experienced more in two days than in his long years at the Compound. But now occurrences he'd dismissed at the time rushed through his mind. He'd been blinded, dulled by the routine of duty he considered now little more than a farce.

"Come with me, Poll. If you don't see the truth of their cause or feel you belong in this fight we'll move on and start our life elsewhere. Either way, these children must be kept safe."

"You would forsake your life here? For me?"

"For you. For the babes. And for me. I have no wish to

remain a bond servant to the Stronghold. As soon as she could fetch and carry our daughter would be bound into service as well. I don't want that life for her."

"Then we'll go. Quickly."

Poll covered her fingers with his on the door handle. Treenie took a deep breath. "We'll pass through this storeroom and follow another passage to a door that opens in the outer wall. Our trek toward the forest, while within sight of the guards, will be shorter from there." She grinned over her shoulder and winked. "I don't wish for you to become overly tired carrying our supper."

Voices sounded from the other side of the door. Scrambling from her cozy nest, Jermanah crouched behind a stack of boxes, lifted her pant leg and drew her knife. Holding the blade before her, she peered around the edge of the boxes. The metal door handle rattled.

She hunched lower and held her breath. She'd stay hidden until whoever disturbed her safety retrieved what they needed and left. Reinforcing what little calm she could muster, she loosened her tight grip on the knife.

The door opened on silent hinges. A young couple entered, carrying a large basket. The woman led the man past Jermanah's hiding place.

She gasped, belatedly covering her mouth.

The couple paused. With measured, casual movements the man lowered the basket to the floor and reached for the sword at his side. Remaining hidden would be more dangerous than announcing her presence, so Jermanah stood. "Poll?"

He paused, head cocked to one side, brows drawn together. With his free hand he gestured to the woman who slid the basket toward the far door.

"Poll? Is it you?" A weight lifted from Jermanah's shoulders.

"I'm Poll. Who are you?"

"Oh." She stepped from the shadows and pulled the cap from her head, letting her braid fall over her shoulder.

Poll dropped to one knee. "My lady."

Jermanah shook her head. "I'm not your lady. Never again." Poll remained as he was with his head bowed. "Stand up. Don't bow to me. I'm only Jermanah."

The woman moved to Poll's side and raked her gaze Jermanah. "So. You're Jermanah. Hmm." She slapped Poll's shoulder. "Get up. You owe her no allegiance. We need to go."

Poll stood and looked sheepishly from one woman to the other. "Yes, I know, Treenie. But my lady—"

Jermanah flashed him a fierce look.

"Jermanah. This place is dangerous for you. I can't leave you here. Come with us."

Treenie's scowl smoothed to a bland expression and she stared past Jermanah. Not understanding the woman's odd reactions, Jermanah said, "No, I must remain here for a time. Where is the babe?"

Treenie stepped in front of the basket and fisted her hands at her hips. "What do you want with a child? Do you plan to give it to the Compound? Bring him to the Stronghold for sacrifice?" She took a single menacing step forward and lifted her fists.

Vowing to be as brave as Kierigh, Jermanah firmed her

spine. She wouldn't retreat before the woman's aggression. "I'd never harm a child. I'm here to see the boy safely from danger. I no longer owe allegiance to the Compound. Nor will I ever return."

Poll knelt again, this time to pull the blanket covering the basket to one side. Treenie cried a denial and Poll took her hand. "I believe her, Treenie. There's a change in her. I can't describe it, but I know. Like the changes of my own thinking."

Treenie turned her face from him. "You see what she wishes you to see. You see her through the eyes of love."

Jermanah caught her lower lip between her teeth. Love? Poll couldn't love her.

His mouth softened to a smile and he kissed the back of Treenie's hand. He caressed her fingers, rose and rested the back of his hand against her cheek. "Perhaps through my vows of devotion, but I don't love her in the way you mean. Treenie. I love you, the mother of my child."

Holding Treenie close, he spoke to Jermanah. "We take the child to the rebels." He motioned for her to look in the basket.

"Two babes?"

Treenie knelt and caressed the fine, soft hair of one of the infants. "She is mine."

Poll covered her hand with his. "She's ours."

Deep longing pulled a wish from within Jermanah. To share life with a child. She sighed. She didn't even know her own place in life, in the world she'd recently discovered. How could she even think to share it with another? Kierigh's relaxed and satisfied smile filled her mind. Perhaps if times were different.

She realized both Poll and the woman were staring at her. Storing away her dream, she said, "Kierigh is in the

Stronghold. Wait for with me and we'll return to the forest together."

Poll paused in thought. "Treenie's plan is better. Two of us will appear as lovers sneaking away. Four could arouse suspicion. Treenie says there's a safe place for us to await the rebels. The rebel can bring you there."

Treenie cast him a grateful smile. When her gaze returned to Jermanah, she was still wary, but the lingering defiance had disappeared. "We'll protect both babes, my lady."

"Please, only Jermanah. And, Poll? The rebel is Kierigh. The man you fought in the forest."

One hand resting where the knife had pierced his chest, Poll drew a deep breath. "I understand."

Treenie covered the basket. "We need to go."

"May I walk with you to the wall? I need fresh air not filled with dusty herbs." As if to prove her point, Jermanah sneezed.

"Can you find your way back to this room?" Treenie's words rang with accusation. So, not all her defiance had been tamed. "All the doors look the same."

Jermanah found a dirty string lying across a box. "I'll fasten this to the handle. I noticed other doors with ribbons or cloth on the handles. Some had knots, others didn't."

Defiance gave way to admiration in Treenie's slight smile. "You're observant. Those rooms without knots are unsafe. Make sure you remove the string when you return."

"I will. You must be on your way. When Kierigh returns, we'll follow. He'll be pleased the child is safe with you."

Jermanah studied their backs as she followed the couple from the musty storeroom. A great depth of feeling lay between them. She wished she'd had the opportunity to know Poll, but the Compound would have punished them both if he'd broken the guards' silence with her.

He wrapped an arm about the woman at his side. They appeared so comfortable together, knowing what the other felt, needed, wanted. Was that a part of the love between a man and a woman?

Love. Did she love Kierigh? Was that the strange churning inside her, the joy when he looked at her? What about the pleasure she received from his gentle mating? She shivered. Was what she felt only desire to repeat the physical act?

No. It was more, had to be more. She needed to talk to someone who would know. Perhaps Grandmother. The old woman's wisdom would help her understand her confused feelings. The Seer's knowledge had been taken from her and she needed someone to turn to for advice. She had no one but herself.

And Kierigh. But she couldn't discuss this with him. How could she explain to him how she felt when she didn't know herself? She studied the way Treenie leaned against Poll as they walked. Perhaps Jermanah could win the woman's trust. They might become friends. Treenie would understand her feelings.

Jermanah's musings ended when they reached the thick wooden door. Poll turned to her. "Return to safety. We'll find you in the forest."

Moving back into the shadowed hall, she nodded. But when a crack of light appeared beyond the opening door, she just had to step outside, if only for a moment, to cleanse the dust from her lungs. She followed the couple into glaring sunlight.

And into a tight ring of lances and drawn swords.

fourteen

Frustrated, Kierigh melted into the shadows and fingered the hilt of his knife. He'd searched every passageway known to him. He suspected there were others, but he'd been unable to discover any entrances. He drummed his fingers against the knife. Where would the child be if not within the Stronghold?

Nor had he found Treenie. One of the other maids told him she'd gone off with a lover. At his scowl, she'd offered herself as a replacement, eying him in what she thought was a seductive manner and running her hands over his chest. Revulsion had shivered over his skin at her touch. A fresh tremor passed through him. He doubted he'd ever find pleasure again. Except with Jermanah.

He'd taken too long for his search and Jermanah would become restless. He'd hoped to present her with the child, or at least the knowledge of where the boy was being held. He pushed from the wall. The return journey through the warren of passageways in the Stronghold would take longer still. Each moment risked their safety.

So he took the direct route, a hidden passage circling

Zigor's main audience chamber. The muted sounds of struggle echoed from a nearby vestibule. As Kierigh stopped to peer through a tiny spy hole into the king's chamber, a tight circle of Stronghold guards pounded their lances against the floor in time to their advancing steps. From the center of the cluster of men, a woman's shrill voice spat obscenities.

Kierigh placed his hands against the wall on either side of the hole. Treenie was always one to speak her mind. Doing so before the king was deadly. His return to Jermanah would be delayed until he freed his friend.

The front of the circle parted for an instant. A tall man stood beside Treenie. Kierigh drew his brows together. This was the guard Treenie had spoken of so fondly? How many times would his path cross this man's? A faint niggling memory tickled his brain. What had the Seer said to him?

Before Kierigh turned from the hole to plan the rescue, the cascading sound of multiple chimes announced Zigor's presence. Kierigh remained in place and snorted with disgust at the grand entrance. Zigor turned and held out his hand until the Highest joined him, followed by a ritually dressed Compound guard. Kierigh rolled his gaze. She dared flaunt her current favorite before the king?

Zigor tucked her hand in the crook of his elbow to lead her to the dais. She perched regally on a low stool at the king's feet, her guard stationed to one side. Zigor spread his robes and sat. He motioned to the clustered guards at the far end of the room.

Pushing the captives and pounding their lances to a raucous chant, they marched forward. Zigor winced, rubbed his temples and lifted one hand to stop the noisy progress. "Quietly."

One guard snickered, receiving a loud cuff of reprimand. The group continued to the dais in silence, opened the circle and pushed three captives to their knees.

The third captive remained hidden from his view, but deep foreboding washed through Kierigh. He trotted to a spy hole located at the side of Zigor's ornate throne.

One glimpse of the multi-hued braid confirmed his suspicions. He slumped against the wall. Why hadn't she stayed in the storeroom? Would she never listen to him? He let a breath huff through his teeth and returned to the spy hole.

The leader of the guards spoke with a grand, overly loud tone. Zigor motioned again for quiet. Kierigh strained to hear. "These three were discovered leaving the Stronghold by the old storeroom gate."

Treenie lifted her head but her defiance had vanished. Kierigh nodded in approval of her meek submission. "My lord, we only wished to share a meal, some time away from others." She curled her fingers around Poll's arm.

Zigor's gaze drifted to Jermanah. The Highest stood to hiss in his ear. He waved her away like an irritating bug. "And what of this other?"

Treenie glanced at Jermanah and shrugged. Kierigh held his breath. "She is a friend who also wished for time away from her duties in the Stronghold."

Arching his eyebrows, Zigor turned to the Highest. "An interesting trio, don't you think?"

The intensity of her urgent whisper brought a glower to the King's expression. He touched her arm. "So you have said. Do stop that infernal hissing. You shall have her—when I am done."

His heavy-lidded eyes turned to Treenie and she shuddered. The king grinned and stood. Pressing his palms to his temples, he took careful steps from the dais. "What dainties are you serving for your meal?"

A guard wrested the basket from Poll and dropped it before the king. Treenie and Jermanah cried out together. Poll lunged for the basket. The hilt of a sword crashed against the back of his head with a dull thwack. He crumpled to the floor. Treenie's gaze bounced from him to the basket, clearly uncertain what to do.

Zigor bent and jerked back the blanket. "Two babes? Which is the child of the Double Moon?"

Defiance once again filled Treenie's face and when Jermanah matched her expression, Kierigh bit his lip to keep silent. Defying the king was dangerous. And deadly.

But Zigor only chuckled and angled toward the women. His voice was soft, belying the evil intent of his words. "No matter. I will sacrifice them both."

With a wordless cry Treenie reached for the basket. Zigor turned his attention from her and grimaced. "Take that wailing woman and that—" He pointed at Poll's inert form. "Take them away. She appears capable. Give her the babes to care for until the morrow." He clasped Treenie's chin and forced her to look at him. "And they will be well cared for, will they not?"

Treenie collapsed in tears.

Kierigh wouldn't have much time to carry out a rescue. At least they'd be together.

A guard jerked on Jermanah's arm to drag her away but Zigor shook his head with slow deliberation. "Leave that one." He returned to his throne and glanced at Jermanah from the corner of his eye while he nuzzled the Highest's neck. Hands clasped before her, Jermanah stood, head down. The king grinned, signaled to the guards and waited until they backed from the chamber. Only the Highest's personal guard remained.

Kierigh gnawed on the inside of his cheek. *Don't look at him.* His silent plea must have reached Jermanah for she angled her head and shoulders from the display on the dais. Despite his assurances, she wasn't convinced she wouldn't turn into a sexual replica of the Highest. Zigor's lewd behavior would only serve to reinforce those fears. Kierigh needed to discover a way to protect her.

But he should also follow the guards so he knew where Treenie and the babes were held. Leaving Jermanah alone with the king and the Highest was out of the question. Her trust in herself was too fragile. No longer able to hear Treenie's cries, he made his decision. He would stay. Pressing his forehead against the rough wall, he tried to think, to plan against the danger and evil his little one faced without his protection.

Jermanah stared at her toes studying the patterns of dust across the nails. Anything to keep from lifting her gaze to meet the evil glint in the king's eyes. Refusing to look at the Highest, she wove her fingers together, squeezing until her knuckles turned white. She found no sense of calm in the way the Seer taught her, so she prayed for Kierigh to find her. Then she hoped he would leave her and save the babes. Oh, she didn't know what she wanted, except to be far from the heated, appraising gaze of the king and the anger shimmering in waves from the Highest.

The pointed toes of highly decorated and polished boots appeared in her vision. Smooth fingers, gentle but insistent, lifted her chin until she was forced to look into the king's bloodshot eyes. An unrestrained shudder of revulsion coursed through her.

The king grinned. "So, this is the pretty acolyte who disrupted our plans."

"Destroy her, my king." Hatred dripped from the Highest's words.

Zigor cast a wave of dismissal over his shoulder. "Patience, Highest. She may well yet serve our purpose. But, never fear, for I shall punish her." Arms folded across his chest he studied Jermanah. "I believe you will enjoy it, Highest. Perhaps then together we may discover a way to succor her wounds."

His heavy hand pressed on Jermanah's shoulder with undeniable force until she collapsed to her knees. Hopelessness and pain swirled with dark sorrow in her heart. She'd failed to protect one tiny child. Now she couldn't do anything to help Poll and Treenie. She couldn't even fight the king's touch. By focusing on anything but the king her mind might take her from this horrible moment. But she refused to think of Kierigh. She might say something in her pain to expose him to the king. She couldn't bear if her rebel was captured as well.

Zigor strolled to stand behind her and brushed her braid to one side. Cold metal scraped against her skin. The back of her tunic parted and slipped from her shoulders. Hot tears of shame burned. She clutched the ruined tunic to her chest in the hope pleading would end this humiliation. She turned her head and lifted her gaze to the king but his cold, icy expression showed only pleasure at her discomfort.

Zigor wrapped her braid around his hand and tugged until her back arched. He pressed a thin knife to her throat and leaned close to her ear. "Drop the tunic."

Clutching the fabric in tight fists, she held her breath. Perhaps he'd make her death swift. Someday Kierigh might forgive her failure. The point of the blade bit into her skin. Only a tiny pain, but the warm trickle of her blood delivered an odd sense of peace. Her spirit would soon join the Seer's.

"Drop it." Zigor gave her hair a sharp tug. Her fingers opened with her surprise and the tunic pooled at her knees.

"Good. You learn obedience." The king stepped away and she lifted her hands to cover her breasts.

"No, young acolyte. You do not have permission to hide your charms from us." With the flat of the knife he pressed against her hands until she let them drop to her sides. "I had thought to allow another to administer your punishment. But now, I find I am rejuvenated by the prospect."

Cool air flowed across Jermanah's skin. Her nipples firmed in the soft breeze and she bit her lip. A hot flush crept up her neck and across her face. Zigor captured her chin and turned her face toward the Highest. "See. She is in anticipation. Her body betrays her supposed innocence."

The Highest glowered at her. The remaining guard leered and licked his lips. Zigor gave a wordless, reverberating growl and pointed at the guard. "Leave. Now."

The man bent to the Highest's ear and whispered, gesturing with one hand. She shoved him away and pointed to the door. His shoulders slumped, but the Highest touched his hand and cast him a wide smile.

Now Jermanah understood the meaning behind that smile. The same intent and promise sparked in the king's eyes.

She ached for death and an end to this torment. She'd beg, if not for the fear of unknown evil that might be meted out to her instead. *Be brave, strong like Kierigh.*

Zigor tapped the knife against his cheek. His brows lowered, but he smiled when the Highest returned her attention to him. “Relax, my dear. I shall present you with a pleasing display of my prowess.” He cleared his throat. “With the whip, of course.”

The Highest clapped her hands and moved from her stool to sit on the throne. One of Zigor’s brows arched at her actions. Then he shrugged and sauntered to a display on the far wall. Touching each piece with a lover’s caress, he studied an assortment of weapons and oddly shaped tools. His fingers lingered on a long, leather wrapped handle before lifting the weapon to test the weight in his hand.

He took the whip from the wall, swinging the falls back and forth. Then he swirled them over his head. Horrified yet fascinated by the dancing leather strips, Jermanah wondered how he didn’t tangle the many ends. Repeated sharp cracks filled the expansive chamber. The king’s breathing grew harsh. Excitement sparkled in his gaze. Silent, he advanced, drawing the tips of the whip through his fingers.

Unable to bear Jermanah’s humiliation or halt the king’s actions, Kierigh turned from the spy hole after Zigor cut through her tunic. Kierigh’s anger grew to a hot, red haze, filling his vision and blurring his reasoning. Steps increasing in speed, his breaths labored, he paced the narrow passage. He jerked to a stop and slammed his fist into the stone wall.

Teeth clenched, he choked back a shout of pain. His reason returned with the pain, but he’d wandered far from the audience chamber. Fool that he was, he'd left Jermanah alone. And at the mercies of Zigor and the Highest, two who held no mercy. Glancing around, he determined his location, turned on his heels and clutched the hilt of his knife.

A hiss of pain escaped his tightly pressed lips. He peered at his fingers, flexed them carefully. He didn't believe he'd broken any bones, but the slightest movement jolted sharp pain up his arm.

A rueful snort helped him refocus his anger. He couldn't forgive his lack of control. So, he ran, Jermanah's pain drawing him recklessly through the maze of passageways.

Jermanah tucked her chin against her chest and clenched her fists. The Highest had leaned forward in eager anticipation as the whip whirled over Jermanah's head. Glee filled the woman's face. The Highest would enjoy her pain, perhaps even join in the giving. But Jermanah vowed she would give them no other pleasure. The reassuring presence of her knife at her calf offered her a way to deny both them both.

Zigor trailed the tips of the whip across her shoulders, stroking gently back and forth. Jermanah bit her lip. She refused to give him the satisfaction of her cries and prayed when the whip fell in earnest, she'd be able to keep silent.

The whip cracked near one ear then at the other. She flinched and covered her face with her hands. Zigor grunted and the whistle of leather above her head stopped.

A deep voice filled the silence. "Do not."

Jermanah tensed, her muscles burning and knotted. Afraid the interruption was a sadistic trick of the king, she kept her face hidden.

Zigor's derisive laughter rang through the chamber. "And why shouldn't I do as I please?"

"You will not harm her. If you must enforce punishment, punish us."

"You offer yourself in her place? Foolishness."

"Not foolishness, my lord. You created within this body the acceptance of punishment and pain. This woman doesn't understand your...needs."

"Why would you do this?"

"Our pain will end on the morrow. Whatever we may endure this day is inconsequential."

"Ah, but you're mistaken. The child has been returned. Along with a second brat also worthy of sacrifice. You'll be with me for yet another cycle."

The whip snapped close to Jermanah's ear, followed by a muffled crack. With a wooden clatter, the handle slid across the floor to bounce against her knee. "We said you will not."

Zigor sputtered. Someone knelt beside her and wrapped soft, worn material around her. After a moment's hesitation, she lifted her head. A man's large body blocked her view of the king. Long, thin scars crossed the man's broad back. Most were old and long healed, others more recent and reddened. She gasped and released the tears she'd fought to hold back, letting the moisture blur her vision and drop to the gray floor. He'd suffered much pain.

The sharp staccato of boot heels retreated. "Take her then. Tomorrow I will have my pleasure. From you. And yes, from her as well."

The Highest's voice rose in irate protest. Zigor silenced her with a harsh command. Stomping and rustling underscored by their muted argument sounded as they exited the room. Jermanah kept her head lowered. Any movement might cause the king or the Highest to return.

The man knelt before her and waited silently. After a long moment, she risked lifting her head. How could this be? Blinking, she cleared the blur from her vision. "Kierigh?"

Concern filled the man's light blue-green eyes and he cocked his head to study her. "We are Daud. Who is Kierigh?"

Intending to cup his cheek, Jermanah reached toward him. He jerked back as if unwilling to allow her to touch his head. So she rested her palm against his shoulder then ran her fingers over the ropes of scar tissue across his chest. He trembled under her touch but remained still.

She stared into the almost familiar face, watching the blues change in vibrant intensity. She had the odd sense someone new looked through his eyes at each breath. Determination not unlike that which filled Kierigh's gaze tinged the depths. But instead of anger, pain fought with determination for dominance.

His hair was the same dark-golden color but cropped close to his skull. Without doubt he was the brother Kierigh had searched a lifetime to find. A bubbling of joy made her smile. "Your brother looks for you."

"We are a child of the Double Moon. We have no family, but for the king who we must serve." The words were a litany, devoid of emotion.

Jermanah shook her head. "You were born a twin. Your brother, who was born before you, has searched for you. He'll save you from the king."

Daud laughed bitterly. His eyes turned cold, a dark, nearly brown green, and stony hard. "It is too late to save us." Then the blue returned and softened. "Come. We must take you to a place of safety before Zigor rethinks his actions. We are not often able to talk him away from his pleasures."

Jermanah clasped his arm and he helped her stand. Disgusted, she kicked at the remnants of her tunic and glanced at the material she held across her breasts. Daud had bared his skin to Zigor's whip—again—to offer her his shirt for cover. She turned her back and slipped the shirt over her head. The hem trailed to her knees.

Warm and feeling much safer she faced Daud. He stared into the distance over her head. "Kierigh is your older brother, born before the time of the moons. He's here in the Stronghold."

"It's too late for us, but perhaps with our sacrifice, this pain will end for others. This is our wish, and our plan." Daud spoke with the barest hint of regret behind his determination.

Then he wrapped an arm about her shoulders and guided her to the far end of the chamber. He was so like Kierigh, yet so different. "Who are these others you speak of? Will they help us free you and the babes?"

"There is another child? We though Zigor meant only to deceive us."

"The child and my friends were taken from here before —" Her words caught in her throat, choking her with the taste of rising bile.

Daud slowed. His fingers flexed against her shoulder. "We will find these others, and the child. Once we lead them from the Stronghold, Zigor will be forced to continue with our sacrifice."

Refusing to go further until he explained, Jermanah curled her toes into a crack between the flooring stones. "You say we. Are there allies in the Stronghold?"

After his failed attempt at encouraging her to move, Daud blew out a harsh breath. “Zigor believes each life sacrificed increases his power.”

“So I have been told.”

“Somehow he learned to create a new life at his whim, at his desire, so he created within this body many, many lives.” Daud’s jaw tightened. The muscles in his neck stood in stark relief. His eyes closed. He blinked and she shrank away from the hate and anger simmering in the dark, now nearly black depths.

Forced through clenched lips, his voice was rough, rusty with sharp, deep tones. “We have a plan to destroy the bastard. He will harm no more of us. No more children. No one. He will use this body no longer for his perverse pleasures.” His eyelids dropped.

The sharp, tense lines of Daud’s face eased. His eyes opened clear, apologetic and pale blue. Jermanah frowned but Daud held out one hand to keep her from speaking. “We are sorry. There are times we can’t contain the angry ones. The many of us are each individuals. Our lives are different, our joys and sorrows personal. Each of us has a private place within this mind.” He gestured to his temple then indicated his body. “All of us inhabit this living vessel.”

Jermanah took a deep breath. “I still don’t understand.”

“Nor do we, even though we share the body. We can only accept the lives we have been given. But on the morrow, we will make a choice. A choice such as we’ve never been given. Come. We will take you to a safe place then find your friends and lead you from the Stronghold.”

“But Kierigh—”

“If there is a brother within these walls, we’ll find him

as well." He guided her to a tapestry, pulled it to one side and escorted her to a dim passageway.

Breathless, Kierigh returned to the spy hole. His chest lifted spasmodically, making it impossible to hold his eye steady at the small hole. Releasing all the air from his lungs, he peered into the empty room. A soft undercurrent of voices whispered from one side. He listened. There. Jermanah. She didn't sound in pain or distress. Relief tempered his breathing. He altered the angle of his viewing.

A tall, partially dressed man led Jermanah through a doorway. A tapestry fell with a dusty thump to cover the opening.

A curse huffed through his lips and he slammed his fist against the wall. Fresh pain shot from his abused hand and he barely kept his teeth clenched against the sounds of dual agony rising from his hand and his heart.

fifteen

Daud settled Jermanah in his small room and gave strict instructions to remain there. From her stiff posture, he knew she'd have difficulty following his advice.

"I want to go with you."

"No."

She offered him a weak smile. "You're just like your brother."

Daud scrubbed his hands through his hair and across his face. She insisted they had a brother. Could that be the odd emptiness he'd experienced from time to time? He'd often wondered how there could be so many and yet still have the sense of something missing. Meeting this supposed brother would perhaps answer many questions. In an attempt to clear his thoughts, he shook his head. "So you say."

"I won't stay here and do nothing."

Daud matched her defiant fists on hips stance. "You shall, and willingly. Or we'll lock the door. We know where Zigor hides the key."

At the mention of the king, she blanched. "He won't come here, will he?"

As they'd passed the king's chambers, Daud had heard the unmistakable sounds of the Highest comforting the king. "He is... occupied."

Jermanah's hands dropped to her sides and she glanced around the tiny chamber. A strange shame at the few things Zigor allowed them to keep burned the back of his neck. "He locks you in here?"

"Often. Because we are not to be seen by others until our sacrifice. And as punishment."

"That's a terrible thing for one man to do to another." She glanced at the high, narrow window. "You'd have to find a way to climb up there to even see outside."

"And so we have. We're not allowed beyond the secret hallways of the Stronghold. A window is our only way to view the world."

"I understand."

Daud arched his brows in disbelief and question.

"I was an acolyte of the Compound."

She angled from him for a moment. He knew little of the Compound other than what he'd seen of the Highest of the High. The woman before him was nothing like how he imagined other women ensconced there. Surprise lifted Daud's pale eyebrows higher.

Jermanah faced him and spread her hands. "We were allowed outside only within the courtyard, a bare area with no grass, no trees or shade. Carrying out tasks there in our heavy robes was unpleasant, hot and dusty. I know how it feels to always be looking through the window, wondering what lay beyond what little I could see. In only two days Kierigh has shown me a world outside the constructs and restrictions of the Compound. A world of freedom and choices."

Daud grinned at the soft pink infusing her face. Her eyes sparkled. From the hidden hallways they'd observed residents of the Stronghold and understood the differences between lust and true emotions. Jermanah loved this supposed brother. And he must care a great deal to face her stubbornness. A rebel and an acolyte. An interesting combination. One Daud wished they had time to know better.

He cleared his wayward thoughts. As it was, there was little time for him to find and return with her friends. "We have books. Perhaps you would like to read while we're gone. We'll return soon with the babes."

"You'll come to the forest with us."

"We will not."

"How else are we to prevent any sacrifice?"

"Must you always argue? We have a plan. We will not fail. The sacrifices will end on the morrow. Shall I lock the door to protect you?"

For a moment Jermanah appeared ready to continue arguing. Then she shrugged and smiled sweetly at him. "I will stay until you return. But don't be long. I'm not known for my patience."

"So we have seen."

Daud left Jermanah studying his small shelf of books. Hoping she would be true to her word, he sighed and moved swiftly through well-known passages to the dungeon level.

The Highest sat demurely at the end of Zigor's bed, hands clasped in her lap. Zigor paced, arms crossed, fingers drumming against his upper arm. He stopped before her and waited. Perhaps he was no longer angry with her.

She licked her lips and lifted her gaze. His eyes were cold, his face stern as if carved of the hardest stone. Angling toward her, he spoke. "We may be done with the issue of the acolyte, Highest. You gained no information from the Seer. And you killed the old fool without learning the location of the book."

"Zigor, I—"

"Silence." He bent until his sharp nose touched hers and captured the back of her head with his hand. "We needed to know the full extent of the prophecy. There must be more than the simple union of the Stronghold and Compound to bring power to the land."

Digging his fingers into her scalp, Zigor shook her head. She twisted from his grasp. "He wouldn't speak. All the man did was smile. I became angry."

"You couldn't have been as angered as I am now." He crushed his lips over hers, the press of his teeth drawing blood. Good, she needed this anger. She sought to extend the kiss, offered him more. He shoved her back on the bed and straddled her. "Shall I do to you as you did to the old man?"

His eyes glittered and he pressed her shoulders deep into the soft mattress. With a half-hearted struggle, she drew breath to scream. He laughed, circling her throat with his large hands. "A scream will do you naught, Highest. You well know screams are not unusual coming from this room. Ah, with just a little pressure and I could snap your neck."

She thought to make a scornful remark at his threats until he squeezed, stopping the flow of air to her lungs. Thrashing against the weight of his body, she scratched at his hands. He leaned as if to kiss her, loosened his fingers and blew air into her mouth.

Gasping, she wrenched her mouth from his. Zigor chuckled and leaned his forearm against her chest. She shoved at his shoulders. Darkness swirled at the edge of her vision. Shifting his weight to his elbows, he allowed her the air she desperately needed. He cradled her head in his hands, and exerted increasing pressure on her temples.

"Or I could crush your skull." He pressed his thumbs deeper, forcing her groan. "But, I won't."

He traced the length of her face with his finger then drew patterns on her skin with the blood from her lip. Ignoring her half-hearted protests, he continued his designs down her neck and across her breasts, topping each taut nipple with a drop of blood.

"We need each other to complete the prophecy, Highest. It will be enough. The book is unneeded, probably only a way the Seer attempted to wrest control for himself. You were wise to silence him. Power will fill the land and we shall rise with it."

Zigor slid his hands to her breasts, smearing his designs. He filled his palms with her. His nails dug deep into her skin leaving flat, red marks. More. She needed more and moaned.

Zigor leaned close to her ear, his thumbs pressed again at the hollow of her throat. "Nonetheless, Highest. Remember my anger. Do not fail me again."

He held her shoulder down with one hand and freed his erection. When he jabbed his knee between her thighs, she opened willingly to him. Anticipation shimmered through her and she offered him her best, sultry smile.

Zigor's brows lowered over his cold expression. He slapped her and her head snapped to the side. Before the pain registered, he entered her in one fierce stroke. His smile grew colder still. "You *will* fear me."

A strange, lost feeling sank deeper in Kierigh's chest with each twist and turn in the maze of secret passageways. He wandered with aimless purpose, stopping at each spyhole lining the way, peering through the tiny openings for the length of a breath. He hoped to see Jermanah, or Treenie, or the babes. But few of the rooms he scanned were occupied, nor apparently even recently used.

Then in one ornately decorated room, the Highest of the High paced, waving her arms while speaking to someone hidden from his view. With his ear close to the hole, Kierigh recognized the swish of the Highest's robes and the sharp staccato taps of her sandals.

Her voice low and simmering with anger, she stumbled over her words. "Damn the Seer to all horrors. I insisted he give me the *Book of Futures* and he smiled. All he did was smile. Now Zigor holds me responsible for our lack of knowledge. I'm not the one who plans to force completion of the prophecy."

Kierigh turned from the spy hole and patted the bag at his hip. So, the book Jermanah risked discovery for was important to the continuation of Zigor's rule. She'd refused to leave the book behind in the cave, even when she had no idea how important it might be. Had she known, she would have insisted on carrying the book herself. And now it would be in Zigor's hands.

He moved along the hall and paused in a sliver of light glinting through a high window. Pulling the book from his bag, he studied the blank cover then flipped through the handwritten pages. He stared at the tiny writing, willing the words of the unfamiliar language to make sense. Hopefully her training with the Seer would allow Jermanah to decipher the script.

He snapped the book shut and returned it to his bag. He struggled to relax enough to access his sense of direction. He had to find Jermanah soon. Judging by the angle of light from the window, the afternoon was well gone and he had no desire to spend the night in the Stronghold's cold passageways.

Jermanah's image filled his inner vision with such clarity he knew she was near. He took a few steps, stopped, shook his head, and spun on his heels to stride in the opposite direction.

The lower Daud traveled through the dungeon levels the more damp cold seeped into his body. The usual rustle and scrabbling of startled vermin sounded with each step. The smell of their droppings nearly overpowered him. Thankfully many years had passed since Zigor had last held them here, yet they remembered every fear-filled moment. Anger bubbled through him and those created by that anger shoved at his forehead and behind his eyes until he was forced to stop. He held his fingers to his temples and concentrated. Finally the Captain and Custodians surrounded the angry ones and led them to a place deep within the mind where they'd remain under control. Until the sacrifice.

Daud took a deep breath, coughed the stench from his lungs and silently thanked the inner helpers. The cool wash of their acknowledgment, along with the assurance their plan would be successful, encouraged him.

He strained to see in the dim light. The babes hadn't been held in the upper dungeons, and this, the lowest, was a dangerous place. Even the guards avoided duty here. Once a prisoner was secured, a guard might visit each day to bring scraps from the kitchen garbage pile. But more often, many died and weren't discovered until the stench of rot rose over the odor of the vermin gnawing on their flesh.

A tiny glimmer of light illuminated the barred slit of a door at the end of the row of cells. He gave a snort of disbelief. The guards had never been kind enough to leave him a candle. He sidled around the piles of unrecognizable trash and droppings.

At the cell door he pressed one hand against the rough, slime-slicked wood for a moment. A woman crooned a gentle lullaby. A child within his body responded to the soft, kind tones and began to weep. A female helper wrapped her arms about the young one and offered comfort. It was never enough.

Standing to the side, he peeked between the narrow bars. A tiny space had been cleared in the center of the floor. The woman sat upon a blanket, nursing a babe. A man lay with his head on her thigh. A second child rested on his chest. The stub of a candle flickered, barely touching the gloom.

A lump lodged in Daud's throat. Despite the filthy surroundings, this was a scene such as they'd imagined when those inside wished for a true family. These children would grow and play in freedom as those of the body had never been allowed to do. These children would know little of darkness, of pain. Daud vowed it. The vow echoed through him as each inner voice added their pledge.

First, these tiny babes must be freed and taken from the Stronghold.

Impatient, yet fascinated, Daud watched until the child finished nursing. Then he scratched on the door. The man jerked, sat, and carefully lay the babe he held in a basket before rising to his feet. He stumbled and clutched the back of his head. Shaking off the woman's restraining hand, he moved to the door.

"Who's there?"

Daud leaned close to the bars so they could see his face in the flickering light. The woman frowned with confused recognition. "Kierigh?"

Daud shook his head. "We are Daud. We are told Kierigh is our brother. Make ready, we will return and release you."

At the meeting of four dank passages he stepped into the guard's cubicle. As usual, the key lay on a small, scarred table. He returned to the cell, unlocked the door and hurried the couple to the main hall. He returned the key exactly as he'd found it. Beyond the table, he wiggled his fingers through the loose mortar between cracked stones and opened a narrow panel.

Motioning for silence, Daud led them swiftly up a steep incline. At each dungeon level he lifted one hand, halting them while he listened or looked through one of the many small holes lining each passage.

Near the upper halls of the Stronghold, the harsh echo of the man's labored breathing forced Daud to stop. He motioned for them to sit then crouched next to the man and glanced into the basket. The two babes slept side by side, tiny arms intertwined.

Daud moved his gaze to the woman. "We recognize you from the kitchen. You're Treenie?" She nodded. Intrigued by the tatters of a formal uniform, Daud studied the man. "But you're not of the Stronghold. A Compound guard?" The man's head bobbed once in agreement.

"Which is the child of the Double Moon?"

Treenie looked away from the basket and the man rested his hand over both children. Daud offered a smile for their concern. "We won't harm either child. We only wish to protect and save them from the king's sacrificial stone. We will be the sacrifice on the morrow. Come now, we'll show you the way from the Stronghold once it is full night. For now, we'll take you to Jermanah."

The man clutched Daud's arm. "Jermanah is safe? The king didn't... did not..."

"Zigor did nothing. We prevented him."

Treenie took the man's hand and caressed his fingers. "I told you, Poll. Her life is charmed."

Daud stood, studied the injured, weary man and reached for the basket. "You're hurt. We'll carry the babes so you can conserve your strength. You'll need energy to reach the forest. We won't go with you then."

Poll nodded and struggled to stand, finally accepting the hand Daud offered. Basket swinging gently at his side, Daud turned and strode down the long passageway.

Kierigh turned a sharp corner into a hallway lit with widely spaced lamps. He paused to consider the change. Most of the secret passages were seldom used and perhaps forgotten by most. This hall was clean and well kept. He puzzled the mystery and searched for clues in the darker corners.

He also considered the book thumping against his hip with each step. He didn't believe in prophecy and accepted no destiny except that he created for himself. What power could a page filled with scribblings of an ancient language hold for one man, let alone an entire land? Why would the Seer insist Jermanah find this single book?

Engrossed in his thoughts, Kierigh grew careless. Until he slammed into a broad chest.

He gasped and stared into his own face.

A muffled thud jerked Jermanah from her reading. She tossed one of Daud's journals aside and faced the door. She'd followed Daud's instructions to stay in the room so far, but the shuffling just outside the door piqued her curiosity.

She firmed her lips, wrapped her fingers around the handle and before she could rethink her impulsive actions, yanked open the door.

Two men stood frozen, nose to nose. She covered her grin with her hand then spoke in the stunned silence. "Kierigh?" His face turned toward her. "I believe you've found your brother."

Daud's gaze fixed on her for a brief moment. "We didn't believe, but now..." His pale eyes shifting in color and intensity, he stared at Kierigh. If there were truly many inside Daud, they all seemed to be assessing their new-found brother.

Kierigh returned the intense examination. Disbelief colored his expression. Jermanah frowned. Didn't he believe now that his brother stood before him?

A slow smile spread across Kierigh's face. He took a quick step to clasp Daud in a fierce hug. "My brother."

Daud flinched then held himself stiff. He found and held Jermanah's gaze with panic filled eyes as expressive as Kierigh's. Sadness settled in her chest. Daud had never been held in comfort or in joy. Even in the harsh strictures of the Compound, with the Seer's compassion, she'd experienced kindness in human touch. If only a portion of what she'd read were true, Daud had suffered greatly only because of the time of his birth.

Daud's ever-changing eyes pleaded with her. She nodded and moved forward to lay her hand on Kierigh's arm.

Tears spiked his lashes. "Jermanah, this is my brother."

"Yes, I know. But gently, Kierigh. He has been through much and doesn't understand your exuberance."

Kierigh jerked back but left one palm resting on Daud's shoulder. Daud eyed the hand, his muscles tensed as though he would spring away at any moment.

Kierigh's lips flattened. Jermanah lifted his hand from his brother's shoulder. Daud's muscles slumped though his expression remained wary. She tugged on Kierigh's hand until he took another backward step. "I know only part of his tale, but it makes my blood run cold. You must be gentle and patient with him, Kierigh."

Kierigh tilted his head to study his brother. Tension

vibrated the air around them. After a long moment he nodded.

Daud blinked twice. When he focused on Kierigh, his eyes were free from fear. "We thank you for your understanding. We are called Daud."

"We?"

Jermanah drew Kierigh's attention with a light touch. "It's part of his tale. But it will be long in telling. Perhaps tonight, when we've returned to the safety of the forest there will be time."

Kierigh shook his head. "First we must find the child."

Poll stepped from the shadows and rested his hand on the basket hanging from the crook of Daud's elbow. "The babe is here."

Relieved Poll was safe, Jermanah asked, "What of the others?"

Treenie moved to Poll's side. She cast an appraising glance over Jermanah and Kierigh, then smiled at Jermanah. "Both babes are safe."

Kierigh's brows arched. "Both babes?"

"Poll and Treenie have a daughter. That's why she's able to feed little Poll. Isn't that wonderful?" Jermanah sighed.

Daud cleared his throat and gestured for them to enter his room. "This hallway is used by none but this body and the king. Zigor has much to consider this night. While we don't believe he'll call for us, we must take care. We'll take you to the gate. It's nearly time for the guards to check the prison levels and it will be discovered you're no longer in the cell."

Kierigh snuggled Jermanah close to his side. "We'll spend the night learning of each other, my brother."

"We would be more at ease if you called us Daud."

"I will. I would know of your life. Of your time here. Perhaps your knowledge will help us defeat the king and bring an end to the sacrifice of innocent children."

Daud reached for the journal Jermanah had tossed on the bed. He thumbed through the pages and touched some of the words with a gentle fingertip. "Such would be our greatest wish. Greater even than the wish for freedom from this room."

He handed the book to Jermanah. "Let him read this, for the words will tell him much about us. We don't have time to explain."

She slipped the book into the bag at Kierigh's hip. "I'm sorry, Daud. If I'd realized sooner how the Compound contributed to your pain I would have—" She paused in confusion. What could she have done? She'd had no power within the Compound to create even the smallest of changes.

Shaking his head, Daud gave her a sad smile. "There would have been nothing you could have done. Now, at the time of our sacrifice, you'll have the opportunity to help the people of this land rediscover freedom and peace."

Kierigh frowned. "You speak as if you'll be sacrificed on the morrow."

"Yes. It is our plan."

"I won't allow it." Hands fisted at his sides, Kierigh faced his brother.

"We've planned for this day since the last sacrifice of a tiny boy. You will do nothing to stop us."

Poll tugged the basket closer to where he sat propped against the wall.

The anger in Daud's voice faded. "There will be no more sacrifices. Zigor created us in the hope our many lives would increase his power as many times. That will not happen. We can't explain everything in this short time. Read our journal. Gain insight and bless our efforts."

He held up one hand to stop Kierigh's grumbling. "It's time for you to leave. We're overjoyed to know we haven't been as alone as we believed. You and your lady will prosper under the freedom we buy with our lives."

Jermanah covered Kierigh's mouth with her fingers. "We'll go to the forest tonight. You'll learn more of your brother through the book." Then, hoping to convince him to use caution with his brother, she stretched to reach his ear and whispered, "We'll return before the sacrifice."

At Kierigh's surprise, she firmed her lips, nodded and turned to Daud. "We're ready."

Treenie assisted Poll to his feet. He stumbled and covered the back of his head with his hand. Jermanah tugged on Kierigh's sleeve and nodded toward the basket. A twitch of his lips signaled his understanding. He took the basket from Poll's weak grip. "I'm pleased you didn't die."

Treenie clutched Poll's shirt front. "Die? Poll, what does he mean?"

Kierigh shifted the basket on his arm. "Another long tale, Treenie. Poll will tell you of it when he's rested."

Poll gave him a nod filled with gratitude.

In a silent procession, the group followed Daud, soon arriving at a tiny alcove. The door in the Stronghold was nearly as thick as it was wide and took the strength of both Daud and Kierigh to open it. Dark fingers of shadows stretched toward them from the forest. A line of scrubby trees and tall rock formations promised safety. Kierigh made a soft sound of satisfaction. "I know this area, but didn't realize there was an entrance here."

As the others moved through the doorway, he turned to Daud. "You *will* come with us."

"We will not."

"I won't lose the brother I've just found. I wouldn't be able to face Grandmother without you."

Daud's sigh was one of infinite sadness. Tears stung Jermanah's eyes. Wistfulness and pain filled Daud's handsome face. "We have a grandmother? Let her read our journal so she will know us as well."

"She will know you. You'll meet her on the morrow."

Daud shook his head. "No. Tomorrow we meet the knife of sacrifice. And we're glad of it. Go now, while it's safe."

Kierigh clasped his brother's shoulder. "I say you'll come with us now."

Seizing the front of Kierigh's shirt, Daud lifted until Kierigh balanced on his toes. Only the stone wall at his back held him upright. Low and menacing, Daud's voice dropped, reverberating as though many voices fought to be heard at once. "We said we will not leave this night. Our plan will succeed in bringing an end to the rule of Zigor."

With little effort he lifted Kierigh higher until Kierigh clutched at his brother's forearms. Daud's eyes flashed. "*You* will go now and leave us to our destiny."

Once Daud opened his fingers, Kierigh's back scraped down the wall until his feet touched the ground. He slipped lower, crouched and gripped his knife.

"No," Jermanah gasped.

Both men focused on her. Daud passed a hand over his face. The angry flash disappeared. "I beg forgiveness." His voice was now soft and filled with sorrow. "We're less able to control the angry ones as the time of our plan's completion draws near. We are sorry." Head bowed, he turned away.

Moving in front of him, Jermanah waited until Daud

looked at her. "You have a right to anger. But sacrificing yourself will do no good. Come with us. Please."

The fire returned to his expression, His teeth clenched. The muscles of his neck stood in sharp relief. "We. Will. Not." His jaw relaxed and his eyes cleared. "Your concern means much to us. We'll rest easier knowing you, the babes and our brother are safe."

Nodding, Jermanah gathered the others and led them from the Stronghold. Listening to the muted sounds of their slow footsteps, she steeled herself against turning back and pleading with the determined man.

Kierigh's reluctance to leave his brother was evident in each heavy step.

Daud needed time inside the mind to finalize plans with the Captain and chosen others. They couldn't risk Zigor calling for them, so Daud stopped at his entrance the king's chambers before returning to his room. He peered through a spy hole.

The king towered over a pair of kneeling guards. "They're gone?"

So, the cell had been checked. Knowing it foolish, Daud sent a thought to his brother to hurry.

"Yes, my lord king. There wasn't no one there when we took food."

Zigor slammed a fist against his desk and Daud grinned. The sacrificial child had alluded Zigor again. Pride in causing the king's foul temper filtered through those inside. His spine straightened. The plan would succeed.

"Traitor. Who is the traitor?" Zigor shook with rage. He wrenched his sword from the top of his desk, whirled and the blade whistled through the air. A guard's head tumbled to the floor.

Daud shuddered. The last time he'd witnessed the king in such rage, an entire conclave of false priests lay dead at his feet. Still, Daud had no fear for their body. The king wanted his power. And so, would gain much more than he anticipated.

Zigor pointed his sword at the second guard then at the crumpled body. "Get that out of here. Then find them. Do not dare return to my presence until you bring me the child. Kill the others, but bring me the child of the Double Moon unharmed."

Retaining his regal posture with the sword extended, Zigor remained silent while the guard dragged his companion's body into the hall and returned for the head. Blood stained a scarlet trail across the pale stone floor.

Grinning, Zigor called after the guard. "Send a woman to clean this mess. No. Send the Highest to me instead."

Daud allowed himself a small grin of triumph. The king would remain occupied with his anger and the Highest.

The body need not fear an interruption during their final planning. Returning to his room, Daud sat on his bed, pulled his knees to his chest and after wrapping his arms around his legs, rested his forehead against his knees. Not the most comfortable of positions, but one that protected the body. He took a deep breath and entered within to meet with the Captain and the assembled volunteers awaiting the final discussion of their plan.

sixteen

Kierigh attached a blanket to small hooks drilled into the rock overhanging the small alcove. He spoke without turning to Jermanah. "I thought you might like privacy since we share the cave this night."

Jermanah smiled at his back. Treenie had surrounded their chosen sleeping place in a similar fashion while Jermanah healed the large bump on Poll's head. Besides the privacy, the blankets also blocked light from the large central cavern, making the alcove secluded and cozy. "Thank you for your concern."

She reached for an apple and turned her attention to the small book in her lap. The Seer called it the *Book of Futures,* and the Highest named it prophecy. Although the writing remained sharp and easy to read, the language appeared ancient. She was able to pick out only a few words but none close enough together to decipher any meaning.

Kierigh lowered himself next to her and squinted at the pages. "Are you able to read the Seer's book?"

"He had only begun to teach me this language, so I know few words. Why would he direct me to this when he knew I wouldn't be able to read it?" She took a large bite of apple, chewed on her thoughts as well as the fruit, and swallowed. "The Seer would frequently present me with a challenge. Often I thought I'd never be able to understand or complete his tasks. Perhaps this is but another of his tests."

"Then you must continue your study. The Highest and Zigor searched desperately for this book. They thought it important enough to murder the Seer when he undoubtedly refused to tell them anything. We'll show the book to Grandmother. She may be able to understand some of the writing."

A lifetime of punishment and fear of another infraction against the Compound strangled Jermanah's recitation of the stricture. "Women are not taught the ancient languages."

The touch of Kierigh's hand on her arm offered comfort and understanding. "When Grandmother was young, she had a beloved, distant cousin who studied the ancient arts. He taught her as he learned, even though it was forbidden. I believe he would have bonded with her had he not been called as a Seer."

"Seers may have life mates."

"Not the Seer of the Compound."

The last of Jermanah's apple fell to the stone floor. "My teacher?"

Kierigh nodded. "He loved Grandmother, but was unable to deny his talents and abilities. Grandmother tells stories of how she lost her mate to a fishing accident before my mother's birth. But I believe she lost her lover to the Compound. She never again mated."

Jermanah thought a long moment on the possibilities. "The Seer was your grandfather?"

"I believe it so."

"I'm sorry." Jermanah bowed her head in sorrow. She'd believed the Seer had been content in his life's work. But perhaps not. His was yet another life that may have taken a happier direction if not for the Compound's control.

Kierigh lifted her chin and kissed her. "Yes, as I'm sorry for the loss of your mentor. To honor his spirit you must learn now from Grandmother and understand what's in this book. If it really is a prophecy."

"I shall. This vow I make to his spirit." She bent over the book and carefully turned the pages, tracing a word here and there with her finger. She would understand what the Seer intended. She *would.*

The awareness of Kierigh watching her lasted a few moments, then he opened his brother's journal. Wondering at his thoughts Jermanah paused in her study. She hadn't read much of the journal, but the pages were filled with writing from many different hands, some flowing and smooth, others cramped and agonized. Many passages appeared to have been written by children, the letters rounded and carefully formed, the thoughts from a young mind. Each was dated and none over a cycle old. She dared not imagine the pain and sorrow Daud's earlier journals might contain. There were so many lining his shelves.

Finally giving up on trying to make sense of words she didn't understand, Jermanah set her book aside to watch Kierigh read. Emotions passed over his expressive face, reflecting how she'd felt reading Daud's words. The horror and revulsion, the pain and sorrow returned stinging tears to her eyes. She wouldn't cry now and sniffed back the tears. How much worse this must be for Kierigh. His brother had experienced each deprivation and humiliation chronicled in the pages.

Kierigh made a harsh sound of denial and slammed the book onto a crate. He winced and cradled one hand in the other. Jermanah narrowed her gaze at the swollen joints and puffy red bruising. Despite his protests, she took his hand in hers and ran her fingers over the joints. "You didn't just do this. What happened to your hand?"

Ducking his head, he mumbled incoherently and attempted to pull his hand from her grasp. She held fast and wiggled his fingers one by one. He jerked in pain.

"I didn't hear you." She allowed herself a grin at his reluctance. He refused to show weakness before her and she cherished his masculine, misguided thinking. At least his fingers weren't broken.

Kierigh took a deep breath and released it slowly. "I became angry when I couldn't prevent Zigor from touching you. I took my anger out on a wall. The wall defeated me."

"Why didn't you show me this earlier?"

"The joy of finding my brother wiped the pain from my mind. We escaped the Stronghold. There wasn't time. It's nothing."

"I'll heal you now."

"You've already healed Poll tonight. I don't wish to tire you."

Jermanah snorted. "Healing brings energy, to me and to the one I heal." She poked his shoulder. "You should remember."

"The Seer gave me a draught to make me sleep. I don't think he wanted me to see you."

She held his wounded hand to her chest. "Perhaps not. It wasn't safe for any to know of my abilities. That no longer matters. Be still now."

When she closed her eyes the familiar power flowed into her so rapidly, the surprise released her control. She stared at Kierigh's hand. The swollen knuckles had returned to normal, the redness gone from his fingers. Confused, she lowered his hand to her lap.

"Jermanah?"

"I've never healed so quickly. I hadn't reached full concentration. I healed without... without thinking. I don't understand."

"Perhaps now that you aren't bound to the Compound the fear of discovery blocking your skill is gone."

"No, I don't think that's the reason. It took a longer time to heal Poll."

"His injury was more severe?"

Doubt cascaded through Jermanah. Questions without answers crowded her thoughts. "I wish I could ask the Seer."

"We'll ask Grandmother. She isn't able to heal but understands much of the magic."

Jermanah agreed and Kierigh pulled her into his embrace. His cheek rested against the top of her head. "Thank you for healing my hand. I was foolish to take my anger out on a wall."

She chuckled. "You were. I trust you won't do so again."

"No."

When she looked into his face, the twinkle in his light blue gaze belied his serious expression. The simple joy of his body next to hers stole her breath. She pressed her palm to his chest, relishing the rise and fall of his breath, the beating of his heart. Their hearts beat the same rhythm.

An ache formed low in her belly. She snuggled closer, attempting to appease the insistent desire. Kierigh stroked her arm and wondrous tingles cascaded over her skin. Even though the need for his touch consumed her, fear kept her wish silent.

Soft giggles echoed across the wide chamber, followed by the low rumble of Poll's voice, then silence broken only by a pleased moan. Jermanah hid her face against Kierigh's shoulder. How did want and fear become so intrinsically entwined?

He stroked her hair and loosened the tie at the end of her braid. "Don't be afraid, little one. Theirs are the sounds of joy. They don't mock love as the Highest does." He pulled his fingers through the braid to let the strands fall free about her shoulders. "Don't fear your feelings, your desires. Or your choices."

"There is darkness in each of us. What if by taking pleasure the darkness is released?"

"That darkness won't touch you, little one. I will not permit it."

If dark desire grew within her like an illness, there would be nothing he could do. For now, she wouldn't argue and ruin their moment of peace. "Truly?"

"So I vow. I would seal this vow with your pleasure." Kierigh gave her a hesitant smile, concern lingering in his eyes.

With her fingertip, Jermanah traced his smile. "And with yours."

Kierigh muted the light with a scrap of cloth before spearing his fingers through her glorious hair and slanting his lips across hers. He tore himself from the kiss and fighting to control his erratic breathing allowed his lips to linger against her cheek. Achieving a modicum of control, he lifted his head.

His little one's wide, luminous eyes watched him. The doubt had faded but fear continued to war with the rise of her desire. Wishing to completely banish the horrible mockery of love she'd witnessed in the Compound, he closed his eyes against the temptation of her lips and waited. Perhaps in this time with her he could also forget the words of humiliation and pain his brother had written. This night would be a cleansing for them both.

Jermanah kissed his eyelids and ran feather soft kisses across his cheek. Warm, apple-scented breath flowed over the sensitive skin below his ear, lifting the fine hairs at the back of his neck. Her fingers tangled in his hair. He'd explode if she didn't cease the innocent torment.

He shook with the need to crush her body against his. To lay her back and show her new freedom with his love. This night he wouldn't rush her. His resolve would remain as firm... as his body.

"Why don't you respond? Don't I please you?" The agony of her questions shattered his resolve into sparks of light behind his eyelids. He groaned and clenched his fists at his sides.

"Kierigh?"

He'd lose himself if he dared look at her. "Ah, little one. You please me beyond all pleasing. Far beyond what I deserve."

"Then why?"

"Hush, Jermanah. I don't wish to hurt you. I wish only to show you pleasure such as two may share. My desire for you is so great, I fear." Hesitant, he looked at her. His desire was reflected in her expression. "I fear."

"What do you fear?"

"I can't say."

Jermanah kissed him. "Tell me."

He held his silence for a long moment then whispered, "I fear to hurt you. I fear I won't give you pleasure. I fear I won't be strong for you. Be what, who you need." *That each time with you will never be enough.*

The soft movement of her lips against his mouth chased his concerns to the far reaches of his mind. The last tattered remnants of resolve faded. He splayed his hands against her slender back and took possession of her sweet mouth. She held his face between her hands and returned the ardency of his embrace.

The combination of passion and innocence in her kisses carried him swiftly to the edge of a dangerous precipice. His doubts disappeared. His thoughts focused on her. Then even those thoughts were gone and he was lost, lost in her eyes.

Jermanah believed she understood Kierigh's reluctance. She was as innocent as he called her. Fearful as well, but determined to conquer both, she wrapped her leg over his hip and settled in his lap. The strong evidence of his desire pressed against her. The persistent swirl of tingles from the contact made her delightfully lightheaded. She savored the taste of his kisses—sharp cheese, apple and man. Her desire grew, danced back to him, matching each stroke of his tongue, each tender exploration with an exploration of her own.

Lips still against her cheek, Kierigh paused. She squirmed against him. The pained hitch in his breath froze her movements. "Kierigh?"

"I must pause, little one, else our time will be over too soon. I wish to pleasure you long this night." A strange desperation filled his voice, but his expression remained closed. Until he smiled slowly, caressed her face and pushed errant strands of hair behind her ear.

He slid his hands under the hem of her tunic and lifted the material over her head, grazing her sensitized skin. Cool air caressed her, followed by the warmth of his palms and teasing fingers. He cupped her breasts and she arched to the slow, tortuous circles of his palms. His mouth replaced one hand, teasing her nipple with his lips and tongue. Her gasp was sharp in the silent cave.

Exquisite pleasure spiraled through her, pooling low, aching for more. She scraped her fingers through his hair to hold him in place and gulped back a moan.

Kierigh lifted his glittering gaze. Promises she'd understand before the night was through filled his sultry smile. Not knowing what she agreed to, but trusting him completely, she nodded.

He stretched beside her on the pallet, caressing her sides with long, smooth strokes. She gasped at the feathery touches and cringed when his fingers circled her navel. The moist heat of his tongue flicked across her stomach. He ignored her encouragement to return to her breasts and nipped her skin before soothing each bite with cool breaths and damp kisses. He swirled his tongue into her navel and she gasped. The tickle of his soft hair across her belly made her laugh.

Taking the drawstring of her leggings between his teeth, he tugged against the tight loops she'd tied. She lifted her head and tried to help him, but he kissed her fingertips before pushing away her hands.

"It would be quicker if I helped."

He grinned. "Yes. But not so much fun."

When he returned to his task, his soft growling reminded her of a small dog that wandered into the Compound when she was a child. The animal had made the same noises when gnawing at the scraps of food she'd sneaked from the kitchen.

After a muffled exclamation of triumph, Kierigh rubbed his cheek against her belly. He took the waistband in his teeth, pulled and tossed his head to work the fabric lower. A mischievous light glinted in his eyes and he slid his hands under her bottom, and lifted to slip her clothing past her hips.

She attempted to wiggle free of the leggings, but he encompassed her hands with one of his and held them against her body. A serious expression flattened his lips. "I will do it."

The ache within her thrummed deep and insistent. The mischief returned to Kierigh's heavily lidded gaze.

He touched her cheeks and lips, caressed her body, easing his fingers across her breasts and over her hips. Then he began again. Each stroke pushed her unwelcome clothing further down her legs. She arched into his hands each time they passed over her breasts willing him to linger. A lift of his eyebrow was the only acknowledgment of her body's mindless pleading.

With a triumphant growl, he dragged the leggings over her feet and dropped them in a wrinkled pile. Jermanah smiled in relief and welcome.

But he didn't return to her side. Bracing herself on her elbows, she discovered him looking at her, his gaze awed and reverent. She shuddered and his gaze met hers in question.

"Kierigh, don't look at me that way. It's how the priestesses and guards look at the Highest." She chewed on her lower lip.

He blinked, lowered his eyebrows and blinked again. "I'm sorry. You're so beautiful, so perfect, I can't help but worship you."

Heat burned across her chest and neck. She looked away from the intensity in his gaze. "Please, stop."

"Then allow me to worship you with my hands. My mouth. My body."

This was what she ached for, needed almost beyond thought. She opened her arms to him. "Please."

"Patience, little one. I must begin my adoration here." Desperation had returned to his expression and twined through his words. Silent and disappointed, Jermanah lay back and stared into the dark above her.

He lifted one of her feet. His strong hands swirled and massaged each toe to bliss. Her eyelids drifted closed.

When both feet tingled he pressed his lips to her ankle. The touch of his tongue trailed liquid fire up the inside of her leg to her knee then back to the tips of her toes. He repeated the swirling patterns up her other leg past her knee, stopping mid-thigh. Her skin burned like flame making her hot, embarrassed and suddenly afraid of what Kierigh planned. Not knowing what she wanted, what she needed, she tossed her head and brought her thighs together.

Kierigh gave a wordless sound of denial, rested his hand just below her navel and settled between her legs. He stroked his thumb over the curls at the juncture of her thighs. His short breaths burst across her stomach, stirring her already tumultuous senses into tangled knots. He massaged and teased, used his thumbs to create a pathway through her curls and blew a soft breath across her exposed desire.

Violent tremors shook her. Then his mouth closed over her. The shock lifted her hips from the pallet. "No."

Barely lifting his head, he gazed into her face. His lips moved against her. "Yes."

The heat of his tongue pressed against her. A cry burst from deep in her soul. Covering her mouth with one hand she pushed on Kierigh's head with the other. "They will know."

Questions sparked from under Kierigh's heavy eyelids. "Who will know what, little one?"

Jermanah took a deep breath and pointed a shaking finger toward the far side of the cavern. "The noises I make. The others will hear. They'll know." Panic filled her chest, stalling her words. They'd think her like the Highest, they would think—

Kierigh moved her hand from his head and kissed her fingers before sucking the tips into his mouth. The caress of his tongue brought another gasp. He tickled the center of her palm with his lips.

"They will hear only the joy of our mating, as we heard theirs. If they spare a thought, they would be glad you have found pleasure. Nothing more." His brows shot high in his forehead. "None would ever believe you to be like her."

Refusing to meet his gaze she shook her head.

"Do you wish me to stop?"

"Yes." She peeked at him from behind her hand. The defeated drop of his shoulders broke her heart. The touch of his mouth there had embarrassed her, but the new ache he created with his intimate kiss throbbed for a completion only he could give. Hesitant, she touched his lowered head and waited until his gaze lifted. "No."

Joy filled his face so she gave him a timid smile. Holding his hand in a tight, fearful grip, she sank back to the pallet. The stroke of his other palm along her side ignited her skin and she relaxed, welcoming his caress. He lowered his head and flicked his tongue against her until she loosened her grip on his hand and clutched the blanket instead. Her hips arched, bringing her closer to his glorious assault.

Exploring, coaxing, his lips and tongue were relentless until she no longer cared in anyone heard her moans.

Stars swirled behind her closed eyelids, whirling her in

a vortex where nothing existed but the heat of Kierigh's mouth and the thrust of his tongue against her. The stars coalesced to blinding brightness. Exploded. Spinning, caught in the vortex, and unafraid, she cried out the joy of her release.

Kierigh cradled her in his arms, softly stroking the heat from her burning skin. Unable to stem the tears trailing down her cheeks, Jermanah hid her face behind her hands. He eased her hands away and waited until she looked at him.

"Don't be ashamed. Aren't tears also a release of emotion?" He caught a tear on his fingertip and sucked it into his mouth.

Fearful of speaking, Jermanah hesitated before nodding. With another kiss, Kierigh drew her into the swirl of renewed passion. She tasted—herself—on his lips and drew back surprised. Hesitant, she touched his lips. The firm, masculine mouth pulled into a lopsided smile. His words tumbled over her fingers. "You are pleased, little one?"

"Beyond anything I could imagine. But what of your pleasure?"

"I am well pleased."

The firm length between them made her think otherwise. She adopted a wide-eyed expression and stroked him. "Truly?"

He stopped her hand, set her on the pallet, stood and stripped. The play of muted light across the strong planes of his body intensified her barely subdued desire. For an anguished moment the fear resurfaced, then floated away on a spiral of need. She closed her eyes and waited to him to return to her side.

The waiting became interminable. Did he no longer

desire her? What had she done wrong? Didn't she respond the way he expected? No, that couldn't be. Jermanah frowned at her doubts and looked for him.

Kierigh sat cross-legged facing her, palms resting against his knees. His erection bobbed and he indicated the space in front of him. "Sit there."

Confusion drew Jermanah's eyebrows lower. He pointed again. "Please."

She sat so her knees touched his. He took her hands and let her fingers rest against his palms.

"Breathe with me. Look into my eyes and breathe with me." He stared into her face and took a deep breath, released it slowly, paused and took another.

Jermanah locked her gaze on his and easily matched the rhythm of his breathing. The technique wasn't much different than meditation exercises she'd attempted to master in the Compound. But why would he wish to meditate when his desire so obviously pointed in another direction? She sighed and broke the established pattern of breaths.

Kierigh squeezed her fingers and she dropped her gaze to his hands. Again he exerted gentle pressure against her fingers. He spoke with the barest whisper, "Come back to me, little one."

Face burning with guilt, she lifted her gaze to his relaxed face and calm, open eyes. His breathing hadn't altered. Had he actually spoken?

Concentrating, she slowed her breathing to match his. When their breaths flowed as one, she sank into the intense blue depths of Kierigh's clear gaze.

Each breath filled her with powerful awareness. She became the touch of Kierigh's palms against her fingers, the rough blanket beneath her. She was the breath flowing between them, the tide of desire rising from the center of their beings.

Kierigh placed her hands on his shoulders. He lifted, then ever so slowly entered her. His thighs tightened around her and he slid his hands up her back to wrap over her shoulders, drawing her closer still. Her delighted gasp faded to a low moan.

"Breathe, little one." Kierigh rocked forward, back, then paused until their breaths once again flowed in unison. The thin skin of his eyelids covered his dark, smoky gaze. He glided slow and smooth within her.

But then he held them motionless. Time faded. Nothing existed but Kierigh, their breaths, the joining of their bodies. Love flowed through her. Her surprised gasp opened a floodgate of clarity, of understanding. Infinity stretched before her, this man forever at her side.

The sensual agony of Kierigh's deep moan rumbled through her. He leaned her back and thrust once. The world exploded, wrenching a cry from the depths of her being. She wrapped her legs around his hips, pressed even closer. He surrounded her, flowed within every cell of her body.

Freed by her fulfillment, Jermanah's spirit floated above the joined bodies trembling with the intensity of mutual release. Warmth and coolness enveloped her. She gazed into Kierigh's spirit eyes. With silent joy she flew into him, merging their energies. Even here he filled her, touched her soul, held her very essence safe. Their earthbound release continued until the air vibrated with visible waves.

Reluctant to end the powerful connection, she allowed Kierigh's spirit to ease from hers and guide their return to their physical bodies. She sighed and collapsed against the strength of Kierigh's chest. They clung together until their breathing calmed.

He kissed her hair then curled a finger under her chin and lifted her face. Surprise and wonder filled his expression. She touched his cheek, his chest, his back, cherishing the minute imperfections her sensitized fingers discovered.

Kierigh caressed her in return, grinning when her nipples peaked with his gentle ministrations. He grew thick and hard within her.

No longer afraid, Jermanah kissed the tip of his nose. She moved from his arms and he slid from her body. His sound of dismay was low, soft and reverberated through her. She lay back on the pallet and lifted her arms.

Delight replaced the disappointment in his beloved face and he crawled forward to enter her loving embrace.

seventeen

Daud slammed to consciousness. The Custodians faded into the dim recesses of the body's shared mind. Except for a slight twitch of one finger, Daud allowed the body give no indication he was awake. The door slid open and an intruder moved across his room to stand over the narrow bed. Zigor was awake early. The anticipation of the day's sacrifice must be great to wake him from his usual sated sleep. They'd let him enjoy the moment.

Feigning sleep, Daud waited. The king hovered over him for many breaths before he sat on the edge of the mattress and rested his hand on Daud's upper thigh. "I know you're awake, Daud."

Daud yawned and stretched, using the movement to pull his light blanket to cover him completely and ease his leg from under Zigor's hand. He turned on his side to face the king. "My lord? You are about early this day."

Zigor grinned, patted Daud's side and stood. Daud snorted to himself. The king expended no sexual energy before a ceremony, the better to insure the potent increase to every aspect of his power. Ducking his chin below the edge of the blanket, Daud hid his relieved smile then sat.

Zigor paced the small room. “I really will miss you. We’ve had interesting conversations.” He faced the bed, a glint lighting his eyes. “And other things.”

Muscles tensed, Daud held his breath. If Zigor went against his usual practice and called for a partner, Daud wasn’t sure he’d be able to regain control. If only they’d learned to avoid the domination of the king’s hands upon their head.

The glint faded from Zigor’s eyes. So, he only waited for a comment. “Yes, my lord. Life with you has been interesting.”

A hearty laugh echoed off the walls and faded into the high ceiling. “An understatement, Daud? There will never be another who pleases me as you do.”

Daud bowed his head, appearing to accept the compliment. Inside anger seethed, leaping from one adult to another until the small ones cried at the intensity. Sensing the Captain barely able to maintain control by linking arms with others to keep the chosen angry ones contained, Daud retreated into the shared consciousness, gave stern words of caution and promise and returned to control the body. He rotated one shoulder to ease muscles drawn tight from the internal struggle. This would be a long and difficult morning.

“I brought you the ceremonial robes. Of course, since you are much larger than the usual Double Moon child, these have been specially prepared for you.”

Grinning, Zigor lifted the glistening robe from the floor, shook out the length and tossed it to the bed. The golden material fluttered across Daud’s legs and he watched his fingers reach cautiously for the shimmering fabric.

The females of the body crowded behind his eyes, cooing over the look and feel of the heavily embroidered fabric. Daud struggled to contain their delight over the smooth flow of gold through his fingers. When they urged him to lift the material to his cheek, he sent a brief negative response, tempered by the gentle promise of later.

Chattering happily among themselves, the females retreated and Daud regained control of his hand. He wanted to roll his gaze and chuckle at the comments filtering into his awareness, but held his calm, outer expression with practiced ease.

Zigor had returned to his pacing and hadn't noticed the fascination with the robe. Now he paused with his hand lifted to the door frame. "Rest now, for I would have you strong at midday. When the sun is half the distance to the zenith, I will call for you."

"Yes, my lord. We will be ready." Daud smiled and let his grin spread when the king's brows drew together in confusion. The confusion turned to suspicion so Daud lowered his head and spoke meekly. "We know and understand our part in this day. All will be done as planned."

Zigor gave a sharp nod, turned on his heels and slid the door closed. Daud glared at the door, and snorted when the lock snicked closed.

Yes, Zigor. According to the plan. Our plan.

Poll insisted on returning to the Stronghold with Kierigh. Despite the protests of both men, Jermanah refused to be left behind. Treenie fussed over Poll until he brusquely shooed her away, but grabbed her hand before she turned and pulled her into a tight embrace. Jermanah grinned and tucked the two infants into their basket.

Kierigh spoke with one of his men. Treenie and the babes would be taken to the camp and placed under Grandmother's care. The man moved to the edge of the clearing to wait. Kierigh cleared his throat. "It's time. Preparations in the Stronghold will have begun for the sacrifice at midday. We must be in place well before then."

Poll gave Treenie a final kiss and moved to Kierigh's side. Jermanah followed.

Kierigh drew breath, but held his words at Jermanah's lowered brows. Poll clasped his upper arm. "You won't win. She's determined."

"Yes." He turned to Poll. "You don't need to return. Stay with Treenie."

Poll's bitter laugh rang through the clearing, drawing Treenie's attention. He smiled at her and shook his head. "I vowed my life to the Compound when little more than a boy. In a short time I've seen how the Highest destroyed the values and good of the women there. The king has proven to be no better. I'll serve neither."

"Then be free. The fight I've chosen against the king is difficult. There is little comfort remaining in hiding or on the run. Still, I'd welcome you as one of our number."

"I'll not have my daughter grow in a world such as this is now. I'll fight willingly at your side."

Relieved, Kierigh held out his arm. Poll wrapped his fingers around Kierigh's wrist, letting his firm grip seal his pledge.

Jermanah strapped her thin knife to her arm and tested the weight. She tugged on her sleeve to cover the blade then wrapped her luscious braid around her head and settled the cap. "I'm ready."

Holding his breath to calm the frantic pounding of his heart failed miserably. Her fierce determination enhanced her beauty. How could he ever fight again without her at his side? Times of peace would be desolate without her. Turning his thoughts inward, he closed his eyes. Was this the love Grandmother spoke of? Could this one, tiny woman, with her great strength of spirit, be the only way to assuage the emptiness of his longing. The light weight of her fingers rested against his arm.

Her fingers. Deprived of all sensation, he'd still recognize her touch. He gazed down at the concern brimming in her golden-brown gaze. What could he offer her? He had nothing. Nothing but love. It wouldn't be enough. He offered a somber smile to ease her worries and pressed his hand over hers.

"Kierigh, we must go."

"Yes."

The Highest paced before Zigor's desk, then leaned over the polished surface on stiff arms. "You've never allowed others to witness the ceremony or take part in the sacrifice. We don't need them. Why begin now?"

Zigor leaned back, pillowed his head on crossed palms and grinned. "It is what I wish."

"Fool. When the people realize the child of the Double Moons is sacrificed—"

"This will be the last. The power gained from Daud renders further sacrifices unnecessary." He stretched and yawned as if bored with her.

She had to make him understand her concerns and

forced her words through tight lips. "Can you be sure? If the power doesn't transfer, you'll show weakness. The prophecy won't come to pass."

"Ah yes, this prophecy concerns you a great deal."

"I never discovered that moon-cursed book. The old man told me nothing. I'm not convinced the ancient scrolls state the complete texts. A single word, a vital phrase missing or out of order might determine a different outcome. The simple fact you're planning to sacrifice a man, not a child... Zigor, what you base this plan upon, what we know, doesn't carry a feeling of completeness."

"This completeness of which you speak will be fulfilled with this final sacrifice. The foolish old Seer knew no more than you or I." Zigor spoke with a confidence that nearly convinced her. He rose, opened a tall, interior door, and strode onto a wide balcony. The Highest joined him and followed his gaze to the specifically constructed, secret courtyard.

A low flat stone angled across one end of the enclosure. A dark stain covered the slight depression in the stone's center. Tall rounded pillars of a similar stone formed a half-circle behind it. The remainder of the courtyard was devoid of color or decoration, the stone floor scrubbed and polished. An inlaid pathway of crushed crystals bisected the area. Soon the light from the midday sun would enter through a slit in the roof and travel the path from one end until reaching the sacrificial stone.

She'd witnessed the past sacrifices of the babes, shared a taste of the power with Zigor when he took the throne from their father. But this time...

Zigor turned to her and dug his fingers into the tight muscles of her shoulders. Forgetting her concerns, she leaned into him. "There is time, my lord king."

Only a breath of space separated them. His heat swirled around her, imitating the increase of power he'd soon acquire. "You forget yourself, Highest. I do not enjoy any pleasures until after the ceremony."

The husky rasp of his words settled low in her body. She slipped her hand through the open neckline of his robe and caressed the flat bud of his nipple. His eyebrows arched and his hands tightened on her shoulders. She tilted her head with a seductive pout. "There is time, and none would know."

Zigor slid one hand to the side of her neck. With the other he clasped her roughly around the waist and crushed her against his hard body. Triumph flushed through her.

His hand wrapped across the front of her throat. "Don't test my anger, Highest," he whispered.

The pressure at her throat made her words cracked and harsh. "I do not forget, my lord king."

Zigor drummed his fingers against her throat.

The Highest drew a shaky breath and closed her eyes. "You are my lord king. As always, your will is mine."

"And the power of my body, Highest? That, too?" He stepped back and chuckled.

Clenching her fists, she glared at the floor. "That too, my lord."

Zigor returned to his desk, snatched up a ragged parchment and shook the page at her. "This is the oldest version of the prophecy. I've followed each step, every instruction without fail. Though I had wished to withhold Daud's sacrifice for another cycle, this choice was taken from me."

"I accept responsibility for the loss of the child." She knelt at his feet. "My lord, will you accept my humble—"

"Get off your knees, woman. Humility doesn't become

you." He stroked her hair. "There's only one reason for you to be on your knees before me."

"My lord?" Licking her lips, she stretched forward, but Zigor shoved her head to the side, toppling her to the floor.

"Get up. The morning draws on. When the sun's path reaches the center of the courtyard we shall begin. I've given instructions for the guards to bring the selected nobles and a handful of trusted servants to the audience hall. Then they will be brought to the courtyard. Assemble your priestesses and prepare yourself."

Arranging her skirts gracefully, the Highest rose to her feet. "There are few priestesses to serve."

"No matter. As with the others they don't participate, only observe. Then all shall carry the word of my power throughout the land."

"Our power."

Zigor curled his lip. "Think you so?"

Without thought she lifted her hand. The slap resounded through the chamber. She stumbled back and cradled her palm against her belly. What had she done?

Zigor covered the red blotch on his cheek and laughed. "As you desire. Our power, Highest."

"My lord. I didn't... I... mean..."

The king held up his hand. "Don't make matters worse. Return to your priestesses and your loving, subservient guard. Prepare. Be in the courtyard at mid-morning."

Anger returned to firm her spine and square her shoulders. She turned toward the door.

The king's soft words followed her from the room. "And Highest? Do not anger me again."

Daud pulled the bed beneath the high window and stood on the sagging mattress to watch the sun's progress across the morning sky. By hanging on to the sill and stretching to his toes, he could see the forest. A deep sigh filled his chest. If only the children had been able to play free and innocent at least once within the safety of the distant trees.

A gentle mind touch brought tears to his eyes. The children understood and didn't mind that they'd never play, never see the sky through the heavy branches of a tree, never feel the grass between their toes. He sank inside and let the tiny hands caress his face and wipe away his tears. By the moons, he should be comforting them.

He hugged each child and sent them to their inner places. He, the Captain and inner helpers would make sure the young ones didn't know the moment the body died. Daud sent a plea into the clear blue sky. He didn't believe, but sent the plea anyway, so the children, at least, would find peace.

Daud glanced at the height of the sun before he sank onto the bed. He erected his seldom used shields and was alone in the stark silence of his mind. He let his doubt surface and covered his face with his hands.

Was it right for few of them to create a plan to destroy the body, as well as Zigor? Did the children deserve such a fate? He sighed. There wasn't an answer, no correct action. Better, perhaps, the peace of nothingness.

Daud listened to the silence. Was this what other bodies experienced? Accustomed to the constant chatter of voices, he shuddered at the emptiness. Would death be like this as well?

A tiny shaft of light crawled along the far wall to

measure the length of the day. Daud allowed his shields to crumble and reached for the robe. It was time.

Many crowded behind his eyes while he dressed. He scanned the small room, lingering on the few belongings Zigor allowed them, especially his precious books and journals. Perhaps they should destroy their writings.

No. Zigor had never been interested in their 'scribblings', and if the plan succeeded, would be unable to harm them, or anyone again. A grim smile touched his lips. Jermanah had taken their last journal. Perhaps later she would think to return to the Stronghold for the remainder of their thoughts and dreams. His brother's woman was indeed a rare creature.

Brother. Knowing their brother had filled the confusing empty space the many hadn't understood. Would that they had come to know of him sooner. With their brother's determination, life might have been different. A little hope traveled far within the many.

Daud ran his fingers over the journal spines then turned away abruptly. The robe swirled around his legs and delighted giggles filled his mind. He allowed the females' to enjoyment flow over the body until with unspoken accord, they retreated to their separate place with soft farewells.

Daud bit his lower lip. He'd not realized how difficult the leave taking would be and wished again their death would bring oblivion for all. But if death were only the silent emptiness, he'd be terribly lonely, a torture far more insidious than any Zigor could devise.

Pausing at the door, Daud jiggled the heavy wood and pushed in the way they discovered slipped the simple lock. With one last glance at the tiny room that had been their world for five cycles, Daud stepped into the hall and paced toward his chosen destiny.

Jermanah understood her two tall companions wished to protect her, but she felt dwarfed and insignificant walking between them. She couldn't match their intense gazes or tightly controlled muscles. Once they entered the Stronghold, her mind wandered and she knew she put them all in danger.

She jerked to a stop. Poll sidestepped to avoid running into her. Kierigh turned back to glare and she shivered under his fierce gaze. "I…shouldn't have come."

Eyebrows arching in surprise, Kierigh's expression softened. "No. But you are here. Perhaps there is a reason. I don't believe in such fancy, but Grandmother sets great store in purpose and destiny."

"As did the Seer."

Poll paced behind her, pulling his sword a few inches from his scabbard then letting the blade slide back into the well-worn leather. "We're wasting time."

Kierigh nodded. "Yes. We're near Daud's room and the king's chambers. If luck continues—"

Fear shuddered through her, chasing her past Kierigh and around a sharp corner. The door to Daud's room stood open, beckoning to her with promises of safety. She rushed through the door and skid to a stop.

Kierigh followed and Poll remained standing outside the door. Despairing, she turned and wrapped her arms around Kierigh. "He's not here."

"No. The room is different. The bed's moved." He stepped on the bed and stretched to peer out the window. "He was watching the rise of the sun to gauge the length of the day."

"Why? Oh. He was marking time until... Kierigh, he means to let Zigor kill him."

Kierigh collapsed to sit on the bed. Jermanah touched his shoulder. "Is it yet midday?"

He shook his head. "Do you know anything about this sacrifice?"

"I thought a male child of the Double Moon was raised here. Yes, despite the hard work, I thought life in the Compound was a blessed, perfect existence. I've learned otherwise. So why wouldn't the Stronghold be home to the same degeneration? What little I've discovered in the book speaks of moral downfall."

Taking her hand, he caressed her fingers. "No matter. We end it this day. Come, we'll find Daud. Perhaps Grandmother's destiny will shine upon us."

"Do you know where the king might do such a thing?"

"No."

She tugged him to his feet. "Then we must hurry."

"Yes."

The trio continued silently down the passage until reaching a terminus where three hallways came together. Kierigh lifted his head like a wild animal sniffing the wind. He turned toward one hall, took a step forward, paused and returned to Jermanah's side. The second hall received the same treatment.

After a deep breath, he stepping into the final passage. He inhaled deeply, tilted his head to one side, then motioned to Poll and pointed a few paces down the hall. Poll knelt at the spot and touched the floor. He nodded, rose and moved forward.

When Jermanah reached his side, Kierigh leaned to whisper, "The air is different in this hallway. Fresher. The way is seldom used, with a fine layer of dust along the edges of the wall. That dust has been disturbed. Perhaps by my brother. Or the king."

Thankful that even now he took a moment to instruct her, Jermanah nodded understanding. Although when they passed and she peered at the spot where Poll had knelt, she knew she would have easily missed the subtle clues. She had much to learn.

They had advanced only a few paces before Poll pointed to a small spy hole set next to the faint outlines of a doorway. Kierigh motioned for her to stay behind him then peered through the hole. She tapped her foot against the cool stone floor, held her breath and waited.

Kierigh motioned them a short distance back down the hallway and spoke in an urgent whisper. "There is a paved courtyard filled with huge stones. Zigor waits there alone. We must find Daud."

The two men softly argued over their next action with expansive arm gestures. Jermanah gazed at the dark ceiling. Grandmother had been correct. Men would talk a plan to death. So, let them plan. She returned to the spy hole.

If the king was in the courtyard, then she would watch for Daud.

eighteen

Standing motionless within the half-circle of pillars, Zigor waited. An array of knives rested on a golden cloth at his feet. A length of the same fabric wrapped around his waist forming an elegant loincloth. A stone pendant hung from a leather strap, to rest at the center of his chest. A thin golden circlet glinted on his brow. He stirred and folded his arms across his chest. Jermanah shuddered and forced her memories to the back of her mind. Her fear and revulsion wouldn't help save Daud from the king.

A narrow shaft of light glared mercilessly on a crystal path leading to a low flat stone. Angling her head, Jermanah sought the cause of rustling to one side of the courtyard. She bit her lip. The Highest of the High led a tight cluster of elderly priestesses and arranged the women to one side of the king.

The Highest lifted her arms and the loose material of her black as night robe gathered at her shoulders. Then she fell to her knees and lowered her forehead to the ground. The other women awkwardly followed her example.

Zigor offered a benign smile, but paid no attention to the few remaining members of the Compound. At the other side of the courtyard guards herded a small group of cowering servants and forced them to kneel facing the priestesses. Weapons held in readiness, the guards stepped back to ring the courtyard.

So many. How would they fight so many?

A cluster of richly dressed men and women entered. From their haughty demeanor she guessed them to be members of the court or nobility. Obeying the guards, they muttered and complained while kneeling before the king. The nobles completed a half-circle matching the pillars. The crystal path remained clear.

Jermanah glanced at Kierigh, who remained in deep discussion with Poll. They took too long, she'd interrupt and—

The Highest's voice rang above the noise of shuffling bodies. "Majesty. Look upon the majesty of Zigor." A single gong sounded. "The time of the king is now."

Kierigh shoved her from the spy hole and squinted through the opening. Jermanah huffed with frustration. Poll paced further down the hall, gave a soft exclamation and leaned into the wall. He'd found another view of the courtyard. She would find one as well.

She turned in the opposite direction and within ten paces found her own observation point. She stood on her toes, discovering she had a better angle to watch the king.

The Highest moved before Zigor and faced the gathering. "Turn your gaze upon Zigor, look full in his wonderful face. For he is majesty. Look then upon the majesty of Zigor."

The voices of the priestesses wavered in the repetition of the Highest's chant. The words swirled through the courtyard, lifting through a narrow gap in the roof. A sparkle of sunlight highlighted the path. "All things of this world grow strangely dim in the light of his glory and grace."

A panel slid open behind the stone pillars.

"Majesty. Authority. Power. Flow now from Zigor's throne."

Dressed in a flowing, gold robe that left his arms bare, Daud stepped between the two center pillars.

Jermanah gasped, turned to Kierigh and pointed toward the courtyard. He nodded without moving from his vantage point and motioned her to silence. Gnawing on her lower lip, she returned to the tiny opening.

"Lift on high the name of Zigor. To him be all glory, honor, praise." As the chant faded to silence, Daud moved to the flat stone and knelt, his expression taut and stony as the pillars behind him. He placed his palms on the stone and caressed a slight depression.

Head bowed, the Highest knelt before the knives. She selected one and held the blade for Zigor's inspection. "Let us rejoice. This is the day the *Book of Futures* foretold."

Jermanah touched the book in the bag at her waist. She hadn't deciphered many words, but she'd discovered no mention of sacrifice. The passages she could read were filled with joy, not anger and destruction. She'd glanced at words near the end of the book. Concern and possibilities were mentioned, but no death. Perhaps a different prophecy told of such an unspeakable act.

"Rejoice and be glad. Rejoice and be glad. Rejoice and be glad."

Zigor dismissed the proffered knife with a slash of his hand. The Highest replaced it on the cloth and lifted another. Jermanah winced at the long, thin blade and imagined the cold metal plunging into her flesh. She must have made some sound, for Kierigh was at her side in an instant. She shook her head at his unspoken questions.

Kierigh kissed the top of her head. "I must find a way to open the door panel." His words stirred her hair. He turned and trotted down the passage, trailing his hand over the wall. Jermanah set her palms against the wall and winced at the scene before her.

Daud had moved to lay upon the stone. He wiggled as if finding a comfortable position then remained still as the stone beneath him. Shallow breaths lifted his chest.

Zigor accepted the second blade, swiping the knife over and over through the air, testing the balance. A thoughtful smile touched his lips before he rested his palm on the Highest's head and leaned to speak in her ear. She dipped her head, the meek posture strange to Jermanah.

Trailing the back of his fingers down the side of the Highest's face, Zigor straightened and moved to stand behind the stone, knife held loose at his side. The Highest rose and pointed to the advancing shaft of sunlight. Sparkling with the light, the crystals shot tiny rainbows about the courtyard. Jermanah winced at the show of beauty in such a horrible place.

Muscles stood in tense relief along Daud's neck and jaw. His hands clenched into tight fists. Despair made her sag against the wall. How would they save him and escape the Stronghold?

A soft, low whistle caught her attention and Poll rushed behind her. He reached back and took her hand to pull her along until they met Kierigh, who pouted to a tiny latch set near the high ceiling. Poll nodded and drew his sword, reaching the tip to the latch. The simple contraption popped from the wall. Kierigh gave a slow push. The panel slid open. But all eyes of the assemblage were focused on either Zigor or intent on the progress of the sunlight. The zenith was very close.

Although Kierigh attempted to hold her back, she eased between the two men. After touching her shoulder, Poll slipped through the shadows in one direction. Kierigh took her hand and followed the shadow-drenched wall in the other. Kierigh motioned for her to stay in the deeper dark of a small alcove, reinforcing his command with arched eyebrows. She nodded understanding and pressed her back against the wall.

Should there be a battle, her small knife wasn't an effective weapon. Insisting on accompanying the Kierigh and Poll may truly have been foolish, but she was here. There would be a way to end this day without Daud's sacrifice.

Expectation filled the courtyard yet she sensed few understood the reason. Daud claimed to have a plan, but how could his death serve any purpose but the king's?

Her thoughts followed Kierigh's progress along the wall... He had to be careful. She loved him.

Kierigh advanced until he reached the nearest end of the semicircle of pillars. He paused, head lowered, his heart filled with the heat of shame and helplessness. His brother lay calm and silent on the low stone slab, staring toward the thin strip of blue sky showing through the narrow opening in the roof.

The Highest began another repetitive chant leading the assembled people in praise of Zigor. Kierigh lifted his head. He clenched his teeth to keep from snarling in frustration. What could he and Poll do against so many? He glanced over the heads of the kneeling, black-clad priestesses. Poll stood directly opposite his position. The man gave a brief nod of acknowledgment and sank into the shadows.

Kierigh's gaze swept the courtyard, resting on Jermanah's hiding place. A small hope had burgeoned in his heart, a hope he could offer her a life by his side. With his brother freed and Zigor defeated, his long life of fighting would end. The peace of a quiet farmstead called to him. Or perhaps a small fishing boat would provide their living.

But if his fight didn't end this day, he wouldn't submit her to the rough life of the rebel camps. Shame enough his grandmother chose to remain where he could provide little for her old age except insecurity. The future, his future depended upon his actions in the next few moments. By the moons he prayed those actions were correct.

The lengthy chant became a rhythmic undercurrent to his tumbling thoughts. Daud lay still. Zigor had retreated a few paces from the stone. Kierigh watched, waited, but his thoughts centered again on Jermanah. She deserved much more than he could offer. Her life in the Compound had been far from luxurious, but still easier than his basic bare existence. He couldn't even provide her with a proper dress. A wry smile touched his lips. Her tunic did little to hide her charms. During the night she'd hidden none of her charms from him. Nor her responses. He would never love another.

He leaned against the wall at his back. He'd whispered the words in his mind, but he couldn't love her. He wouldn't. His shoulders slumped. He did. How he felt with her, his thoughts when she wasn't near, how she frustrated and delighted him. All these were dreams he'd never imagined for himself.

The scar at his shoulder tingled and grew warm. Jermanah poked her head from the shadows searching the length of the wall. Did she look for him? She stared at her hand, then lifted her fingers to her lips. The tingle deepened to a pleasant vibration. He inched forward, angled toward her and caught her eye.

Jermanah cradled her hand with the other against her heart. After giving him a wondrous smile, she slid back into the cover of the shadows. Kierigh returned to his place and rubbed his shoulder. She was a remarkable woman. Hope filled the emptiness in his chest. Dare he hope she returned even a portion of his feelings?

He took a deep breath and mouthed the words, 'I love you, little one.'

The chanting ceased. In the sudden, expectant silence, guilt chilled his skin and he jerked his attention to his brother. The path of sunlight touched one end of the stone slab.

"Majesty. Bow before Zigor's majesty and power. We call upon the power, upon the majesty of our king. Bow. Bow now before him. Now." The authority of the Highest's words rang through the courtyard. The people bowed lower, ducking their heads as if fearing to look at the king.

Zigor smiled with benign satisfaction then bent to peer into Daud's face. His soft words were clear to all. "You offer me the power of your lives. When the midday sun fully encompasses you, that power will be mine. But, I find I am unable to wait even this short time. I must taste of the power now."

Zigor straightened and grabbed Daud's arm. The knife flashed. He opened a short slit along a vein in Daud's wrist. Zigor dropped to one knee and pulled the wound to his mouth. He lapped greedily at the welling blood then covered the cut with his lips. The sounds of sucking filled the silence.

Horror widened Kierigh's eyes. His hand clenched around the haft of his knife. The observers shifted nervously but dared not lift their heads. There wasn't a better time to attack the king.

Daud's face strained as if he attempted to remain impassive. Anger filled Kierigh's chest, matching the rage burning in his brother's tight expression. Pain flowed down Kierigh's arm and settled at his throbbing wrist. He took a deep breath. Now.

Daud turned his head, his gaze landing on Kierigh's hiding place without hesitation. Daud's expression changed many times in each breath until determination set his jaw and, though his lips barely moved, Kierigh understood the simple plea. Kierigh's anger railed against the decision, but he would, for the time being, honor Daud's bravery and not interfere. For the time being. He would not, however allow his brother to sacrifice his life to the evils of the king.

Though he had no idea how to accomplish this task, he gave Daud a sharp nod. His brother returned a weak smile and turned his face again to the sky.

Zigor's moan reverberated with ecstasy. He stood and gently rested Daud's bloodied arm across his chest. Daud bit his lip but a soft groan echoed the king's joy. Zigor wiped his mouth daintily with the hem of Daud's robe. A faint glow like the shimmer of heat over sand surrounded the king. He turned to the Highest and held his hands before him.

"Observe the power. Ah, you should feel it, feel the new strength flowing through me."

The Highest stood and touched Zigor's arm. She jerked away and sucked her fingertips into her mouth. "You are hot, my lord. You've burned me."

"Yes, Highest, yes. The strength burns, charring away the old and filling me with golden power." His eyes widened, awe filled his voice. "I don't know if I can contain it." He laughed. "Yet, I shall. For I am king and all power is mine."

The Highest swung her hand toward the sunlight. "The zenith sun nearly covers the source of your power. May this sacrifice fill you with the heat of the sun, the power of the heavens. All glory and majesty are yours, oh Zigor."

Staring into the sky, Zigor lifted his arms and turned in a slow circle. He stopped, faced Daud and reached for the fallen knife. His gaze fixed on the path of the sun, he shoved the robe from his victim's shoulders to fully expose Daud's chest. Leaving a trail of deep red blood smeared down his side, Daud's arm fell heavily to the table.

Kierigh held himself in check with aching determination. Every muscle screamed to rush to his brother's defense. He spared a glance toward Poll who leaned forward, sword held at ready, focused, waiting for his signal. Kierigh shook his head, understood Poll's surprised denial and silently reinforced his command. Poll frowned but lowered the tip of his sword enough Kierigh knew the man would continue to follow his lead. Whatever that might be.

Stunned he didn't rush to destroy Zigor, Kierigh eased back as well. The wishes of a brother he barely knew bound him to inaction. His emotions careened out of control.

Tearing his gaze from Daud, he glanced at Jermanah. No. She'd moved into the courtyard. Highlighted by sunlight, her hands lifted toward the stone. Tears trailed down her cheeks and when she looked at him, her anger burned his skin.

He winced, realizing her anger wasn't aimed at him, but for his inaction. He fingered the sharp edge of his knife.

Even though he didn't understand his own reasons, he'd given Daud his word. He would not interfere. Yet.

Once Zigor—Kierigh dared not even think the words—Kierigh would kill him. Glowing power or no, his brother and the sacrifices of many children before him would be avenged.

Every head in the courtyard angled to follow the final length of the sun's advance over the stone. Time slowed. The light crawled over Daud's feet, sparkling up the gold of his robes until the soft glow covered the crown of his head. A collective sigh filled the courtyard.

The Highest lifted her arms and shouted, "Glory to Zigor. Give all glory to Zigor." Her gaze fell hungrily on Daud's face before rising to meet the triumph of the king's expression. Her voice fell to a harsh whisper. "Glory. Glory. Glory."

This was Kierigh's last opportunity to stop the sacrifice. He clenched his knife and stepped forward. Daud didn't turn his head, but his lips moved with silent words. Kierigh understood. "No. Do not... brother."

Burning filled his eyes. He couldn't swallow past the lump blocking his throat. "Farewell," he whispered. "You are honored. I will avenge—"

"I know." Daud smiled.

Bright and feverish, Zigor's eyes glittered. "So, the additional witnesses to my power at last make themselves known. The others may come forth from the shadows. I've knew of your presence at the moment Daud gifted me with partial power."

"He did not give. You took. You stole from him." Jermanah skirted the prostrated people to stand at Kierigh's side.

Eyeing her dispassionately, Zigor shrugged. "Give, take,

what does it matter? The power is mine to do with as I will."

Poll moved to Kierigh's other side. "I think not. No child will again fear your knife."

"That is true, guardsman. Very true." Zigor rested his hand on Daud's chest. "With Daud's gift I'll no longer need to supplement my power. Watch now, then stand in fear before me."

Zigor's knife hovered high, centered over Daud's chest. The Highest forced the continued chant from her priestesses. The nobles and servants cowered, hiding their faces.

Kierigh ignored the witnesses. The sheep would be no help. But neither would they hinder Zigor's death.

Jermanah clutched Kierigh's outstretched arm and attempted to step around him. He shook his head, continued to hold her back and lifted his knife toward Zigor. Confusion darkened her expression. Kierigh hated denying her, but neither could he deny his brother's last wishes.

Daud drew an audible breath. Amazement arched Kierigh's eyebrows at the intense hatred flaring in his brother's eyes.

Daud angled his face to the king. "Take what you have created." The sound of many voices issued from his throat, forced through lips moving against clenched teeth. The ragged sound challenged the chant, forcing the priestesses to silence. A young priestess cried out and fell unconscious. The hair on his arms lifted and Kierigh cringed. Jermanah covered her ears.

The knife plunged toward Daud. Jermanah screamed in denial. Startled, Zigor jerked and the blade missed the heart of his sacrifice, burying to the hilt in Daud's chest.

A wash of dark heat flowed up Zigor's arm and swirled

around his head. He turned to the Highest, his fist lifted high. "The prophecy is true. I am filled. I *am* power."

"Filled, Zigor. Not with power." Daud's words were raw, a rasping whisper. "Look inside. See what...we've given you."

The king's gaze narrowed. "What folly do you speak? You'll die and every portion of the power you possess will flow into me. I will be invincible."

"We die, yes. But we keep power. Our gift is... another." Daud's words trailed to silence, his breathing shallow and labored.

Glowering, Zigor swept his arm indicating the cowering people. "Look at me, fools. Ah, you know not what you fear to witness. So go. Out. All of you. Await my coming in the audience chamber." The nobles and servants stumbled to their feet, falling over each other in the rush to escape the courtyard. The timid crawled after their companions. The guards hesitated until Zigor glared at each man until he backed through the doorway.

A brief surge of satisfaction lightened the horror surrounding Kierigh. At least now there would be few witnesses to the king's death, no one for him to fight but Zigor. And the Highest. He had no doubt the woman would be a formidable opponent.

As if in answer to his thoughts, the Highest spoke with gruff authority. "The Compound must remain to verify the truth of the prophecy." The exiting priestesses froze at the calm, cold command and huddled together at the far end of the courtyard.

Zigor reached for the knife rising and falling with Daud's shallow breaths. His hand jerked, halting inches from the hilt. Strain corded the muscles of his neck and forearms. Beads of sweat broke upon his brow. "I... can't..."

The pain tightening Daud's mouth softened to a serene smile. "Then we... successful."

A roar of rage burst from Zigor. He lurched forward, shoving Daud from the stone. The muffled thud of Daud's limp body and his weak groan were loud in the silence.

Shoving Kierigh's restraining arm aside, Jermanah fell to her knees at Daud's side. She carefully turned him to his back and pressed her hand to his cheek. His eyelids fluttered before he looked at her and smiled.

"Don't grieve. Defeating Zigor... our destiny. We are... I am... at peace. Anger gone."

"No. I won't let you die. Kierigh has just found you."

"Ah, my brother." Daud's dimming gaze searched for Kierigh. "Had we known..." His eyelashes brushed his cheeks, the tense lines of his face relaxed.

"Kierigh?" Jermanah lifted Daud's head to her lap. Frozen, Kierigh stared at the king. Now was the time. Jermanah slapped Kierigh's calf. "Daud needs you. Pull the knife from him."

He dared not move his focus from Zigor. Unfortunately, he'd been witness to many wounds such as this and shook his head. "He will die from shock and blood loss if the wound is opened."

"He will surely die if you don't. I can't heal him with that evil thing in his chest. I don't have the strength to remove it."

Losing his brother filled Kierigh with agonizing pain. His gaze bounced between his brother and the king. He had to do something, make some decision. But what? Why couldn't he decide? Act?

A strange voice issued from the king's mouth. "Help the body. If the body still lives, those remaining must be given a chance to be free."

Jermanah circled her hands around the protruding knife and pressed lightly on Daud's chest. Her voice wavered. "He lives. Kierigh, please. Let me heal him."

Poll faced the tight cluster of priestesses, his gaze skittering between the entryway and the king. "Be quick about it, man. I won't be able to hold back the guards for long if they return. I'll watch Zigor."

Lowering his gaze to Jermanah, Kierigh knelt. A faint glow surrounded them in a halo of light. The sun's path had passed the midday point yet still highlighted Daud and the ornately carved wooden haft embedded in his chest. His brother's chest. He wrapped his fingers around the knife, shivering at the touch of the cold, metal guard. Jermanah released a long, slow breath and nodded.

Kierigh sent a silent plea for forgiveness into the air, grunted and yanked the knife from Daud. As the tip of the blade left his flesh, Jermanah pressed the edges of the wound together. A thin trickle of bright blood oozed between her fingers. Slowed. Stopped.

Captured between Jermanah's palms, Daud's skin knitted together until only a thin, white scar remained. Then she curled her fingers over the gash in his arm, healing the cut.

Jermanah spoke without raising her head. "He has little will to live, for he doesn't believe he can." She moved her hands to his head and lightly touched his temples. "Daud, stay with us."

Daud tossed his head as if trying to avoid her hands. Determination filled Jermanah's words. "You will live, Daud. You'll know your brother. Your grandmother waits to meet you. Stay with us."

Daud's chest lifted with a deep breath and he angled his head from under Jermanah's hands. She touched his shoulder before clasping her hands on her thigh. "He's in distress, but he will live. He needs sleep to complete the healing."

Unwilling to leave his brother, Kierigh shook his head. "Not here. Can we move him? Take him to the forest?"

"Yes, but it's not the wisest action."

"We won't remain here. Once I'm done with Zigor—"

An elderly priestess had inched from the others to stand nearby. "You healed him? It is prophecy come to life before my very eyes. I did not believe the good would appear in my lifetime." She stretched a gnarled hand toward Jermanah. "The Compound will honor you, bless you for the changes you bring."

The breath caught in Kierigh's chest. This old woman offered Jermanah the opportunity to return to the life she knew, the ways she'd held dear. Why should she choose a life with him, little comfort, little safety over the life and honor of the Compound? He angled from her so he couldn't see the joy filling her face, yet strained to hear her words of acceptance.

"I am no longer of the Compound."

The priestess cackled. "You are. You'll purge the evil of the Highest."

Amazed at Jermanah's calm denial of the Compound, Kierigh rose. Movement flashed behind the king. Forgotten during Daud's healing, the Highest lifted a long knife in each hand and lurched toward them.

Pulling Jermanah beneath his body, Kierigh curled over her and steeled steeling himself to take the blows. Air whistled over his head disrupting the Highest's warbling scream.

Cautious, he kept Jermanah tucked in safety and lifted his head. The upper third of the Highest's body lay before him, neatly sliced from the rest. Blood pooled on the stone pathway, dead eyes stared into his. He held Jermanah's face against his chest to shield her from the gruesome sight.

She struggled and moved from his embrace. She shuddered, shrank back against him then straightened.

"Jermanah?"

"I'm... it's..." She shuddered again. She touched his hand and he realized he shook as well. "Kierigh, it's done. Can we speak no more of... her?"

A sword dropped with an eerie clang between the separated parts of the Highest. Poll wiped his hand on the front of his thighs and mumbled, "I won't touch that contaminated metal again." He draped one arm about the shoulders of the stunned old priestess and guided her back to the other women.

Zigor laughed. Kierigh tensed then eased to his feet, his knife held at ready. "You are the next to die, Zigor. Join the Highest."

The king continued to chuckle. Kierigh attempted a step forward but a firm grasp circled his ankle, holding him in place. He spared a quick glance toward the ground. Daud held him. Trying to free his leg, he ground out his order, "Let me destroy him."

"Kierigh, my brother." Daud's voice was weak, but the passion in his words made Kierigh pause. "Zigor no longer controls that body. He's contained deep within. He will never escape. He's been effectively destroyed."

Keeping his focus on the king, Kierigh knelt at Daud's side. "I don't understand. The things he did to you and you don't want him to suffer?"

Jermanah tugged on his sleeve. "He must be quiet and rest."

Daud grinned at her then at Kierigh. "Your woman is very persuasive."

"Yes."

His voice growing stronger as he spoke, Daud continued, "We heal more quickly than other bodies. Perhaps as a way to hide the numbers within and the pain inflicted on us."

Poll returned and pointed a plain, undecorated sword in the king's direction. "The nobles and guards have scattered. I don't imagine any wish to return. What about him?"

Kierigh shook his head and pressed on Poll's forearm until he lowered the sword.

The Zigor-body spoke. "We will continue the tale so Daud's body may heal. Listen then. When the child was sacrificed at the last Double Moon, we began to form our plan. With Daud's assistance, I, the Captain..." The Zigor-body saluted and clicked his bare heels together. "We began to gather those who wished to attempt our plan."

Now the voice issuing from the king changed every few words, a chorus speaking one after another. Anger and sorrow filled the many male and female voices. Shock froze Kierigh's muscles upon hearing the voices of children as well.

Both Poll and Jermanah stared with slack mouths and wide eyes. Kierigh struggled to keep his own astonishment under control and believed himself successful until Daud winked at him. He spread his hands. "But how?"

"We planned the entirety of this cycle, fully intending our body would be destroyed. Many within were grateful to choose the oblivion of death. As always, we do all we are able to protect the innocent children. Others of us chose to become the power Zigor sought, to fill him and in that way punish him as he punished the body. To create in him the fear he took pleasure in creating in so many of us."

With jerking and awkward movements, the Zigor-body paced. His eyebrows wiggled and he lifted his hands to touch his lips and cheeks. "It may take some time for us to become accustomed to this body."

He circled the stone to kneel at Daud's feet. "The one known as Zigor will never again control this body. Those who remain with you need not fear. We will destroy this body before Zigor could ever gain control."

Daud closed his eyes. "There is emptiness. You will be missed."

"We think not. Miss the anger, or the fear that prevents joy? You will know we're gone, but in time, we won't be missed. There are others who need you now, Daud. Care for them. Show the children a world outside these walls. Allow them to be children."

Kierigh knelt as well, touched his brother's arm and waited until Daud looked at him. "Come. We'll go to the forest. Grandmother will be overjoyed."

Disbelief warred with hope in Daud's expression. "All of us?"

"Yes. She'll help the children and love them deeply. She's a wise woman." He stood and offered one hand to his brother, the other to Jermanah.

Daud shook his head and despite Jermanah's concerns, struggled to his feet without assistance. "We don't easily accept help that too often comes with a price. One we no longer will pay."

"I'll never ask a price of you, my brother. Jermanah?"

She took his hand with both of hers and he assisted her to her feet. Not content to have her merely stand at his side, he took her by the waist and lifted until her feet dangled above the ground. Her arms snaked around his neck and he kissed her. Daud's words resounded through the rush of a sensual haze. *Your woman.*

Joy flooded his chest. His quest to find his brother was complete. Life stretched before him, cycles to spend learning more of the unique combination of those within Daud, and cherishing the woman in his arms. They'd return to the forest. This night he'd take Jermanah to the springs. He sighed into her kiss. And tell her there. He loved her.

Kierigh reluctantly lowered his little one to her feet. The Zigor-body touched his arm and he jerked as though burned. Spreading his hands in apology, he turned to the body that had once been king. In only a few moments so much had changed. He must be changed as well, for how else could he accept how many personalities lived within his brother and that some of them now controlled the king's body?

The Zigor-body shrugged. "Your reaction is of no consequence. We understand. However, you must stay. The others will take Daud. There is more we must tell you, things we've discovered hidden deep within Zigor's mind.

"No."

"You must." The Zigor-body stood rigid, barely containing the anger flashing in his eyes. The shoulders relaxed and he mimicked Kierigh's apologetic gesture. "We find it difficult to remember we no longer need the anger to survive. Many of us are only anger, some only fear. We don't always know how to interact with others, for that duty belonged mainly to Daud."

Kierigh's curiosity urged him to discover Zigor's secrets. In doing so he might learn more about his brother. But not now. There would be time enough later.

The Zigor-body continued, "There are things you must

know before you leave the Stronghold. Stay a short while only. Let us explain. We now understand much and will assist you in piecing together the evil you fought so well."

Jermanah wrapped her arms around Kierigh's waist. "Poll and I will take Daud to Grandmother. Although he grows stronger with each passing moment, I don't wish to compromise his healing. You need to learn as much as you can. Listen to what he has to say." Pink suffused her face. "Perhaps then, when you return, we could visit the springs?"

Ah, how her thoughts echoed his. She knew him well, for he was curious and would worry over imagined dangers if he didn't stay. "Then I'll stay. For a short while. I'll return to camp before darkness falls." He leaned close to her ear. "Yes. We'll go to the springs."

She blushed a deeper red and kissed his cheek. After lingering a moment gazing into his eyes, she turned to Poll. "Will you escort me once again, guardsman?"

"As always, my duty and my honor, lady." His efforts to slide the plain sword into his narrow scabbard failed. He canted his head toward the king and handed Kierigh the sword.

She shook her finger at Poll. "I am only Jermanah." She cast her smile on Daud. "Are you ready to face your new life?"

"Such is a dream I never dared imagine. I truly never hoped to leave the Stronghold, except as an empty shell. We'll lead you again to avoid the curious." He took a few eager steps then stopped. Slowly, he turned back and gnawed on his lower lip. "My books. My journals."

Jermanah skirted the blood and the Highest's body. "We'll need to pass your room, won't we? You can gather whatever you desire to take with you so you'll never have to return."

"A wish, a dream. Come." To Kierigh he said, "Take care, but fear not. You may trust them. Don't be long. Please."

The Zigor-body stepped over part of the Highest. "He will be gone from here before the afternoon fades. We'll be swift in our telling."

Kierigh watched his love and his brother cross the courtyard then turned to the Zigor-body. "Tell me. What can be of such great importance to me?"

nineteen

Shaking off Jermanah's supporting hand Daud led her and Poll from the courtyard. He paused and glanced around the wide audience chamber, but only the group of priestesses remained, speaking in agitated whispers.

Jermanah moved in front of him. "They won't stop us."

The old priestess gestured in her direction and the group advanced quickly across the polished stone floor. A lump of fear and misgiving coiled in the pit of Jermanah's stomach. The fierce urge to run enveloped her. Drawing on a newly discovered force of will, she held her position against the determined advance.

As one the priestesses knelt and lifted their voices in joy. "Praise and glory to the Highest."

Jermanah whirled. Had the Highest somehow joined herself together and followed them?

With a grave expression, Poll leaned close to her shoulder. "They mean you."

No. The strength fled her legs. Poll took her arm and she crumbled against his support. Her gaze darted from him to

Daud to the priestesses then lingered on the courtyard doorway. "I can't return to the Compound. I won't."

The elderly priestess crawled forward and clutched the hem of Jermanah's tunic, but looked at Poll. "We are without a leader. Blessings upon this man for cutting down the evil the Highest brought upon us." Her age clouded gaze shifted to Jermanah. "You have the gift of healing. It has long been said when all-encompassing evil is destroyed, a healer will come. She who will come is destined to heal all the Compounds. No, in truth, she will care for and heal the whole of our land."

The priestess bowed her head. "As a young woman I studied and discovered there was more to the prophecies. But evil in the guise of the Highest and the king came to power and the words were hidden before I could learn what was needed to bring about the completion. Only the Seer knew how to discover the truths. But he is gone."

Unsure if producing the Seer's book was the correct action, Jermanah hesitated then pulled the thin book from her bag. Soft light from the high, arched windows illuminated the volume. Tiny dust motes floated around the worn leather like a dance of joy.

The priestess gasped. "It is the book."

Jermanah stroked the binding with reverence. "The Seer directed me to discover this book, but I've been unable to decipher the pages."

"You *are* the one." The old woman signaled to a young priestess who assisted her to her feet. "You will return with us now to the Compound and take up your duties."

"I go to the forest." Jermanah turned from the woman's greedy gaze. Daud waited patiently, his head cocked to one side. She rested her palm against his chest. "I must take this man from the Stronghold."

"Ach, let the other man take him." The old priestess lifted one hand, her fingers moved, counting off the points of her argument. "It is your responsibility to lead. Such is your destiny. You have the book. You are a healer. You were trained by the Seer."

She cackled at Jermanah's surprise. "Yes, I know many things. I've not attained this great age by letting the world merely swirl around me. I know when to keep my own counsel. The Highest didn't learn of you from me. Come. Return now and set things right."

Poll sidestepped in front of Jermanah and reached for his sword, but his hand dropped from his empty scabbard and he sighed. After clearing his throat his words were sharp and determined. "Jermanah says she's going to the forest."

The priestess rounded on him. "Fool. She must come to the Compound. She spent her entire life preparing for this moment."

Daud stepped forward, a solid comfort at Jermanah's other side. "My life was spent preparing for sacrifice. Preparations do not destiny make, old woman."

Moving away a few paces, he and the priestess debated the concepts of training and destiny. Jermanah found it difficult to follow what seemed to be good natured arguments. Daud grinned. He enjoyed verbal sparring, but shouldn't tire himself. She needed Kierigh, but he had his own discoveries to make.

Along with the man, Jermanah ached for the forest, for the comfort of the open sky and breeze upon her face. But her deeply ingrained sense of duty and loyalty to the Compound also called to her. She knew what life expected of her within the security of the Compound.

Kierigh had offered her nothing.

Except freedom and choice. Such a precious gift. Perhaps her destiny was to take that gift and make a new life for herself. But was that life within the Compound or with him? Alone? All her life she'd been given orders, been told what and how to think, the correct way to act. Without those orders, she wasn't sure what direction to take. Making choices was so new.

Poll paced restlessly. How he must miss Treenie. Was he counting the moments until they were together? Jermanah ached for Kierigh, for a taste of the passion she found in his arms. Leaving those feelings behind by returning to the Compound held no appeal.

Might there be a way to do both? The *Book of Futures* vibrated in response. If she read the rest of the book, perhaps she would find a way to be with Kierigh as well as heal the land. She'd seen, and experienced, so much pain and sadness in these few short days. Her heart was drawn to finding a way to ease the lives of all the people of the land. To do so, to find that meaning—she sighed—she needed to return to the Compound.

But only for the time needed to send the Seer to his final, honored rest. If she couldn't learn the complete prophecy perhaps she'd discover clues to some meaning or opportunity for discovery. Anything else could be accomplished from the forest with Kierigh at her side.

Kierigh. She'd made her decision, now she could only hope he understood. She worried her lower lip. He would. He had to. His life had long been filled with purpose and the duty to see those he cared for safe and protected. Surely that sense of duty would help him understand her decision to do much the same.

She glanced at his brother. Would Daud understand? And Poll? They were all so protective, but unneeded now.

She must find a way to convince them to leave her with the priestesses and return alone to the forest camp.

Stepping between Daud and the old woman, she waited until Daud looked at her. "I pray you to understand. I must go to the Compound for a short time."

At the sharp intake of the priestess's breath, she held up her hand. "I said for a short time. I go only to learn more of this prophecy and to perform proper rights for the Seer. When I have learned what I can, I'll come to the forest."

Daud remained silent a moment before nodding. "We understand. If you desire, we'll attempt to aid in Kierigh's understanding as well."

Relief settled over her shoulders like a warm blanket. "Thank you. He'll need you now."

Closing his eyes, Daud lowered his head in assent. "We all have much to learn."

Poll made a sound deep in his throat and rubbed a spot just below his heart. "I don't wish to face Kierigh when you aren't where he expects to find you. I don't think you should return to the Compound alone. Together we can take Daud to the camp then I'll return to the Compound with you."

"No, Poll. You'll be needed in the camp. And I don't want to keep you from Treenie or your daughter. I'll be safe enough. Though Kierigh may chose not to believe it, I have learned from him and will keep myself safe."

Jermanah turned to the priestess who sobered a triumphant grin and nodded. "You'll be safe enough, even without guards. Most have run off by now. The people fear the Compound, as they do the Stronghold and will not approach the gates. Come, we must return now. There is much to be done."

"Patience." Jermanah stood on tiptoe to kiss Daud's

cheek. "Please don't let him be too angry with me. Or with you for letting me go."

"He is a man of strong emotions and will be very angry. But, we will try."

Poll slapped his palm against his thigh. "I don't see why you're insistent on returning alone."

"I won't be alone."

He snorted. "A bunch of women? Jermanah, use what sense you have."

She tugged on his arm until he bent to her. A quick kiss graced his cheek. He lifted his fingers in surprise to cover the spot. "My lady?"

"We all must do as we deem right. It's painful, but it's also right for me to return to the Compound now." The truth in her words settled around her like a warm blanket. "I'll come to Kierigh as soon as I'm able."

Daud wasn't sure he did the right thing by letting Jermanah go without first talking to Kierigh. They'd had so few interactions with others. Perhaps this was the way people in love behaved.

For his brother loved Jermanah. And he was fairly certain she returned the feeling. Daud sighed. How could he tell when he didn't even know what love was?

Poll turned to him. "It appears we must eventually face the man without the woman. I don't look forward to the prospect."

An unaccustomed chuckle rose from Daud's chest. "We agree. Do you think Treenie might help?"

"At least with binding our wounds. We need to return before Kierigh, if for no other reason than to warn the others. I anticipate the camp will then be nearly empty by his return. I don't care for how this day continues to develop."

Silent in his agreement, Daud led the way through the hidden passageways to his tiny room. In a few moments he'd gathered his books and journals, tying the small bundle in a worn bed covering. He stripped off the blood-stained robe and dropped the gaudy fabric to the floor. Dressed in a simple shirt and loose pants, he took a final look around the room that had been his prison for so long. He would never return.

The door closed with a satisfying click.

After a short but animated discussion, and full of misgivings, he led Poll through the public areas of the Stronghold to the main gate. But most of the guards had truly disappeared, leaving the hallways and gathering rooms deserted. The few guards they encountered either turned their backs or found something of interest in another direction.

Instead of exiting the gates immediately, Poll led Daud across a wide bailey to a line of open stalls. Huge war beasts hung their heads over the gates and watched them pass. Poll gave a sharp whistle and a shrill whinny returned from the far end of the stalls. He grinned and trotted along the narrow walkway.

Daud eyed the huge beasts when they stomped and snorted at his presence. This close the animals were far larger than they'd imagined when they'd been able to see one through a distant spy hole. He reached where Poll stood caressing a huge, dark brown head. The animal nuzzled Poll's shoulder and he chuckled.

"Patience, friend. I have no apples. Take us swift and sure to the forest and there will be apples aplenty." He patted the animal's nose. Daud's fingers itched. The children were close, watching, wanting to know if the pale nose was a velvety as it appeared. Poll opened the wide gate and the animal pranced from its confinement.

Daud pressed his back against the empty stall. The beast snuffed at him then turned its head away as if disinterested. "You don't smell like apples either," Poll said. "Baran would do anything for apples."

As Poll fitted a leather halter to the large head, he rubbed the arched neck. "As he will do anything I ask of him, even without the bribe."

Gathering a handful of stiff mane, Poll pulled himself onto the beast's high back. He leaned sideways and held out his hand to Daud. "I won't leave my companion to the whims of the Stronghold. And riding will return us to the forest much faster."

The children crowded behind Daud's eyes, both curious and afraid. The animal grew larger, and Poll's hand shrank away from him. Daud shook his head and his lower lip pushed out into a pout. "We 'fraid. Not go on big animal."

Confusion filled Poll's expression and his brows drew together.

Fascinated in their fear, the children fought Daud's attempt to regain control of the body.

Then Poll took a deep breath and gave a slow nod. He leaned further until his face was level with Daud's. "Don't be afraid. Baran can be a fierce war beast, but we don't ride to war. He'll carry us swiftly and safely to the forest. Would you like to go to the forest?"

Daud nodded rapidly. "We can play?"

"Of course." Poll's easy grin showed relief. "What games do you like to play?"

"We not play. Not come outside 'fore." Tears welled and one rolled down Daud's cheek. What must Poll think of him now?

"I'll teach you games, if you like."

Again Poll received an emphatic nod.

"Let me help you on to Baran's back so we can go. You can give him an apple when we reach the forest. Then, we can play."

Daud's hand lifted until Poll closed his fingers around it. "When I pull on your hand, jump up behind me."

The great beast stood without moving while Poll helped Daud mount and settle stiff and awkward behind him. "Hold tight to me. We're going to ride fast. Do you understand?"

"We fall?"

"No. Baran will never let any fall who I ask him to bear."

Daud's arms tightened around Poll's waist when the animal moved in an easy walk from the Stronghold. Once they reached open ground, Poll allowed the anxious animal to run.

When the children gathered together in excitement over the ride and prospects of play Daud slipped back to the surface of control. He relaxed his stiff muscles and loosened his death grip on Poll's tunic.

Poll turned his head, arched one eyebrow and shouted, his voice carrying to Daud on the wind. "Welcome back."

Kierigh perched on a hard wooden bench and leaned his forearms on his thighs. Weariness tightened his muscles. "Get on with it. What was hidden in the perversities of Zigor's mind that could ever be important to me?"

The Zigor-body chuckled and bent to retrieve a loose robe crumpled on a low table. He slipped the garment over his head and tugged until the hem fell to the floor. "You would be amazed. We'll tell you only a portion—for now. You'll learn more as we do." He pointed to his temple. "There are many secret places here."

Kierigh slid to the end of the bench allowing the other man to sit then angled to study the subtly altered face of the king. Without the tense lines of anger and power-filled desire, the Zigor-body appeared as a gentle man just past his middle years.

"Do not relax your guard despite any changes you may witness. The evil still wars within this body. We contain him only with our rage. This outer shell merely binds all together. Such is a fitting punishment for him."

Kierigh narrowed his gaze. "Then how am I to trust what you say?"

"I, the Captain, now control the body. I'm not one of the angry or vengeful. My thoughts are unclouded by revenge. I assisted in creating the plan and am in charge of this phase of the undertaking. I'm to give you facts untainted by emotion."

"Don't you hate Zigor?"

After a long moment of contemplation, the Captain spoke. "I am angered by his actions, for I, too am a result of his machination. But I feel no direct hate. Although Zigor didn't create me directly, I came into being to form the plan and see it to completion." He gazed across the chamber. "Our time is short. There may be a guard or noble who actually wishes to seek out the king."

Unable to imagine how anything the Captain would say was more important that returning to the forest and Jermanah, Kierigh released a slow breath. He'd said he would listen, and so he would. But not for long. The others were on their way by now. He'd follow soon.

The Captain cleared his throat. "This body will no longer rule the land."

Kierigh grunted. "He never did. He forced and controlled, but did not rule."

"Agreed. Now there must be another to follow. The transition between rules must be sanctioned by Zigor. He must name the successor."

Ah, this he could do. Relief relaxed Kierigh's shoulders. "And I am to find this successor for you?"

"No. You *are* the successor."

Kierigh surged to his feet and whirled to face the Captain. "You wouldn't. I'm no leader."

"What of the men and women who look to you within the rebel camp?" The Captain grinned at Kierigh's surprise. "Zigor watched the growth of your small rebellion with curious interest. He didn't know you, but discovered and catalogued much. He did not, however, know you to be Daud's brother. That surprised him greatly."

The Captain's eyes seemed to focus inward. He blinked twice then focused again on Kierigh. "You are the man this land needs to prosper once again."

"Me? I have no desire to rule. I wish only to live in peace."

"Get to know your brother? Raise a family? Remain unknown? You will not be able to fight your destiny."

"I don't believe in destiny. I've created my life on my own and will continue to do so."

Under arched eyebrows, the Captain grinned. "So you think. You shall lead this land. If not destiny, then your own belief in what is right will bring you to this decision. You won't be able to hide in your peaceful existence when the world around you struggles in disarray."

"You claim to know much about me."

"We know Daud. You're not so different."

Silent, Kierigh sat. His mind worked rapidly to discount the accuracy of the Captain's words. He couldn't stand aside and allow the people to fall further in despair. If he had any amount of power or some ability to improve the quality of life for all, he had to try. Didn't he?

But what about Jermanah? He'd still have no peace or security to offer her. Would she be willing to stay at his side when the future hung around him in confusing shreds? At this moment, he didn't even want to be himself. He couldn't make this decision alone. He desperately needed Jermanah's, logical, calm mind to assist him.

"I can't give you an answer. I need to speak with—"

The Captain lifted his hand. "There is no time. We had originally planned to hold the rule ourselves, but our new knowledge of you is fortunate. For Zigor continues to fight us. He is very strong. We must transfer the rule this day. Soon this body will appear as a madman. You must be in control before that time or the opportunity may be lost."

He stood, wavered then paced across the chamber. "Now. We must go. Then this body must be hidden until our control is complete. The body will live, although Zigor will have no life but for our revenge."

Ducking his head, Kierigh rubbed the back of his neck. He couldn't make this decision. This wasn't only about himself. His decision and choices would affect the life-paths of many. Especially his loved ones. The grand scale of this decision shouldn't be made in a brief moment.

The fear and poverty of so many of the land flashed through his mind. The pain he'd witnessed when joy was stripped from the people under Zigor's rule filled his chest. He could accept this new challenge and make an even greater difference.

In reality, there was no choice.

Resignation replaced the pain. He lifted his gaze to the Captain. "Tell me what I must do."

Compassion filled the dark eyes studying him. "We do understand the difficulty you face. We wish there was more time so we could assist you during this transfer. But internally we remain locked in battle with Zigor. He was more powerful than we anticipated. But come. The king will announce his successor. We believe most will welcome the change."

Kierigh followed the Captain into the large audience chamber. At the sound of a small bell, single guard entered, drew his sword and marched forward. The Captain halted the man's advance with the lift of a finger. "Go. Find others. Bring the nobles."

"My lord king, many have already left the Stronghold."

"It matters not. Bring those who remain. Now."

The guard whirled. While the Captain moved to stand before the ornate throne, Kierigh remained in the shadows. He crossed his arms and drummed his fingers against his tight muscles. That monstrosity would be one of the first things to go.

Grumbling and protesting, nobles entered followed by a hand count of guards. The Captain waited until an awkward silence fell. Kierigh didn't listen as the Captain spoke, the words weren't important to him. The how and why of what he'd agreed to do settled in the pit of his belly. In truth, what would he be able to accomplish? What differences could he make?

First, he needed his family at his side. As always, Grandmother would be the voice of reason in this insanity. It pained him to think of asking Daud to return, but he needed his brother. Daud had experienced Zigor's perversions and would be able to give insight in the healing of others.

Healing. Would the healer stay with him? By the Moons, he loved Jermanah. Any life, in the Stronghold or forest, was unimaginable without her. Now all he could offer her was another ordered life to replace the one she'd left in the Compound? Her new-found freedom might be treasured more than what he could provide. Love might not be enough to bind her to him.

A sudden, expectant silence intruded on his thoughts and he lifted his downcast gaze. The Captain motioned to him. Kierigh took a deep breath and stepped to the king's side.

Zigor's imperious voice flowed from the body. Startled, Kierigh took a step back, but the king turned to him with a slow wink. When Kierigh cast him a questioning look, a raised eyebrow was the answer. With a deep breath, Kierigh schooled his expression.

"This man, Kierigh, takes now the throne in my stead. I grow weary of rule and pass the care of this land to him. You will follow him as you have followed me. The divine right of his rule will be revealed in time and, more importantly, shown in his actions, in his care of what I leave to him. Honor him as you have honored me."

Despite the confused glances from one noble to another, the gathered people knelt. In one voice they offered allegiance to the new ruler. The Captain gave a satisfied nod before he lifted the circlet from his brow. "I pass then, to Kierigh, ruler of the land, this, the symbol of his rule."

He held the brightly polished, entwined metal circlet toward Kierigh who shuddered and gave a minute shake of his head. The Captain glared and nodded once toward the floor. Kierigh caught back a sigh and knelt. He hadn't agreed to this and bending a knee to Zigor lifted the hair on the back of his neck, even though the vicious king no longer controlled the body. Kierigh desired no symbol of rule, needed none, but he'd accepted the challenge. He bent his knee and lowered his head.

The Captain hovered over him and placed the circlet, speaking low so only Kierigh could hear. "You need only accept this now. Whether you wear it in the future is of no consequence. The rule in not in the metal upon your brow, but in your thoughts and actions."

Taking the offered hand, Kierigh rose, allowed the Captain to clasp his shoulder and turn him toward the gathering. "Greet then your king. May he bring prosperity to all who dwell within this land."

The enthusiastic nobles responded by surrounding Kierigh, touching and congratulating him. He answered relieved smiles with his own. But the people crowded him, trapping him, until his muscles burned with the need to run. He called upon the strength of his determination to remain where he stood.

Finally the chattering nobles moved to the far end of the long room and the Stronghold guards stomped forward. Kneeling before him, each offered his sword as a pledge of loyalty. With the Captain's encouragement, Kierigh touched the hilt of each blade and noted the men who didn't look him in the eye when they offered allegiance. Later he and Poll would discuss how best to deal with the guardsmen. Despite these first, easy moments, the transition and acceptance of him as ruler would not be as simple as the Captain hoped.

He glanced at the Zigor-body. Subtle tremors jerked his arms. A tick throbbed just under his left eye. He grimaced and spoke through clenched teeth. "We must go. The body is exhausted. If we don't rest, we may lose control." A shudder shook the whole body.

Kierigh turned to one of the guards who seemed to have offered true allegiance. "Send runners throughout the land. Tell the people there is a new, uh, ruler. Those who are able to travel will come to the Stronghold within two seven days. This land stand at the beginning of a new adventure. A new era of peace."

The Captain plucked at Kierigh's sleeve. The new king spared a glance at the trembling hand and backed from the dais. He set his features into a glare, looking at each person in the chamber. "I will be away from the Stronghold this night, but will return upon the morrow to take up my duties."

Biting his lip to keep his wry chuckle contained, he barely believed he'd speak his next words. "Dare not think to defy Zigor's wishes."

Taking the Captain by the arm, they strode from the chamber. Away from curious eyes, the Captain collapsed against the wall. "Take us to Daud's room. We'll show you how to secure the door. We'll need nothing until you return. The body will continue to function, but will not respond should anyone speak to us. When you return, call for the Captain." Head lolling to one side, he slid down the wall, collapsing in a boneless pile.

If the weight of the day's happenings hadn't come crashing down around him, Kierigh would have laughed at the strangeness of lifting the ex-king carefully in his arms. He stumbled, righted himself and strode forward. He had no idea what to do, how to lead an expansive land filled with folk of all sorts. His only experience was leading an ever-changing small group of men and women who'd joined his rebellion. Now he wasn't even sure if he'd led a true rebellion of simply used the concept in his personal search for his brother. He hadn't thought beyond finding Daud.

No, he'd been committed to ending the oppressive rule from both the Stronghold and the Compound. The small band had been successful in disrupting the flow of violence casting darkness over the land.

His perseverance and beliefs brought him to this moment, to a time and place where he could finally make positive and permanent changes. He didn't know how to make a dream a reality. A plan. He needed a plan to set in place.

First he'd root out those remaining loyal to Zigor or the Highest. Determining how to deal with those who would be the new rebels— He chuckled. He'd never imagined being on the receiving side of a rebellion. But what would he do? Despite the life he'd pursued as a rebel, he had no taste for killing.

At the door to Daud's small chamber, the Captain lifted one hand to point to a small crack in the stone wall. Kierigh placed him on the narrow bed and returned to the hall. He found a tiny key within the crack and closed his eyes in sorrow. His brother had lived locked away in this room for so long.

The Captain barely nodded when Kierigh brandished the key. "Daud has returned here. He's taken his journals. Leave now. Apparent madness will come with the weakness but none will hear our battle with Zigor here. By the morrow we will once again be in complete control. Don't forget us." He managed a bland smile.

"I won't. I'll do as you say. For now." When he turned to slide the door closed, Kierigh remained a moment watching the body jerk and tremble until only the barest lift of the chest indicated the body lived. Could Jermanah heal this one? He decided not, simply because the Captain wouldn't risk losing control or allow anyone to prevent their revenge.

After locking the door, he returned the key to the crack and leaned his forehead against the thick wood, allowing confusion to dominate his thoughts. Those now controlling Zigor's body had once inhabited the body of his brother. How were such things possible? He no longer doubted the many living within Daud, nor that some of them now controlled Zigor's body. But how? He doubted he'd ever completely understand.

He left those concerns with the Captain and trotted down the hidden passageway to exit the Stronghold from the small side gate. The sun dipped to touch the tops of the tallest trees. He'd remained too long and now the forest beckoned to him.

He had much to discuss with Jermanah. The springs weren't far from the second camp so they could easily visit the pools. Her gentle touch would do much to ease his confusion. Her image before him and his love for her drawing him on, he ran through the growing twilight.

twenty

Jermanah pulled her knees to her chest and rubbed at the chill bumps dancing along her arms. She'd forgotten she'd taken her blanket to the forest and her empty room was cold. When she attempted to replay the day, her thoughts circled again and again to the man she'd left at the Stronghold. She glanced out her narrow window. Full dark. He'd be in the forest now. A knot tightened in her belly. And she hadn't been there to greet him.

Would he consider her returning to the Compound a betrayal? She hadn't willingly returned, but had been pulled here by her sense of duty. Surely he'd understand.

The old priestess had insisted she move to the chambers of the Highest but Jermanah refused to even set foot on that level of the Compound. Instead she asked the remaining priestesses to clear the rooms of books and parchments. In short order those volumes and many others from the library filled a covered cart. On the morrow, or the next day, she'd take the cart to the forest camp where she could study and think more clearly. Too many disturbing memories haunted the Compound.

She hadn't convinced herself to return to the Seer's chambers until late in the evening. Slipping away from the overly attentive priestesses offered her only a short time to gather an armload of scrolls. She'd avoided glancing at the empty vessel of the old man's body, pretending instead he had simply left his rooms on some private errand.

She'd juggled the scrolls and paused just outside the doorway to renew her vow to properly honor her mentor and release his spirit.

Returning her thoughts to the dark night and her lonely room, she imagined discovering the answers locked in *The Book of Futures.* One of those answers would surely point her toward her place in the world, to where she truly belonged.

In her heart she knew that place should be with Kierigh, but what would she do if destiny set path her in another direction. She curled herself into a chilled ball, thought of Kierigh's warming touch and let exhaustion carry her to a restless sleep.

When he neared the thick ring of undergrowth surrounding the forest, Kierigh whistled then listened for the sentry's response. The reply came immediately so he jogged the relatively short distance to the second camp. He paused steps into the clearing and, with his hands on his hips, fought to catch his breath. Small groups clustered near flickering campfires, but he received no welcome. No one even looked toward him. Had word of his kingship reached the camp before him?

A figure rose and, silhouetted by firelight, walked toward him. Poll didn't meet his eyes until standing before him. Sorrow filled the guard's face.

Fear tightened Kierigh's chest. He clutched the man's upper arms. "Has something happened to Daud?"

Poll shook his head. "He sleeps comfortably. Treenie and your grandmother watch over him."

"Then what's wrong?" He angled his upper body but kept his fists clenched at his sides.

"Kierigh, I..."

"What?" Dreading Poll's response, Kierigh steeled himself for the confirmation of his fears.

Poll drew a slow, deep breath, and held the air in his lungs before speaking in a rush. "Jermanah returned to the Compound with the priestesses." His eyes widened and he took a quick step back.

Anger and betrayal flared in Kierigh's heart. He struggled to contain the frustrating urge to strike out at something. No innocent tree would pay for his anger. He swallowed past the rising pain, flexed his fingers and stalked away in silence.

Knowing Daud was well cared for, Kierigh left the camp, wandering aimlessly along little used forest paths. His steps faltered. He pressed his forehead against the trunk of an ancient tree. He didn't feel the rough bark. He felt nothing, for even the anger and pain had faded.

Humid air filled his nostrils. Without realizing a destination, he'd come here. Jermanah said she wanted to return to the springs. Instead she turned her back on him at the first opportunity. She'd returned to the Compound.

The joyous, bubbling of the water dancing against rock wound through his heart, easing into the jagged cracks and breaking apart the ragged pieces. He'd never come here again. He wandered to the hot spring and sat on the low rock. He'd never be able to forget how she rose from the steam with an innocent invitation shining in her eyes.

He turned his head. And there, the soft grass crushed from their bodies when she said he showed her choice and freedom. He clenched his fists. The choice to turn from him when it suited her. He'd vowed never to hurt her. She'd broken him, but he wouldn't give her the satisfaction of his pain. He bit the inside of his cheek to turn his focus from the stinging burn behind his eyelids. He would not.

Soft, slow footsteps drew his attention. Faint hope rose in his chest but he dashed it away before glancing at the intruder. Grandmother paused a few steps into the glade and waited.

He rose and motioned for her to take the rock seat then sat at her feet as he had as a child. The fading moonlight glittered in the silver of her hair and the bright blue of her wise eyes. He touched her hand. "Do you know any of what transpired this day?"

She nodded and wrapped his hand in hers. The familiar comfort eased his soul. "Poll and Daud have told me much. Daud's full tale will be long in the telling, for he is reluctant to name his pain."

He'd feared as much. Thankfully, Grandmother would be patient with Daud. With them both. "Do you understand the many within him?"

"As much as I'm able. We will all learn more when he's comfortable and feels truly safe."

Kierigh held her dry palm to his cheek. "I doubt I would have been able to survive as he has."

"The life-spirit is strong. One never knows how much can be survived until faced with adversity." She patted his cheek. "And he says much the same of your life, of the things you've done. You and your brother are more alike than either of you realize."

"Were you told part of him transferred to the king?"

Silver brows drew together before she nodded.

Unsure how to continue, Kierigh took a breath for calm. "Those others maintain a tenuous control over Zigor. The Captain, the one who spoke to me, says they have discovered many of the king's secrets. And in order to continue their control, they, as Zigor, had to name a new ruler."

Grandmother's easy smile confused him. The soft twinkle in her eye faded for a moment then returned. "And somehow they named you as successor."

"I don't understand why, but yes. Despite my better judgement, I allowed them to make me the new king. I've given my word. But what am I to do? How do I lead an entire land?

"We never know until we must know."

Kierigh fought the need to roll his gaze to the sky and lost. Grandmother knew he hated her proverbs and odd sayings. He huffed. "Why me? I desire only to live a quiet life. To provide a safe home for you, and now for my brother as well."

"For us alone?"

Unable to form an answer, he rested his cheek against Grandmother's Knee. As she had when comforting him as a boy, she stroked his hair. Her skirts muffled his anguish. "Why did she return to the Compound?"

Silent, Grandmother continued to stroke his head. He shuddered and allowed her comfort draw repressed pain from his soul. His tears soaked the rough material under his cheek. Drained but calmer, he lifted his head.

"I love her, Grandmother."

"I know. Does she?"

"I planned to tell her this night. In this place." Safer than sorrow, his anger returned. "She turned her back on me."

"Today you accepted a destiny you never imagined would be yours. Perhaps she also has a duty to fulfill. You may yet be together."

Kierigh ruthlessly tamped down a rise of hope and snorted his disbelief.

"Patience, Grandson. The king and the Compound will draw near once again."

Terror squeezed his heart. "Don't call me king. Yet, if I must be, I will make sure the Compound won't be one such as I fought for so long."

"You'll change the relationship. And I believe, with Jermanah's assistance."

Wanting to believe, yet doubtful, Kierigh caressed his grandmother's weathered cheek. "You are ever the hopeful old woman. Come. We should return to camp before the moons' light is gone. I'll deal with... all this on the morrow."

She shook her head. "Bide with me for a while longer. There is a tale I must tell you."

Weariness settled across Kierigh's shoulders. "Grandmother? It's late."

"So much has been hidden for too long. Perhaps in my telling you'll learn something to help you in the coming days. Most of all, I pray you to understand what I must tell you."

Settling more comfortably at her feet, Kierigh searched his grandmother's beloved face. She stared into the distance over his head as she did when sorting her thoughts. When her gaze lowered to his, she began without hesitation.

"When my distant cousin trained in the mystic ways, we became lovers. The stolen moments we shared were the greatest joy of my life. Until the happiness brought to us by the birth of our child. But after your mother's birth, our secret was discovered. His mentor appointed him Seer of the Compound. Although we weren't directly punished, we were forbidden to even see each other at a distance."

Kierigh reached into the small bag at his waist then pressed the amulet he'd taken from the Seer's room into her palm. "Grandmother, I—"

"You fear to tell me he is dead?" She touched the amulet to her lips before looping the cord around her neck. The stone lay against her breast and shimmered in the moonlight. "I knew the moment his life-force passed from this world. He waits for me in another lifetime. Such is life. And death. Hush now. I must continue.

"Even though we couldn't meet, he sent messages and watched our daughter grow. She was such a beautiful child and grew into a lovely young woman. We were so proud of her.

"But she caught the eye of the prince. He seduced her and left her with child. With children, for you and Daud were born of that union. I believe the prince timed his seduction so his child would be born under the Double Moon conjunction.

"Your mother told me the prince believed words he'd found in an ancient scroll. A prophecy perhaps, or simply words the prince took to mean what he wished. Words that insinuated a father would gain power beyond imagining from a son."

Kierigh interrupted. "The Seer directed Jermanah to a book, what she called the *Book of Futures*. Perhaps this is where the words came from."

"It's possible." Grandmother leaned forward, curiosity filling her expression. "Has she read the book?"

"She isn't able to decipher many of the words." Kierigh paused to worry over this new puzzle. Zigor believed he would gain power through sacrifice. He had created many others within Daud to increase the power gained through a single sacrifice. But that meant—Kierigh gasped a sharp denial.

"Now, you understand. You and Daud are Zigor's sons."

"No. That can't be. How could mother have been so deceived by him?"

Jermanah's smile filled his inner vision. Despite his pain and doubt he refused to place her actions and reasons next to Zigor's.

"He wasn't always outwardly evil. As a young man he was charming and persuasive. Once he wrested the throne from his father, he became more powerful with each passing cycle. He visited your mother from time to time, taking great joy in tormenting her with the details of Daud's sacrifice. He physically abused her to show his power. Unlike your brother, your mother took the path to madness to protect herself." Grandmother dabbed tears from her eyes.

Kierigh had been so young when madness claimed his mother. He hadn't understood her pain, only his own at her unknowing rejection.

Grandmother cupped his chin and lifted his face to capture his gaze. "You were born before the conjunction and hidden from your father. He never knew of you. Never suspected. Even at her most desperate times, your mother never spoke of you to him. I didn't return soon enough after concealing you. Zigor and the Highest had arrived. Once Daud was placed in his arms, he spared no glance to the woman he'd once claimed to love.

"A cycle later, we learned Zigor didn't sacrifice Daud. He bragged to your mother, laughed about how he abused their son. Her madness increased until she discovered a way to withdraw from life. Her death pains me still. I couldn't protect her."

"How could that man be my father? Daud's father? How could he do such things to his own child?" Kierigh expelled a series of sharp breaths. "Why did you keep this from me?"

"The quest for power will change a man although the depths of change depend upon the strength and the heart of the man. Perhaps the change may be for good. This is the difficult path. The way to evil is easier, the rewards more glorious. Zigor excelled on this path."

He feared the answer to the question burning through his heart. "Does Daud know?"

"Yes. When the others entered the king's body, Zigor's mind wasn't shielded and they knew. They passed the knowledge to Daud. Strangely, he's not surprised."

Kierigh scrubbed his hands over his face. "When I first met the Seer, I imagined him as my grandfather. That truth is welcome. But now I must also believe Zigor is my father, and as such, I'm rightful successor to his rule? This is more than I can comprehend this night."

"I regret I dared not tell you sooner."

His chuckle was raw and desperate. "I suppose not. Grandmother, are there more secrets I need to discover before I return to the Stronghold on the morrow?"

"Only that I know you'll find the strength you need in

your heart. This knowledge will serve you well as you begin your rule."

More of her proverbs and sayings. "You sound like a prophet. The words make sense but the sentences do not."

"You're overly tired, Kierigh. So much had occurred this day, bringing extreme changes to our lives. You'll need a rested mind and body to face the coming days." She tugged a short torch from her worn bag. "Here, this will light our way."

Kierigh held Grandmother's hand on the silent walk to camp. His thoughts weren't on his new-found brother, or the myriad of duties and concerns he would face as a new ruler. His thought were only of Jermanah. He would find no peace or rest this night.

Jermanah halted the short procession of priestesses at the edge of the forest. A relieved, collective sigh rose from the women as they dropped the thick ropes used to pull a heavily laden wagon. Speaking encouragement to each woman, Jermanah poured water from a heavy skin into metal cups. The previous day she'd released the priestesses and remaining acolytes from their vows. Many had returned joyously to their homes with her blessing. The remaining women followed her here.

A young acolyte smiled shyly and took the skin from her, so she wandered to the cart and tucked a length of waterproof canvas securely over the pile of books.

She scanned the forest, confident they'd arrived near one of the sentry lookouts. She'd wait—impatiently—until someone came. She both hoped, and dreaded to see Kierigh striding toward her. The short days since she'd left him in the Stronghold weighed heavy in her chest.

Several of the older women dozed in the warm afternoon. Others discussed what the future might bring. Jermanah sat in the shade and attempted to read, but concentration remained allusive. Even with the minimal assistance from the elder priestess, she wasn't able to decipher any meaning, so she closed *The Book of Futures,* stood and stared into the distance.

"Jermanah?"

She whirled and stumbled into Poll's arms. He held her until she steadied herself then stepped back. "Welcome, lady Jermanah."

Ignoring his use of an unwanted title, she glanced around. "Is Kierigh here?"

Poll angled his face from her. Raw and stretched tight, her disappointment sharpened her tone. "Poll, where is he? Hasn't he returned to the forest? No, he isn't being held in the Stronghold, is he?" Terror for him destroyed the disappointment and she clutched the front of Poll's shirt.

"No, Jermanah. He's not being held, but travels freely between the camp and Stronghold." He pried her fingers from his clothing. "He should return later this afternoon."

Relief flooded through her. "We've seen runners sent in all directions from the Stronghold, but none came to the Compound. Tell me what's transpired. Why did Kierigh return to the Stronghold?"

Poll stared at her, his mouth opening and closing soundlessly before he cleared his throat. But still he didn't speak.

"Is something wrong? Is Daud well? What, Poll? What?" She reached again for his shirt.

His large hands surrounded hers and he leaned closer. “You don’t know?”

“What? What don’t I know? Tell me.” She stamped her foot raising a tiny swirl of dust.

Poll shook his head and turned to forestall her further questions. “It’s not my place. Both Kierigh and Daud are well and you’ll see them soon. Come, I’ll lead you to camp.” He turned back with a smile. “Treenie will be happy to see you.”

Jermanah glared at his back as he moved toward the wagon and roused the women. At his whistle, additional men appeared from the forest to pull and guide the heavy wagon. The women followed with weary footsteps.

When Poll moved past her, she drew breath to speak, but his face had settled into a guard’s blank expression. Knowing she’d obtain no further information from him, she sighed. At the rear of the procession, she offered her arm to the oldest priestess. Thankfully the old woman was too tired to talk, even though the distraction might have been welcome.

Jermanah imagination flared. What need did Kierigh have to return to the Stronghold? Fear numbed her thoughts. While decisions concerning the Compound and the women there had been easy, she’d avoided any personal choices. Even though she’d been caught up in her plans, she should have sent a message when she first arrived at the Compound. Or in any of the days since. Now she’d pay for that mistake.

Daud sat in the center of a small clearing. Jermanah watched him make piles of small stones, knock them down, giggle, then start again. His face filled with unabashed joy as he began a stack of tiny sticks next to the stones.

Jermanah crouched next to him in the small spot of sunlight.

His hand froze, holding a trembling stick suspended above the pile. "Who you?"

"I'm Jermanah."

"Oh. Daud know you." He returned to his sticks, taking time to choose the next to add to the pile.

Ah, this was one of Daud's children. She had no experience with small children, so she studied his intent expression. At least he wasn't afraid of her. "What's your name?"

"Jimi."

"How old are you?" Would these inner children have any concept of age or time?

Jimi lifted one hand, the last three fingers held straight, his first finger bent at the knuckle.

"You're three?"

Jimi shook his head emphatically and used a tiny twig to point to the bent finger. Jermanah crossed her legs to sit and thought a moment. "And a half?"

His head shake turned to a happy nod.

"Three and a half. You're nearly a cycle old." Jimi gave her a tentative grin then bent his head over his small constructions.

Jermanah picked three small wildflowers and wove the long stems into a braid. She added more flowers when the stems grew short until she had created a long, flowery chain.

"Dat?" Jimi pointed at the flowers.

"I made chains like this when I was a little girl. Would you like to learn how? I think you're old enough."

"I can do. Show me."

Hidden by the shadows at the edge of the glade, Kierigh studied his brother and Jermanah. They sat close together, heads bent over the flowers in Jermanah's lap. Daud crawled away, picked a few more blossoms and returned to Jermanah's side. Their delighted laughter eased the tight control Kierigh held over his emotions and he smiled.

He longed to forget the past days and sit beside the woman he loved in a sunlit field. He wasn't jealous of the fact his brother could, not really.

Daud touched Jermanah's hair and held the long braid to the light. Then he took the chain of flowers and placed it on her head. The chain slipped over one eye and they laughed again.

Daud glanced up, saw him and cringed against Jermanah's side. "Who dat?" His words were a child's confused whisper.

Jermanah angled her face toward Kierigh. His heart leapt at the joy sparking in her expression. Until she hid that delight behind a mask of apprehension and a soft frown. She touched Daud's arm to gain his attention. "That's Kierigh. He's Daud's brother."

"'Righ? He good? Not hurt?"

"No, Kierigh won't hurt you. He saved you from Zigor. He saved me, too."

The child's gaze traveled from Kierigh's feet to the top of his head while he remained motionless under the intense scrutiny. "He big."

Jermanah chuckled. "Yes."

Grandmother appeared at the other side of the clearing and motioned to Daud. "Are you hungry?"

Jimi's eyes widened. "Yes. Have yellow fruit?" At Grandmother's nod, he clamored to his feet and waved at Jermanah. After a quick, wary glance at Kierigh, he tottered off to take Grandmother's outstretched hand.

Kierigh winced. The child in control of the body took tiny steps. Daud's legs must ache after such confining movement. Allowing the children a chance to play had been one of Daud's prime concerns, so perhaps the aches meant success to him.

Jermanah remained sitting with her gaze focused on the flowers she twisted in her hands. She nibbled on her lower lip. Kierigh groaned. How could he not love her? He moved closer.

The garland slipped further over her eye. He tentatively tucked the flowers behind her ear. Finally she looked at him and his breath caught at the base of his throat.

In that moment he realized he'd turn from the vows, his honor and duty if she asked him. He also knew she would not. Honor and duty were an integral part of her. That duty must be the reason she returned to the Compound.

Except now she'd brought a cadre of priestesses and acolytes to the forest, begging for refuge. He needed answers from her to understand the whys of her actions.

He needed—her. Sitting so his knees touched hers, he stilled her restless hands, willing his body to forget the last time they sat in the same position. She watched him with luminous eyes. A faint rosy tint crept across her cheeks. So, she remembered as well. Before he explored the memory with her, he had much to explain, much to discuss. But first, he had to know.

"Why didn't you tell me you wanted to return to the Compound?"

She opened her mouth but no sound emerged. When she swallowed the soft length of her throat mesmerized him. "I didn't wish it, but it was my duty."

Nodding, Kierigh said, "We've both been the victims of duty."

"The old priestess was waiting for me outside that...place. She said I was the healer foretold by ancient prophecies. I needed to discover the truth of her words, of her insistence I'm somehow able heal this land. I don't know how, but in my heart I know I must try. Somehow. The priestesses have named me the new leader of the Compound." She shuddered. "I refused the title of Highest."

An unexpected rush of relief poured through him. He lifted her fingers to his lips. Dreading her answer, he asked, "Will you rebuild the Compound?"

"No. I released the women and guards from their vows. Many returned home. Those with me now either had no homes or felt themselves too elderly to begin again. I hope Grandmother will help me find a place for them. There is no reason for the Compound now that the Highest has been destroyed."

Holding her fingers against his lips, Kierigh thought for a long moment. Then he leaned forward and captured her gaze. "Perhaps. Despite the evil that festered there, many still look toward the Compound in their belief. I think beyond that, the new ruler may require assistance from the leader of what was once the Compound."

A deep wrinkle appeared between Jermanah's brows. "There's a new ruler?"

Kierigh dropped her hand. "You haven't heard?"

She shook her head and the flowers slipped to the

ground. "Daily we witnessed runners leaving the Stronghold, but none came near enough to the Compound to bring us news."

Foolishly, when he'd heard she returned there, his anger had prevented any communications. He continued to stand in his own way. With the luck of the moons, she'd forgive him for this. And much more. "Will you walk with me?"

Jermanah nodded and allowed him to lift her to her feet. Stretching her cramped legs, she fell into step beside him. He was preoccupied. During the twists and turns of the past turbulent days she'd found it difficult to remain at one task for any length of time. Except for loving Kierigh. Her one constant and her only strength.

They walked in silence. Jermanah held tightly to Kierigh's hand and he rubbed his thumb across the back of her fingers. This was where she wanted, needed to stay.

At her sigh Kierigh gathered her in to a tight embrace. His desire-dark eyes glittered before he slanted his lips across hers. Her low moan met the insistent dance of his tongue. He lifted until her feet dangled and she slid her arms around his neck. The world around them faded. This was where she belonged.

Kierigh cupped her bottom to press her against the rise of his desire. She wrapped one leg around his thigh and pressed closer still. He trailed frantic kisses along her jaw. Accepting the unspoken invitation of her arched neck, he traced patterns with his lips and tongue under her ear and down to the hollow at the base of her neck.

His warm breath ragged against her cheek, he lifted his head. His embrace loosened. Pain and uncertainty filled his expression. "I must tell you of the new ruler."

"Now?"

"Yes." His fingers flexed against her sides as he allowed her to slide down the length of his body. Her knees barely supported her but he supported her before stepping back and shaking his head when she reached for him. Taking her hand, he held himself at arm's length.

His eyes flashed with an internal battle before he settled his face into a neutral expression much like that of the Compound guards. "Zigor had a son."

At his bland statement, all thought fled Jermanah's mind.

A shout rang through the forest. Head cocked to one side, Kierigh listened to the repeated call. He stared at Jermanah. "The Compound?"

"Is it near dusk already? I must go. I must see the Compound." She whirled in a frantic circle. Which way?

Kierigh caught her elbow then took her hand. "This way."

She rushed them through the trees until they reached the thinning forest nearest the huge Compound. The priestesses and members of the camp gathered in a tight group. Jermanah stopped at Grandmother's side and acknowledged Daud. Kierigh stood behind her with his hands resting on her shoulders.

Thin columns of smoke rose from the buildings before dissipating on the light breeze. Doubting her decision, Jermanah took a deep breath. Grandmother sniffed softly and Daud wrapped an arm about her shoulders.

Kierigh's fingers dug into Jermanah's shoulders. She rubbed her cheek against his hand until he relaxed.

Treenie moved beside them and lifted both babes from their basket. She held them cradled in her arms and pointed with her chin. "See, there is your papa."

Relieved the woman had claimed the tiny boy,

Jermanah shielded her eyes with one hand and squinted toward the Compound. Smoke roiled along the ground, surrounding the buildings with a thick haze. A large war beast raced toward them. Poll had been successful. The Compound would be no more.

Kierigh whispered in her ear, "Little one, what have you done?"

"I honor the Seer. I bring down the Compound. Nothing remains of the Highest." A surge of satisfaction warmed her cool skin.

"The stones will not burn."

Watchful silence encompassed the observers. Even the birds fell silent. Poll drew his beast to a skidding halt and slid to the ground. He took one of the babes from Treenie, wrapped his free arm around her and turned to face the smoking Compound.

A deep rumble shook the ground. Jermanah leaned back, accepting the safety of Kierigh's arms. The stone walls swayed, crumbled. The buildings collapsed in upon themselves. Nothing remained of the Compound but a pile of rocks and rubble.

A cheer rose from the gathering. After a long moment the cluster of women began a chant of praise. Jermanah stepped from Kierigh's arms, shrugged and looked at him over her shoulder.

"The Seer taught me a mixture of herbs that when burned a certain way would cause stone to fall."

twenty-one

Speaking quiet memories of the Seer, Grandmother and Jermanah turned back to the forest. The others faded into the dim light under the trees, leaving Kierigh and Daud to watch the dust and smoke settle over the pile of rubble.

Kierigh scuffed the toe of his boot in the dirt and ripped up small clumps of grass. “Why didn’t you tell her?”

“This isn’t mine to tell.”

“No. Do any of the camp know?”

Daud shook his head. “None but Grandmother, Poll and most within this body.”

The difficult question he needed to ask Daud weighed heavily in Kierigh’s mind. And in his heart. Closing his eyes allowed him to prevaricate a few moments longer. “I watched a child at play today.”

“We know.”

“It was disconcerting to witness how your body appears to grow smaller. Your face wasn’t like an adult pretending to be a child. You looked like a child.”

“We’ve known nothing else, so the change in our

appearance is as natural to us as for you to hear only one voice in their head. We are as we are."

"Have you enjoyed these days of freedom?"

The joy of Daud's smile filled his expression. "Yes. With Grandmother's and Poll's help, the children are learning the joys of play. Some already begin to trust. Ah, Grandmother. She's remarkable. We learn much from her. No matter who controls this body, she gives each the love and understanding they are able to accept."

Hesitating, Kierigh ground a clump of grass into the dirt then stared at his feet. "Do you trust me, Daud?"

"You are my brother."

"That's no answer."

"I trust you with my life and with the lives of those within this body."

Sounds of celebration rang from the camp. Daud stepped closer to Kierigh. "You must tell your followers before word reaches them from the Stronghold. You've been lucky thus far, but only because no one but you and Poll have come to the forest. You could lose their support if they believe you hid such an important occurrence from them."

Wrapping one arm across Kierigh's shoulder, Daud continued, "You must tell Jermanah first." He bent to smile up into Kierigh's lowered gaze. "Trust us, brother. She'll accept your new life."

Kierigh nodded but didn't raise his head. "I must ask something difficult of you."

"We can't imagine anything you'd ask which would be more difficult than the life we've already survived."

Fear of alienating his brother so soon after reuniting with him kept Kierigh's gaze on the ground. He cleared the lump from his throat. "Will you return to the Stronghold with me?"

Daud's silence lingered long enough Kierigh was forced to look at him. His brother crossed his arms over his chest and lifted one hand to cup his chin. His index finger tapped against his cheek. The smile still crinkled at the corners of his eyes. "Of course, Kierigh. Why do you need us there?"

Relief released much of the tension tightening Kierigh's shoulders. "The Captain wishes to speak with you. I need to map and destroy the secret ways through the Stronghold. I value your opinion on many things." He paused. "I need an adviser."

"What of Poll? He knows the land, the people. We only know the Stronghold."

"Poll has already agreed. I need you both. I don't have the knowledge or the understanding to rule alone." Kierigh spread his hands. "As my brother, you are the logical choice."

Daud clasped Kierigh's upper arm. "You must tell Jermanah. I won't go with you until you do."

Kierigh accepted the rousing congratulations of those gathered around the fires wry humor. The pledges of these brave men and women meant more to him than the prostrations of the nobles. Even the women who had once been priestesses supported him. But what of Jermanah?

She sat with her head lowered, refusing to meet his gaze since the moment he'd spoken the words, 'I am now the ruler of this land'. Agreeing with his brother's suggestion, he'd planned to tell her before the others, but there'd been no chance. Her shoulders lifted and dropped with a deep breath.

His chest filled with a responding sigh. He hadn't named the shame of his new life, exposing he was Zigor's son. He wasn't concerned with the camp's reaction for they knew him as the man he was. But would Jermanah turn from him in disgust? He had come to understand her overwhelming fear of becoming like the Highest.

When he was able to escape from those pledging themselves to him, he crossed the clearing and knelt beside her.

She lifted a stunning smile to him. "I'm so happy for you, Kierigh. You'll be the leader to take this land from the despair Zigor and the Highest created." She rested her hand against his cheek.

He placed a kiss in her palm. "Will you walk with me again? There is more I must explain to you."

Her eyebrows arched before she nodded. They rose and slipped from the renewed celebrations.

Kierigh took her hand, a lifeline, an anchor in his new reality. He couldn't imagine attempting to lead anyone ever again without her at his side. Comfortable silence surrounded their walk to the springs.

"We've returned." She twirled in place, her braid whipping around her. When she stopped, she opened her arms to him.

Holding himself still, he shook his head. "I must speak first."

She sank to the ground, one hand still extended toward him, confusion dulling her smile. He sat and tugged her hand to his lap, caressing her fingers with long, soft strokes. The hitch in her breathing nearly made him forget the words he needed to say.

"There is more to the tale of my kingship. I don't wish for this to be commonly known, but the knowledge won't remain hidden long. My future depends on your reaction."

"My reaction? Your future?"

"You may grow to hate me."

"Hate you? How could I—"

"Please, don't speak, little one. Hear my words." He paused, lay her palm against his thigh and covered her hand with his. This way she could remove her hand easily, while he still had the comfort of her touch. Fearing her reaction, the darkness over her shoulder held his gaze while he spoke.

"When Zigor was yet a prince he seduced a young woman. She bore him twin sons. One he took to the Stronghold, while the other remained hidden from him."

Unable to gauge her silence, he chanced a quick glance at Jermanah. Her gaze sparkled in the dim moonlight, a tender smile graced her lips. Unable to read her expression, he drew a deep breath and continued in a rush. "Jermanah, little one, I am one of those sons. Zigor is my father."

She slipped her hand from beneath his and cupped his cheek. "And so, the son will be a much better ruler than the father."

"Perhaps." He hadn't anticipated her easy acceptance. He'd worried over and planned for a more negative response. His next words could still alter the tide of her emotions. He struggled to name his fear in a harsh whisper. "If the power of ruling tempts me, I could become like him."

"As I feared becoming like the Highest?"

He nodded and Jermanah's warm palm slipped from his face. A chill skittered down his spine. She didn't—

"Look at me, Kierigh." She waited until he complied with her soft command. "You have no evil within you."

"Do you believe you know what lies within me?" After the rage and hatred he'd felt toward Zigor, he wasn't sure himself.

"Yes. For you have taken me to a place where I touched your soul. There's as much darkness in you as you discovered within me."

He jerked and stared at her. "I found no darkness."

"So, neither of us has the will, the desire to follow an evil path. You aren't Zigor. Your life has been spent fighting the corruption of his rule. How does that change when you know he's your father? And what of Daud? He is also Zigor's son. He experienced, and survived, that pervasive evil. Yes, Zigor caused a darkness to grow within your brother, but those in his body channeled that evil toward good. Daud is also free of darkness."

With a suddenness that left him breathless, Kierigh's fear dissolved. Jermanah's soft smile banished the remnants of doubt and concern and his muscles relaxed. He leaned forward and touched his lips to her forehead. "You are the constant in my life. My ray of light. You tell me what I already know but can's see for myself. I love you, Jermanah."

The soft caresses of her sigh warmed his cheek before she sat back. The muscles at the base of his neck knotted. Catching the inside of his cheek between his teeth, he waited. Waited for her words of denial or soul-destroying laughter.

"As I love you, Kierigh." Her voice was soft and filled with joy. "I believe I always have. I feared you didn't care for me."

"How could you imagine—? How could I not love you? As you have seen my soul, so you *are* my soul." He gathered her close and nuzzled her neck.

"And you are my life." She braced her hands against his chest to initiate a sweet kiss. She sighed into his mouth then captured his groan and danced her tongue along his.

A low growl of impatience rumbled from Kierigh as he ripped his shirt over his head then grabbed the hem of her tunic and tossed it to join his in a rumpled pile. The rest of their clothing followed before he lay them back on the cushion of fresh, sweet smelling grasses.

Soft, reverent, insistent, he touched her. He cupped her breasts and circled her nipples with his thumbs. The arch of her back and her desire-laced pleas tempted him to draw tangled patterns with his tongue down the swell of her breast.

Jermanah's hands roamed his back then rose to tangle in his hair. With impatient tugs she lifted his head to return his lips to hers.

Rolling so she straddled him, Kierigh splayed his hands at her hips. She captured his hard length in her hands, caressing, pausing then beginning again. Kierigh clawed handfuls of grass from the ground and thrust against her downward strokes. The silk of her hair ignited him, each strand burning sensation and need against his skin. Her kisses scorched his soul, branding him to her. With an arch of one eyebrow he rolled again to settle in the cradle of her thighs.

A rumble of thunder vibrated the air around them as he eased into her welcoming body. His shout of joy challenged the skies.

Jermanah clutched at his buttocks, delighting in the play of his muscles when he thrust into her. Joy, pure and right flooded her body, her heart, her soul.

Large, wet drops fell onto her closed eyelids. Kierigh slowed until he barely moved within her. Her inner muscles clenched and she grinned at his vocal response. His mouth hovered close to her ear. After the brief caress of his tongue, he whispered, "It's raining. We should find shelter."

His voice was breathless, raw with desire. For her. She wrapped her arms under his and up over his shoulders to keep him deep within her. "No. Let the rain wash away out fears, our concerns, and bless our love. In this moment we begin to purify the land."

He chuckled and she pressed her breasts to his chest to capture the sensations. "You sound like a prophet."

"Did I read that in the book and not remember? The words don't feel like mine." She lay back and drew her brows together.

Kierigh kissed the tight spot between her brows. "Weren't they?"

He circled his hips, beginning a slow withdrawal and return. She couldn't form an answer. The tight spiral of sensations chased words, thought, everything but him and their mating from her mind.

Large warm drops fell around them, lifting tiny poofs of dust. The fresh, rain-wet aroma filled her with a surge of hope. The hope swirled with her desire until she no longer sensed the grasses beneath her or the rain-washed air. All became Kierigh. Kierigh and the joining of their bodies. Their hearts. Their souls.

He whispered to her ears, to her mouth, and to the amazingly sensitive skin of her forehead. His words entered her as he did, the rhythm building, growing higher, stronger. Him. "I love you."

The world couldn't contain the intensity of her joy, the bursting of her pleasure. A streak of lightning split the night sky. Echoed by thunder, Kierigh's cry joined hers.

Much later they donned their wet clothing and returned to camp. Dawn had brightened the sky, but the people remained in their shelters. Canting his head, Kierigh listened to the silence. "We'll let them rest. The celebration must have gone long into the night."

"Yes." Heat rose to fill her cheeks.

Grinning, he chased the heat with a finger. "We'll return to the Stronghold. You'll be at my side to help me make decisions for the rebuilding of the land."

She'd dreaded this moment, knowing the time would come ever since she'd noticed him watching Jimi at play. Deep sorrow lay like a stone in her chest. His hopeful, loving expression faded with her prolonged silence. Their future depended on his reaction now and her determination to follow her resolve. What she did was right. For her. Her life. And their love. Finally she drew a short breath and spoke to the ground. "I can't go with you."

He clutched her shoulders and she lifted her gaze. "Why? I need you, little one. I want you by my side. For my lifetime."

The pain etched deep in his expression ripped a jagged a fissure through her soul. Too much time had been lost already. "I wish that as well, for my lifetime. But I can't. Not until I understand the *Book of Futures*. I must know what prophecy is hidden in the words, what clues, what knowledge may line the pages. This is my duty, Kierigh. My destiny."

"You are my destiny."

Feeling a traitor to that destiny, to their love, she returned her gaze to her toes. "It may be so, but I can't, no, I won't leave here without knowing what the ancients predicted." Desperate for him to understand, stared into his eyes, nearly lost in the deep, sorrow-filled blue. "There may be knowledge you need. I won't leave you to find your way without this assistance."

His gaze narrowed, hiding his thoughts from her. "You'll study at the Stronghold."

He was sure of his words, convinced she would acquiesce to his statement. A determined leader. A good man. Disappointing him broke her heart. If she broke his as well, there might never be a way to repair the cracks and distance she now set between them. "No. I don't understand the reason why, but I must remain here. The priestesses will continue to assist me. And as you said, Grandmother may have knowledge of the language. I'll need her help as well."

She stood without moving, watching Kierigh's expression alter with his effort to contain anger and remain calm. His voice cracked with the effort. "She will come to the Stronghold with you."

"Do you really think so?"

After a glance at Grandmother's small, round tent, he shook his head. "No. Perhaps only when all traces of Zigor are removed."

"If she agrees, we'll come together. I hope soon."

"I love you, little one. How can you refuse me?"

"It's because of that love. I don't know how, but I'll use any means to protect you. And through you, this land." Stunned by the determination and truth of her words, she paused. "Perhaps I, too, am meant to be a leader. I don't know. I must discover that possibility before I join you."

"But—"

She covered his lips with her fingers. "This I vow. I'll do all I can to be with you as soon as I'm able. For you are my life."

He'd never seemed so lost, so alone. She feared for him, his safety and his life if she didn't discover everything she could from the book. Turning away was one of the most painful things she'd ever done, but after a sigh, she gave him her back. "May joy be with you, my love."

Kierigh caught her hand and held her fingers in a loose grip for a moment. If she turned back at his slight tug on her hand, she'd undermine her determination. Squaring her shoulders, she waited. Cool lips touched the back of her hand. Then he walked away. She angled and watched from beneath her lashes. He stalked to the edge of the clearing, gave the sentry an abrupt signal and disappeared into the forest.

Once he calmed and could think rationally, he'd understand. He had to. If not, she had no life, no reason or purpose. She hurried to her tent, shaking away the dire thoughts. The sooner she learned what the book had to tell her, the sooner she could go to Kierigh.

She paused with one hand on the leather tie holding open the entrance. If he would still have her.

Kierigh believed time would pass slowly without Jermanah, but each decision spurred the need for more plans, more decisions. The Captain provided a wealth of information and assessment. Kierigh didn't care to understand how, but those within the Zigorbody had been resourceful in gaining information the old king struggled to keep hidden.

Finding an odd irony in the orders, Kierigh sent his men to scour the land for new rebels, those few who remained loyal to Zigor's ideals. After long, tiresome meetings filled with fear and pleading, the nobles had begun to understand the new king's leadership didn't mean they had to give up their opulent lifestyles as long as they agreed to work themselves in order to hold what they had. The common folk rallied to him, their support a balm to his aching heart.

When Jermanah had refused to join him, he'd considered destroying the Stronghold as she had the Compound. But the numbers of people who lived and worked to keep the huge structure functioning made the idea impractical.

Instead of merely mapping the hidden passageways, he began to tear down the stones, discovering walled-off rooms and stores of goods. A team of scribes was charged to catalog the riches and hidden treasures. Much of those goods he planned to return to the people. He gathered books and scrolls together in one large room, employing carpenters to create large tables for study and shelves to hold the new library. As each volume was shelved, he wondered if—no, when—Jermanah would arrive to enjoy the growing collection.

Daud and Poll worked tirelessly at his side. Kierigh grew to know both men well and valued their opinions more than he imagined. When leading his small group of rebels, he'd made decisions alone. Having others to consult with eased the strain of decision making. Surprised, he realized he'd become a more competent leader.

Despite the busy days and his personal accomplishments, he was empty. The narrow walkway at the top of the walls became his solace. From there he'd watch the forest, imagining Jermanah deep in study or relaxing at the springs. No one brought him news of her, nor did he ask. He spent long hours standing in the sun and wind, forcing himself to consider the decisions he made daily. More often, he'd simply stare across the plains to the trees, his mind numb.

Then Daud or Poll would come to physically lead him from the battlements and he'd return to himself and to his duties.

Days of study merged into one long blur. Jermanah struggled from dawn until long past the setting of the sun to interpret the book. The old priestess remained diligent at her side, recording the decoded words, until she fell asleep over the pages, snoring softly. With kind words of appreciation, Jermanah would send the old woman off to her tent then review the day's progress.

Because she assumed her actions would be as the Seer intended, she remained determined to understand as much as she could by herself. She ignored Grandmother's hovering and persisted until she could read nearly all of the first handful of pages. The remainder of the odd language resisted any attempt at deciphering, so finally, she turned to Grandmother.

"These first pages are nothing more than a recounting of the history of the land. Most of this I knew and now I no longer care which king did what, nor how the people reacted. There are passages that will be of help to Kierigh, but no prophecy." She placed the open book in Grandmother's lap and jabbed her finger against the irritating pages.

"But I can't read these last pages. None of the priestesses recognize the language. Why a different language? Is this the prophecy?"

She allowed her frustration to carry her around Grandmother's chair. She paced, turned, paced again, twisting the end of her braid through her fingers.

Grandmother lifted a leg in Jermanah's path to halt her restless wandering. "Sit next to me, dearie. I can't think with your frantic movement. Come, let's see together what these pages contain."

Jermanah sat with a huff then rose to her knees to give Grandmother a hug of apology. Settling on a thick rug at Grandmother's feet, Jermanah rested her palm on the book. Despite knowing Grandmother might be able to help her, it was still difficult to release her possessive need to understand.

Grandmother looked at the page. Her eyes widened and she drew in a sharp breath. Wrenching the book from under Jermanah's hand, she lifted the volume closer to her face, angling the pages toward the bright sunlight. She chuckled.

"What is it, Grandmother?"

The old woman laughed until tears trickled down her wrinkled cheeks. Gasping for breath, she patted the book. "Oh, Jermanah. If you'd come to me sooner, so much time would have been saved. You see, dearie, the Seer and I had to hide our love, so we developed a secret language to send messages. He'd send the loveliest messages." Pink tinged her wrinkled cheeks.

"But what does that have to do with *this* book?"

Grandmother stroked a line of the bold handwriting. "What you're unable to read is in that language. If you wouldn't have brought this to me, I doubt you'd ever gain understanding. Come, young woman. I'll read this to you."

Embarrassed, Jermanah ducked her head. She'd been stubborn and prideful, wanting to prove herself worthy by reading the book with no assistance. Asking for help wasn't a weakness. She let out a long breath. She could have gone to Kierigh sooner.

"Don't berate yourself, dearie. When one is suddenly given a position of power, it's often difficult to allow others to help you. You felt you needed to prove yourself. Such is the nature of all people. True leaders are those who understand they aren't able to do it all. Now, the book." Grandmother held the book at an angle so she could point to the words as she read. Jermanah leaned forward to clearly hear her low tones.

"The writing starts with a personal message telling me of his love. He knew if I read this, he would have passed to another lifetime. Ah, he affirms he'll await me there." She read silently for a few moments.

"Ah, here we are. This is what he says. 'I have recorded in this volume the history of our land. It is my hope the new rulers will learn from the past and avoid the mistakes of those times. Now, I record my seeing. I have analyzed my visions and share here what I have learned, but not the complex tangle of images that confused me for so long.

"'I am saddened I was unable to tell you, but I saw the madness in our daughter long before her birth. The love I bear for you wouldn't allow me to turn from that destiny. I also knew the pain to be borne by her sons. The younger—few could bear his pain. His father planned his suffering even before his conception.'"

Grandmother paused to wipe sorrow's tears with the hem of her sleeve. Jermanah's mind whirled. If the Seer knew about Daud, why... She sighed. Because there were always plans within plans, visions within visions. And choices within destiny.

Grandmother continued to read. "'The elder will make a fine ruler—if he heeds the advice of his brother. In this does his strength come. And also comes understanding and knowledge to bring the land to peace and prosperity once again.

"'Also by the ruler's side stands one of the Compound, one who denies the Compound. I have trained her in many ancient ways, but I am unable to see the extent of her skill. In order for her to stand with the man, she must heal. Heal the son. Heal the brother. Heal self. In all this, she will heal the land.'"

Jermanah made a soft noise of frustration. "What does he mean? I've healed both Kierigh and Daud. That I understand. But how do I heal myself?"

Shrugging, Grandmother lowered the book. "I don't know. Even as a young man the Seer often spoke in riddles. Even when he believed he spoke clearly, he muddled the minds of others. Hush now, I'm almost done. Perhaps there will be an answer or two to come."

She angled to book in the morning sunlight. "'I have seen my own ending, but I don't fear that time. Our love will remain strong within our grandsons and their children. And so it will be for all of time. There is no prophecy, though claiming one has been a useful tool to set events in motion. As always, what I've seen is only one possibility in many. The minds and wills of our grandsons create their future. For this lifetime and beyond.

"'Farewell, my love...'" Grandmother paused and cleared her throat. "The rest is for me only."

Jermanah surged to her feet and faced the old woman with her hands fisted at her hips. "There's no prophecy? Then how... why? I don't understand."

Offering a gentle smile, Grandmother closed the book and patted the purple leather cover. "Go to Kierigh. Listen well to your hearts. They will lead you. If you leave now, you'll be with him by mid-afternoon. "One thin eyelid lowered in a knowing wink.

Jermanah drew breath to speak but Grandmother waved her to silence. "Go, young woman. Don't waste any more of your precious time."

Once again the Seer's words and logic had defeated her, yet she didn't mind not understanding. She saw possibilities and hope. Nothing could keep her from Kierigh. She bent to give the old woman a fierce hug. "I won't, Grandmother. Thank you."

Once in the clearing, Jermanah motioned to a man lounging by the fire. "Will you take me to the Stronghold?"

He glanced around and hesitated.

"I must speak with Kierigh," she explained.

The man brightened and nodded. Heads peeped out from tents, smiling as they passed. Jermanah returned the smiles and shook her head. Had everyone been waiting for her to go to Kierigh?

twenty-two

Within moments Jermanah and her guide left the camp. She held hope tightly in her heart. With no prophecy to harm Kierigh, no mystic words stood between them. Love for the tall rebel—the new king—burned through her. He'd forgive her. She sobered. If she hadn't waited too long and lost his love.

They crossed the wide open plain at a quick pace. The last time she'd surreptitiously approached the Stronghold faded from her memory as she studied the remarkably beautiful structure. Had the walls and high towers always appeared so, or was the change because of Kierigh? Flags snapped merrily from the high battlements drawing her attention.

A lone figure stood silhouetted against the sun. Kierigh. When they drew closer the figure moved from view. Aching to run the final distance to the open gates, she held herself at a stately walk.

Kierigh appeared at the gate and shook his head. Did he forbid her entry? Then he ran forward and her heart leapt.

She paused, waiting for him to come to her. If he planned to deny her, better now with an easy escape than once she was within the walls.

He skidded to a stop ending his headlong rush a few feet from her. He spoke between deep, gasping breaths. "Why are you here?"

Her heart lodged in her throat. He didn't want her. She'd tell him what Grandmother had read then return to the forest. After that, she didn't know.

"With Grandmother's help, I understand the book."

"You've learned the prophecy?" He took an eager step closer.

"There isn't a prophecy, only possibilities. The Seer recorded a history of the land then sent a message to Grandmother in a language only they understood. He stated you are to rule. Daud must stand at your side."

Kierigh nodded but doubt and worry tightened his expression. "Any you? Where do you stand?"

"You are my life." The words were her only truth.

He lifted one hand to cover his heart and swept the other back toward the Stronghold. "You will stay with me? Help govern this land?"

"Yes. If you'll still have me."

The doubt faded and his eyes grew dark. The familiar glint of desire sent thrilled spirals of need racing through her. Kierigh bounded across the final distance and gathered her in his arms. He crushed her lips with a fierce kiss.

She returned the burning passion, welcoming the twining of his tongue against hers. A quiet moan tightened her throat when he angled back to gaze at her. Glistening moisture spiked his thick lashes.

"I would have you with me every moment, every day for the rest of my life. And beyond, into many lifetimes if that were possible." He kissed her again then swung her in a circle until she grew dizzy.

A cheer rose from the Stronghold and from the man who'd guided her. Men and women lined the top of the wall and crowded the gates. Kierigh lowered her to the ground, wrapped an arm around her shoulders and turned her to face the Stronghold. He swept his other arm toward the gate. "Welcome home, my lady."

She punched him lightly in the stomach. "You, my lord, should know better than to call me that."

He sighed. "I wish we could be only Kierigh and Jermanah. But the challenges I've accepted, and you choose by loving me, dictate the occasional use of titles."

"I know. But when we're alone?"

"Let us then be only Kierigh and Jermanah."

Proud of his accomplishments, Kierigh showed her the many changes he'd already instituted within the Stronghold. Their progress was followed by an ever-changing group of well-wishers Poll tried valiantly to keep from them.

Jermanah admired the subtly larger rooms and knelt to peer at the floors, unable to identify where the walls hiding the secreted ways once stood. "But where are the stones? I saw no rubble outside."

"There's only one level of dungeons now. Poll made sure the lowest levels were filled in first. Come." With her hand resting in the crook of his elbow, they walked across the audience chamber. He stopped before the panel leading to the hidden courtyard.

She jerked and violent shudders shook her body. "I won't ever go in there again."

"I must show you the courtyard."

"Please, Kierigh, don't make me."

"Only for a moment. You must find peace with what happened there. Each of us, Daud, Poll and I, have faced the horrors. You won't feel safe in the Stronghold or wish to remain within these wall until you understand what we've done. Please, little one. Soon we'll permanently seal the courtyard. Except for a view from the room the Captain now occupies, maintaining the sight as part of their control and revenge over Zigor."

Belief in his words and her own curiosity overcame Jermanah's fear. With a deep breath she clutched Kierigh's arm and peeked around him. A massive pile of stone rubble filled the area, mounding high to one side, close to a second floor balcony. The columns, the sacrificial stone, the glittering pathway were all hidden beneath the rocks. She hid her face against his sleeve and whispered, "What about her?"

Kierigh eased Jermanah into his embrace. "The Highest was not moved. When the courtyard is filled, all entrances will be sealed, covered and forgotten. No one will remember. She wasn't honored."

"May we leave now?"

Kierigh lifted her and carried her into the audience chamber, sat on the dais steps and cradled her in his lap. "You don't need to fear, little one. I'll keep you from harm."

"Truly?"

"I don't lie."

"I know." She rested her cheek against the strong, comforting beat of his heart.

They were wrapped in the comfort of simply being with each other, silent, until Poll stepped forward and cleared his throat. "A delegation from the far west has arrived and insists on speaking to you immediately. I've already put them off for some time and can't delay much longer." His face contorted as he attempted to hide his pleased grin then he shrugged and let the smile light his face.

Resignation reverberated through Kierigh's sigh, echoed by a Jermanah's soft, sorrowful hum. The moments of comfort had been more precious to her than any declaration or promise. He stood her on her feet and helped her straighten his tunic. She pushed stray hairs back from his face then her fingers lingered against his shoulders. He bowed to her. "I would be unpresentable if not for your care."

With a final soft brush of her palm against his cheek, she snorted and moved to the side of the dais. Kierigh shook his head and extended his hand to her. "No. You will stand by me."

She narrowed her gaze at his pompous tone and he grimaced.

"Please. Today we begin to show the people the promises of the future."

Promises of the future. His unspoken words and the love in his light blue eyes spoke many promises made only to her. Jermanah moved to his side and took his hand. As one they turned toward the broad, grand entrance to the audience chamber.

A tight knot of ragged men advanced in silence and stopped before Kierigh. One man, dressed in a slightly more ornate—and clean—tunic moved forward and bowed his head. "We come before the new king to offer allegiance."

"I accept your offer."

A second man slipped from behind the first. He whipped a knife from under his tunic and rushed forward. "Allegiance to Zigor."

Denial blasted through Jermanah and she leapt in front of Kierigh. The knife sliced down and pierced her chest. Ripping pain tore through her. She stiffened with shock then collapsed into Kierigh's arms. Praise to the moons, she'd saved him.

Fumbling for his knife with one hand, Kierigh knelt with Jermanah's limp body held against his chest. Helpless anger burned, blurring his vision. The assassin leapt back, turned and impaled himself on Poll's blade. The man's screams were silent compared to the agony raging in Kierigh's chest.

Jermanah's breathing grew shallow, labored. No, that wasn't the rattle of death. He couldn't let her go now. Not ever. Without her there was no need to fight. He would die with her.

Weapons drawn, others of the party advanced on Kierigh, success gleaming in their wild, twisted expressions. Poll planted himself before Kierigh, sparing only a short glance filled with sorrow. Sword held at ready, he waited for the attack.

"Hold."

The assassins halted, turned as one to the Zigor-body and dropped to their knees. The leader lifted his blade. "Hail, Zigor."

"Silence. What foolishness brought you to the Stronghold?"

"We come to return you to power."

The Zigor-body advanced. His voice dropped to a harsh

whisper. "I named my successor. Willingly. I placed the circlet upon his brow. Willingly. You misjudge my desires. He will not be destroyed."

"My lord?" Confusion filled the man's expression as he glanced at his compatriots for confirmation of his words. "Our orders were to kill any who attempted to hold power while you yet live."

"Ah. But, I no longer wish to rule. This man is my choice to govern the land. Honor him. Obey him, or die. You, and your clan."

"I follow none but Zigor."

Pointing at the men, the Zigor-body nodded to Poll. "Then you will die. But not today."

At Poll's shouted order, guards rushed in from the hallway, surrounded the now cowering men and dragged them toward the dungeon.

The metallic clang of Poll's dropped sword echoed as he stumbled to Kierigh's side. He fell to his knees and took Jermanah's hand in his. When he lifted a stricken gaze, Kierigh gave a minute shake of his head, answering the unspoken question.

The Zigor-body commanded, "Find Daud." One of the many guards that now filled the chamber dashed across the floor and through a narrow doorway. The remaining guards shuffled back to the hallway, followed by Zigor. He shut the door behind them.

As if holding her tighter would keep the life within her body, Kierigh eased Jermanah closer. "Don't leave me, little one."

Her lips curved. A glaze of pain dulled her eyes. "I'll wait for you."

"You won't go. Isn't there anyone else who can heal?"

"Don't believe so." Her words grew softer, mere breaths of air. "Seer said... I was the only..."

Daud slid to a stop and dropped to his knees. He touched her forehead with the tips of his fingers. "Then you must heal yourself."

Her eyelids fluttered. "I... don't..."

Daud touched the knife and a flash of silent agony twisted Jermanah's lips. Kierigh struggled to not shove his brother away and clutched her even tighter. She was his, in life. In death.

Daud leaned closer to Jermanah's ear. "We didn't wish to live, yet you pulled us from the edge of oblivion. We thank you and wish to return the gift of life to you." Daud's words sank through the haze of despair circling Kierigh. Might there be hope? He had to believe.

Jermanah's head shifted. "No strength."

Kierigh kissed her damp forehead. "As you are my soul, I will be your strength. I will not accept your death."

Despite the pain tensing her jaw and forehead, she still offered him a serene smile. "Accept? Little you can do."

Daud eased her hand from Poll's and placed her fingers at one side of the knife. He placed her other hand so her fingers and thumbs touched around the weapon. He took a deep breath and focused on Kierigh. "I will take the knife. Brother, you and Poll must help her close the wound." His voice dropped to a harsh, agonized whisper. "Jermanah, you have healed these three bodies. We all will be your strength."

Kierigh accepted his brother's plan. He had to. He nodded, then after Poll's silent agreement, placed his hand over Jermanah's. Poll's fingers trembled when he covered her other hand. Daud gnawed on his lip then carefully grasped the knife. "Now."

The renewed sharp agony tore an echoing cry from Jermanah. The sound faded in the now empty chamber allowing Kierigh's urgent whispers to swirl around her. "Now, Jermanah. Now. Concentrate. Take power, strength from me. From each of us. Heal yourself. Jermanah, don't fail the Seer."

She tried to concentrate. For him. But the peace calling from the end of the darkness was so beautiful. She didn't fear the warm darkness surrounding her. It pushed the pain from her body. She floated. A vague memory lightened the dark. Another time… place… pain. Why would she stay in such a pain-filled place?

Intruding on the peace, the darkness, a low voice pushed, urging her to listen. "Little one, stay."

Curious. She should know that voice, know why it intrigued her. Yet there was no strength within her to pursue the thought. She allowed the voice to float away. Sharp pain penetrated each breath. Stop the pain. Don't breathe.

The voice returned, urgent, compelling. "Breathe Jermanah, breathe with me."

The pain wasn't so great if she took shallow breaths.

"I love you, little one."

Love? Who loved her? Kierigh. His voice wanted her to stay. At the edge of consciousness, she touched the welcome darkness and realized it held false peace. Lassitude flowed from her. She remembered. Who. Why. How. The tingle of rising power made her gasp. The power concentrated in her hands, her chest. Her skin began to knit together around a bloody wound.

Too much pain. Her concentration failed and the wound stretched and gaped open. A second voice. Similar.

Different. Then a child called to her. "Stay 'Manah. We make flowers with the pretty lady."

A third voice. A friend's voice. "Jermanah, heal yourself. We need you."

Kierigh's presence loomed closer. "This land needs you, the people. But not as I need you. Stay, love."

Her fingers burned. Unable to resist the calls so filled with love, she concentrated, furrowing her forehead. The wound closed. From a far, beauteous distance came another voice. No words, but approval and love. A touch on her brow from the Seer reduced the pain to a harsh memory. Cautious, she took a deep breath and forced open her eyelids.

Three male heads bent over her, pain reflected in each set of tear glistened eyes. She fluttered her fingers to move the hands pressing hers against her chest. She tried to smile but was so tired. "I'll live. I wouldn't, but for the strength you gave me. Each of you."

Daud and Poll each kissed her cheek then rose and moved out of sight. Kierigh lifted her and stood with slow, exaggerated care. "You will rest."

"Yes. I won't heal as quickly as Daud." Her eyelids drifted closed. The easy, rolling movements of Kierigh's steps lulled her to moon-blessed, healing sleep.

The sweet and pungent aroma of warmed herbs surrounded Jermanah. She stretched and tested the pull of the new scar on her chest. Rubbing the raised tissue, she fingered the length of the wound. Then she opened her eyes.

Hands folded in her lap, Grandmother sat in a thickly padded chair next to the huge bed. "Ah, finally you're awake. It's been four long days. I've been at odds with both Kierigh and Daud, who wished to be at your side at all times. Thank the moons Treenie kept Poll occupied, else I'd have been forced to tear out my hair. Men do worry so when they love you."

Grandmother rose and tucked the blanket securely at her waist. "You're not to rise but to stay abed for another day at least."

"I feel fine now."

The old woman plumped and arranged the pillows behind Jermanah. "I know. And as a healer, you understand why it is unwise to rush your return to health. I must let Kierigh in now. He's worn a path in the stone outside the door with his pacing."

Jermanah held the old woman's hand to her cheek. "I'm so glad you're here."

"Yes, dearie, I know." She patted Jermanah's cheek and leaned to peer into her face. "The Seer's words have come to pass. You have healed yourself."

"Yes, and now I must help heal the land?"

"That is your choice, child." Grandmother straightened slowly, a mischievous twinkle in her eyes. "Are you ready for the onslaught of worried man?"

Jermanah chuckled. She could imagine how Kierigh must have hovered while she slept. Grandmother paused at the door and winked. Seconds later Kierigh rushed in and stumbled to a stop at the foot of the bed.

"Are you—"

"I'm healed and well, although Grandmother says I must stay here another day."

A relieved grin pulled at his lips and he crawled into the

bed, settled next to her and pulled her close. Jermanah sighed. "I think she meant alone."

"What Grandmother doesn't know pleases me greatly." He stroked the shorter hairs around her face back behind her ears. "You're truly healed?"

"How could I not be when you wouldn't let me go? You gave me the encouragement, the strength and power. You are my life."

She snuggled closer and looked at him from under her eyelashes. "This is such a comfortable bed."

His loving gaze darkened with promise. "That Grandmother would surely forbid. And she would know, for I'm not to stay with you long. This time." He took a deep breath. "I would have you at my side always. I love you, Jermanah. Would you honor me, little one, would you be my life mate?"

Why did he even have to ask? The cautious hope in his expression brought her tears of happiness. "I will join with you forever. For this lifetime, and more."

He lifted her into his lap. Their first kiss was tender, his lips lingering, soft against hers. "And more." His mouth possessed hers. His hands drew circles on her back, pressing her closer to deepen the kiss. She was lost, happily lost in the swirl of their love.

Grandmother peeked through the doorway, backed into the outer chamber and closed the door with quiet deliberation. Knowing what her words would be, but still anxious to hear the confirmation, Daud bounced on his toes. He'd not known how excited those within him could be at their brother's happiness.

They were difficult to contain, and he didn't really want to suppress their joy and so felt many crowded behind his eyes.

Taking his hand, Grandmother matched his wide grin. "Your grandfather's words have come to pass.

"The healing is complete."

dear reader

With today's world of vast reading choices, word of mouth is the best advertising. So please let others know about this book. Tell your friends, relatives, acquaintances, the book reading stranger on the bus. Even your dog. Hey, you never know... By sharing a good book, you may discover a new friend.

Readers like you spark the energy needed to tell these tales. Again, thank you. Your reviews help readers discover and connect with new authors. Every review is important to me and is greatly appreciated. Please consider leaving an honest review of Double Moon Destiny at your favorite review sites or at any or all of these places.

Goodreads

Bookbub

*the *starr library*

THE KELTIC MULTIVERSE

Double Keltic Triad Collection Box Set

The Double Keltic Triad is a series of interconnected, stand-alone fantasy romance novels. All 6 books, and a bonus 7th story are included in this set.

It ain't easy being fey...

About the books:

By Keltic Design Allyn Keely, Celtic artist and friend of Faerie, finally finds a man she can love. But she's older than he is and faces the insurmountable task of helping him realize his destiny in the Faerie Otherworld.

Fires of a Keltic Moon Lara Zeroun needs something in her life, so she opens a portal in time and travels to the ancient Highlands. But, how can she become involved with a dark, mysterious man who belongs to another time?

Keltic Flight To the Faerie Gentry of the Otherworld, the fairy wee folk are but a myth and legend. Until the fairy Korin falls in love with a half-Gentry maid. Forced to bargain with an evil king to woo her, he risks discovery, and his life, to fulfill the conditions.

Wild Keltic Carouselle Falling in love was easy. But demons of the past and evil-doers intent on destroying the present tear Carrie and Bryce from their newfound love, throwing them into a world of deception, lies and revenge.

Keltic Dreams A spiritual quest throws Bard, naked and alone, from his world to the desert Sahara. Each grueling step through the shifting sands only adds to his questions and confusion. What did the seven Guardians mean for him to learn in this strange place? Will Kaelea help him discover a way home?

A Faire Keltic Renaissance It ain't easy being fey... and the subject of prophecy. Three worlds are in peril. A pieced together ancient prophecy might defeat the separate evils, but will it also bring Jayse and Lucidea love?

Bonus story: Prince of Dark Ness An ill-prepared fey prince struggles to protect two worlds and a newfound love from the evil of an ancient fire elemental.

Purchase the books separately

By Keltic Design: *Double Keltic Triad 1*

It ain't easy to be fey when you don't believe in fairy tales.

Fires of a Keltic Moon: Double Keltic Triad 2

Can love find a way through time?

Keltic Flight: *Double Keltic Triad 3*

What does she need to believe in love?

Wild Keltic Carouselle: *Double Keltic Triad 4*

Falling in love is easy, the possibilities endless.

Keltic Dreams: *Double Keltic Triad 5*

Passion blazes hotter than the desert sun.

(Author's note: The action of the book *Prince of Dark Ness* takes place between Triad books 5 and 6. While it's not necessary to read *Prince of Dark Ness* here, it does give background into Lucidea's life prior to meeting Jaysson.)

A Faire Keltic Renaissance: *Double Keltic Triad 6*

It ain't easy being fey... and the subject of prophecy

MORE FROM THE KELTIC MULTIVERSE

Prince of Dark Ness: *Keltic Mulitverse*

A romantic fantasy

(Author's note: This story takes place between books 5 and 6 of the *Double Keltic Triad* and introduces the heroine of book 6.)

An ill-prepared Alfar-Sindhu prince struggles to protect two worlds from an ancient fire elemental.

Blue Keltic Moon: *Children of the Triad 1*

Can a place filled with despair and loss also be a discovery of love and redemption? Perhaps... only under the blue Keltic moon.

Just My Imagination: *Children of the Triad 2*

Can his magic save her reality? And will their truths lead to love or destroy any hope they've forged?

(Author's note: This book is also a part of the Aspen Gold Series 18)

Candy Guy and the Chocolate Brownie: *Keltic Mulitverse*

A Keltic Multiverse short story

Who better to assist a struggling chocolatier than a Brownie?

FANTASY ROMANCE

Double Moon Destiny

Can a rebel and an acolyte set aside pride and differences to find a lost brother, defeat evil, and discover their prophecy fulfilling destinies?

CONTEMPORARY ROMANCE

Birds Do It!

A search for truth, switched babies, and a threat from the past

Macaws as lovebirds?

SHORT STORIES

Written in Stone: *'Structs in the City 1*

Will working with the sexy agent to keep the city safe be too dangerous for her heart?

Dead Lily Blooms: *At Death's Gates 1*

Someone wants vampyre Lily dead, and a bargain with Death has been struck.

This short story originally appeared in the anthology ***Tales From The Mist****. This re-release has had minor corrections from the original edition.*

Death and the Dryad: *At Death's Gates 2*

What's Death to do when a dryad appears at his gate without her soul?

*This tale appeared originally in the **Martini Madness** anthology and this re-release has had minor corrections and additions from the original.*

*lizzie also enjoys creating journals and guided workbooks for authors and other creatives. Look for them on her website.

a special series

Once upon a time a group of writer friends got the grandiose idea to create a continuity series. We threw ourselves into developing characters, fashioning families, dynamics and a setting, which evolved from one member's love of all things Colorado.

Years after the initial idea, we rallied again to write the stories, now hoping readers will feel the same intensity and appreciation for this project as we do. We welcome you to join these families, laugh in their good times and cry in their sad times, follow them as they solve mysteries, expose secrets, recover from their pasts, reach for their goals and, most importantly, as the residents of Spencer Colorado fall in love.

These Aspen Gold books are independently published by the authors. We thank you for your support, and we take pride in giving you quality books and excellent stories. We're thankful you've chosen to follow us and be part of the AG community.

The Aspen Gold Authors

Want to know more about Spencer, Colorado, and the Aspen Gold Series? Be sure to follow all the Aspen Gold Series updates at:

Aspen Gold Website
https://www.aspengoldseries.com/
Aspen Gold Twitter
https://twitter.com/@gold_aspen
Aspen Gold: The Series on Facebook
https://www.facebook.com/AspenGoldSeries/
Rocky Mountain Rumors, the newsletter
https://www.subscribepage.com/n9n7p3

*LIZZIE STARR'S ASPEN GOLD BOOKS

Ryder's Heart: *Aspen Gold Series Book 3*

Ryder discovers an intriguing woman in his bed...

She can't allow secrets to steal love from her...

Neither can start a new chapter in their lives until they stop rereading the old ones. Will acceptance overcome their secrets and show them their Rocky Mountain path to love?

For Keeps: *Aspen Gold Series Book 4*

Hiding the truth is like denying the sun.

Will two people who once shared a heartfelt love, allow their lonely secrets to consume and define them? Or will they help each other, forgive each other, and build a future together—For Keeps?

(Author's note: Barbara Gwen was one of the original authors who created the Aspen Gold Series. When I joined the group and planned my own story, we discovered our heroes were best friends. When Barb left this world much too soon, how could I not finish the book of her heart. **For Keeps** is by her and for her.)

Speechless: *Aspen Gold Series Book 8*

How many peonies does it take to get married?

Vianna Harrison and Ryder Barlow would love the honor of your presence as they celebrate their marriage.

Also includes;

The Child in the Cellar

The Christmas Portrait

Fortunate Cookie: *Aspen Gold Book 11*

This woman. Wearing Frosting. And nothing else...

Some Days are Diamonds, is a short story included in:

Yesterday's Promise: *Aspen Gold Series Book 16*

A high-stakes poker game, first meets, a dog rescue, loves lost and rekindled, and life-altering choices fill the history of Spencer, Colorado.

Just My Imagination Aspen Gold Series 18

Can his magic save her reality?

Will their truths lead to love or destroy any hope they've forged?

(Author's note: This book is also a part of the Keltic Multiverse: Children of the Triad 2)

a new writerly me...

There's another writerly me who specializes in... sparkling hot short stories with happy endings! Check out LizAnne's shelf in the library.

Makin' History : Turquoise Creek Ranch

A chance meeting with a sexy biker turns into a night of passion hotter than the summer sun. Will they make their own history... together?

Makin' Amends: Turquoise Creek Ranch

How can he make amends when he doesn't know what he did wrong?

More titles in this series coming soon.

Watch for the Auction Babes series in 2023!

Want to keep up with LizAnne's books? Visit her website at www.lizanneaxtel.com to sign up for her newsletter and get a free short story.

about the author

*lizzie always made up games and stories to keep her company. So, a cunning witch lived in Grampa's weather research station and was only held at bay by waving a certain weed. An ancient road grader morphed into a boat carrying wild adventurers to islands filled with fierce lions and dangerous cannibals, which really looked a lot like sheep.

Now filled with fantasy, love, and romance with a sparkling twist, the stories of her imagination swirl their way into the mundane world.

*lizzie recently retired from her more routine life of being *the Lunch Lady* at a private school. According to the kids, she was 'the best cooker!' Yes, she misses the students and teachers, but is delighted now to start her days by telling stories rather than opening cases of chicken nuggets and counting milk cartons.

Her tag line of *Author and lunch lady~~what a combination!* no longer holds true (which makes her sad because she really liked that one.

Now you'll know *lizzie by her tales of...

~~Romance with a sparkling twist~~

Want to keep up to date with all of *lizzie's worlds?
Sign up for her newsletter on her website:
www.lizziestarr.com

facebook.com/authorlizziestarr
twitter.com/lizziestarr
instagram.com/lizistarr
amazon.com/*lizzie-starr/e/B003F33Y0W
bookbub.com/profile/lizzie-starr
pinterest.com/lizziestarr

www.ingramcontent.com/pod-product-compliance
Lightning Source LLC
LaVergne TN
LVHW030917080826
845145LV00013B/2929

* 9 7 8 0 9 9 7 7 5 4 2 8 5 *